MIDNIGHT LOUIE

"Midnight Louie is one heavy dude. Gourmand, ladies man, and world class dog baiter, this feline detective attacks crime tooth and nail. But if he lays a paw on my lasagna, he'll tangle with a *real* heavyweight."
—Garfield, as told to Jim Davis

ADDITIONAL PRAISE FOR *PUSSYFOOT*

"Move over, Koko and Yum Yum (and Sneaky Pie too): Midnight Louie's back, prowling the sin-soaked streets of Las Vegas once again." —*The Purloined Letter*

"An excellent followup to CATNAP." —*Mostly Murder*

"Midnight Louie's off his leash for the first time since CATNAP with his own superbly funny side of the tale..."
—*Mystery News*

AND FOR *CATNAP*

"Midnight Louie stands out as the coolest cat of all...no doubt about it, Carole Nelson Douglas has hit the jackpot again, with her nifty new sleuth and his intrepid investigations."
—*R*A*V*E Reviews*

"CATNAP glitters and snaps like the town that inspired it."
—Nora Roberts, *New York Times* bestselling author of DIVINE EVIL

CAROLE NELSON DOUGLAS

PUSSYFOOT

A MIDNIGHT LOUIE MYSTERY

FORGE®

A TOM DOHERTY ASSOCIATES BOOK
NEW YORK

This is a work of fiction. All the characters and events portrayed in this book are either products of the author's imagination or are used fictitiously.

PUSSYFOOT

Copyright © 1993 by Carole Nelson Douglas.

Cover art by Joe DeVito

A Tor Book
Published by Tom Doherty Associates, LLC
175 Fifth Avenue
New York, NY 10010

www.tor-forge.com

Tor® is a registered trademark of Tom Doherty Associates, LLC.

ISBN-13: 978-0-7653-3473-2

Library of Congress Catalog Card Number: 92-43705

First Edition: April 1993
First Mass Market Edition: January 1994

Printed in the United States of America

P1

For the real and original Midnight Louie:
nine lives weren't enough

Contents

PUSSYFOOT

Prologue

The Life That Late He Led

Even the darkest day begins with a dawn.

This one starts with me lounging on the third-story patio of my pied-à-terre as the sun rises over Muddy Mountain. Clouds shift against the distant peaks like Sally Rand's famous ostrich fans teasing the notorious foothills of her form. Fading shades of pink and blue reveal the sun's naked red eye opening to scorch the already-browned sands. Good old Sol has been up all night, just like the folks on the Las Vegas Strip, only he did his usual disappearing act while smiling on the other side of the world. Smart fellow.

It is early July, and soon the sands will be hotter than a sizzling lucky streak on a craps table. I allow my eastward-gazing mind to picture Lake Mead as a bright, London-blue topaz in its dusty desert setting. Hundreds of carp glitter like sunken gold along the shoreline, carp apant for the daily influx of tidbit-bearing tourists. I have never seen this treasure hoard of panhandling carp in person, but I hear plenty about them. I share the tourists' fondness for carp, although my tastes run more to feeding on than feeding to.

I expect a tranquil day. Miss Temple Barr, my doting room-mate and a freelance public relations specialist, is between assignments. While I dream of vistas of wild game, my civilized heart awaits the *grrrr* of the can opener. This happy sound precedes the dollop of some rich aquatic concoction into the banana split dish that my little doll has deemed fitting for, and large enough to accommodate, my healthy appetite.

It is not a bad life I lead of late, during this age of Aquarius. Much is to be said for domestic bliss, especially by one who not four weeks ago languished on Death Row in the local animal pound. It is true that my presence there was by design: I went undercover as a common homeless dude, a transient as the sociologists put it, in order to solve a murder at a booksellers convention. Yet this environment in which I now bask—a ray of not-yet-searing sun, a dry desert breeze and Miss Temple Barr hovering with the can opener—appeals far more nowadays than the edge-treading loner's life-style I have been wont to lead.

So I slip into the languid snooze my kind is famous for, a happy laid-back dude expecting no more at the moment than the atten-tions and comforts I have earned over the course of several of my lives.

My personal sun-spot has shifted into shade when I next come to, awakened by the click-click of two dainty high heels arriving at my side. Gastric juices begin doing a tap dance on my rib cage as I lazily cock open one green peeper. I do not wish my famous, devastating stare to bedazzle my little doll before she is com-pletely awake.

But Miss Temple Barr is more awake than I think, or than she should be at this early hour.

''No breakfast for you, Louie,'' she announces with puzzling cheerfulness.

My still-drowsing senses are then jolted by yet another out-of-custom shock. Something thumps down beside me. Before I can open my other eye to study the phenomenon, Miss Temple

PUSSYFOOT

Barr's long-nailed hand (she has irresistible attractions for a fellow of my sort) scoops under my midsection.

"Come on, big boy. Whew, what a handful."

While I enjoy the personal contact, and before I am fully awake, I am prodded into an ambience I know all too well: four bland-blond walls that reek of plastic.

A silver grille snaps shut on my blinking, disbelieving eyes. I have been herded into a portable cell. All I can see through my steel meshwork is Miss Temple Barr's shapely ankles, today propped atop a pair of deep purple pumps. (Some so-called experts claim that my breed is color-blind, but what do they know? Certainly their conclusions are not based on personal testimony.)

I know that I see pure red as the reality of my situation impresses itself upon me; mostly it is the grille that is impressed upon my body hair as I turn frantically in the cramped space. I also express my opinion in words not fit for the company of a lady, but then Miss Temple Barr's entrapment scheme is less than ladylike.

"Hey, don't growl, Louie. It won't be so bad."

My portable cell is swooped aloft to the accompaniment of Miss Temple's anguished "ooof." Then I am swaying helplessly beside her as she trots into the condominium, pauses to grab her tote bag and car keys and vamooses out the door. Some say that ocean voyages produce seasickness. I say that bouncing about like a captive clapper in a molded plastic swinging bell is worse.

At last I am slung onto the sun-warmed front seat of her Geo Storm. I feel like last week's refuse being heaved into the belly of the trash truck. Miss Temple Barr hops behind the wheel and starts the car. Moments later the air-conditioner grilles spurt a stream of hot air directly into my big green beads.

I sigh, turn my posterior to the door of my cell, and settle onto my stomach, which has now joined me in making soft, intermittent growls of protest. The aqua Storm darts through the early-morning traffic like the winged insect known as a darning needle. It was a knitting needle that iced the book dude, I recall as I contemplate using that weapon on Miss Temple Barr. Is this the thanks I get for solving the ABA murder and getting her fat (what little there is of it; she is more than somewhat petite) out of the fire?

At last the car stops and Miss Temple Barr leaps out. I am extracted in my cage and taken into a low building that smells of disinfectant, indiscretions of a liquid nature and dogs. I cannot believe my nose! I have been returned to Death Row, although the betraying scents seem muted now.

"Oooh, he's a hefty one," a feminine voice chirps as I am flung atop a counter, case and all. "A real heavyweight."

"Yup," Miss Temple Barr admits with little concern for my feelings and the truth.

I am solid, it is true, but this is all muscle and bone.

"What is his name?"

"Midnight Louie."

"Cute. Is he black all over?"

"I think so. I haven't looked everywhere."

"Then you do not know if he is fixed or not."

"Er . . . no."

I have never heard my little doll sounding so uncertain, and a trifle guilty.

"Last name?" the chirpy chick prods.

"His . . . or mine?"

"Yours is his now."

"Oh. Barr. But Midnight Louie *Barr* doesn't sound right."

"It is just for the records. We had better weigh him," Miss Chirpy suggests.

At last! The grille swings open and I am swung out in my little lady's loving arms. Not for long. I am swiftly deposited like an errant hairball on a black rubber carpet.

"Eighteen—nineteen. Nineteen point eight." Miss Chirpy's tone drips with syrupy admonition. "Time for an improvement in diet."

This ambiguous statement suggests that some chow is headed my way, at least. I growl approval as Miss Temple Barr lifts me again with a graceless groan, and follows the white-coated female into a private chamber.

PUSSYFOOT

I have heard of such places, though I am not sure if this is the kind of joint that arranges forced assignations between two individuals of the opposite sex who have never before met. I have never been party to such shenanigans in the past, being perfectly capable of finding my own lady friends.

"I am sorry, Louie," Miss Temple Barr croons while chucking me under the chin. I have never known it to fail that a person chucks me under the chin when playing Benedict Arnold, or is it Roseanne Arnold these days? And didn't her last name use to be *Barr*?

I only have time to scan the ceiling for spiders, study a cabinet filled with bottles and boxes of a pharmaceutical nature and observe that I am sitting atop a slab with a monolithic base not unlike a sacrificial altar. (I have seen my share of old movies when the TV remote and I are the only active things in the living room.)

The hair on the back of my neck rises as the door opens, then closes just as quickly. I glimpse another white lab coat.

"Dr. Dolittle," another strange female announces herself. I am feeling surrounded. I look up and would blanch, were that possible. I am staring up at an exceedingly thin, tall doll with a face that would do a hatchet man credit. I have never before seen such a personage, but it is clear that Midnight Louie has joined the vet set, not by his own inclinations.

"Is he purring or shaking?" this female Dr. Death inquires, laying a bony hand upon my shoulders. I do not think much of her diagnostic skills; any fool could see that the frigid air-conditioning is giving me an ague. This doctor doll reminds me of every villainous or supposedly expert human female known to man or tomcat.

"I doubt he has seen a vet before," Miss Temple hazards, rightly. "He is a stray I found. He used to be unofficial house cat at the Crystal Phoenix Hotel on the Strip."

"Hmm." Dr. Leona flicks back my eyelid so that all I see is her hairless hand before my eyes, then pulls my jaws open and leans forward to look at my teeth. "He is lucky that he was not picked up and sent for a three-day stay at the Hotel from Hell— the animal pound."

My tail lashes while I weigh the benefits of sinking a fang into the vet's disgusting, white nose so temptingly within reach. Miss Temple Bar would no doubt find such behavior, however much an act of self-defense, embarrassing, so I restrain myself. I permit myself a low, warning wail, however.

"Eight, maybe nine years old, I would say." Dr. Imelda narrows her eyes. "Nice shoes," she adds approvingly, glancing at my erstwhile friend's feet. She presses my palm until my digits spread. "Nails could use clipping. You ever do that?"

"Only my own," Miss Temple answers.

"Well." The vet sticks a cold hand under my nether parts and pulls me to a standing position. I have never been so humiliated in my life. "He will need all his shots, of course. He is a bit old for declawing, but we could neuter him at the same time. Do you let him outside?"

"Actually, Louie lets himself out."

"Oh?"

"I leave a small bathroom window open. If I do not, he has been known to unlatch the French door to the patio."

"Quite a talented scamp," Dr. Natasha says with a feeble laugh that I do not like. "And he will have to go on the latest scientific formula diet, of course. The out-of-shape senior variety."

I twist angrily out of her grasp and berate her with a few choice words, which she ignores as if they were Urdu.

Miss Temple Barr forlornly strokes my head. "I do not want to overwhelm Louie," she says with the wisdom and sensitivity I have come to expect from her superior sort of person. "Just the shots and the food today."

"But if he wanders, you cannot want him impregnating all the female cats."

"No, but maybe he has slowed down."

Fat, excuse the expression, chance.

"I really advise you to at least fix him," Dr. Ruth suggests with a cheerful leer. "If he goes out, he might need his claws, but he certainly does not need his procreative powers with four out of five kittens born doomed to die within a year."

"No . . ." Miss Temple is waffling.

PUSSYFOOT

I huddle, preparing to hurdle atop the cabinet. When the two shout for help in retrieving me, I will bound down atop the rescuer's head, and out the door before you can say "sold downriver."

"At his age he could get pretty badly beaten up in a fight with another tom," Dr. Death says.

Name one! Or even a Dick or Harry who could cream my corn!

Miss Temple regards me in sad perplexity, even her perky red curls drooping.

"I have never seen him injured," she puts in. "Maybe he is too big to get hurt."

"Now that you have brought him indoors, he could spray the furniture. Males are messy, you know."

Here I cannot restrain a snarl. I do not deny that I am a gentleman of the road, but my indoor manners are impeccable. Even outdoors I am a model of civic responsibility, and go out of my way to make my deposits beside, rather than on top of, the flora.

"Spraying . . . ? He has not done that yet," Miss Temple murmurs in my defense, but her tone is troublingly indecisive.

Clearly, some unmistakable action is required, and I take it. I yowl plaintively and rake my front fingernails across the gray Formica.

This protest shakes my little doll out of her funk. "Just the shots, please," she says. "I will see about getting some special food on the way out."

My triumphal self-congratulations prove premature when this Dr. Dolittle doll instructs Miss Temple Barr to "hold him."

While I squirm, a series of indignities are performed on my posterior with a hypodermic that, while I cannot see it, seems about the size of the previously mentioned knitting needle.

"Does he bite?" this latter-day Madame Defarge inquires a trifle tardily, removing her needle to pick up another.

Not the hand that feeds him, I think as I restrain my fury, although if Miss Temple Barr is planning on switching her current brand to the aforementioned scientific sludge for seniors, I may reconsider that resolve.

Chapter 1

Electraglide in Black

Temple pulled the aqua Storm into the shade of a spreading oleander bush and paused, her hands clinging to the
steering wheel. The Circle Ritz's condominium and apartment building's white marble facade looked cool and calm
in the blazing July heat.

She eyed the flat Timex watch that almost covered her
wrist. Punctuality was essential to Temple's work. She
had no time for fancy, deceiving little watch faces that she
couldn't read accurately at a glance. Good. Only twelve-
twenty.

She got out, clicked around to the passenger's side and
finally wrestled Midnight Louie's carrier through the gaping car door. Her credit card might be a hundred and forty
dollars lighter, but she could swear the carrier was heavier
than before. Perhaps this was the result of passive resistance; Louie had been silent and ominously still all the way
home from the vet's.

Tilting to balance the carrier's weight, she struggled toward the condominium's back gate. Three steps took her into silk-searing sunlight. Temple could feel her hot pink top bleaching and the crown of her red hair fading to pink.

She was a tiny woman who didn't like to be reminded of it, not even by herself. So she gritted her teeth and took one laboring step after another, counting each one. The high heels didn't encourage efficient locomotion while toting overweight cats, but elevation was enough of an issue with her that she didn't mind. Three, four, five steps . . . uh. Maybe Matt Devine was by the pool working on his tan and his physique, both already perfect, but why stop now? He could help her with Louie. No, she could make it herself. Eight, nine, ten steps. The gate. Ah.

She eased the case to the hot concrete and sighed as her shoulder joint assumed its normal alignment. The vet was right; Louie desperately needed a diet.

A distant droning she took for bees in the honeysuckle vine draping the pierced concrete wall grew louder. Temple frowned and eyed the cat carrier. Was Louie growling again? He had not accepted his trip to the vet in the best of graces. The noise increased into a surflike roar.

Temple peered through her sunglasses toward the side street as the roar crested, then slowed into a chatter. Something large, silver and meaner-looking than a robotic junkyard dog, Terminator-style, turned into the driveway and rolled directly toward Temple.

She felt the nasty little twinge motorcycles had inspired since *The Wild Bunch*. They conjured visions of Nazis and Hell's Angels. Today's anonymous riders, now helmeted with obscuring black visors, did nothing to improve the image.

This motorcyclist wore a black nylon windbreaker and rolled its mount right up to Temple, the engine still clattering.

Temple eyed machine and rider, ready to dash through the gate should it or he/she jump either the concrete car-stop or her person. Then she read the hot-pink words emblazoned over the smoked-Plexiglas visor.

"*Speed Queen?*" Temple articulated incredulously.

The engine died with a final clank as the rider's ankle-boot-clad feet hit hot asphalt. One hand lifted from the handles and whipped up the visor.

Electra Lark's genial sixtyish face peered past the bowling ball of silver metallic paint that covered her head. She was grinning like a Halloween pumpkin.

"Just me. And wait a minute. You gotta see this." Electra slung a leg over the long black leather seat and engaged the kick stand as soon as she stood on her own two feet.

Temple watched nervously as the older woman stepped away from the motorcycle. It tilted but did not tumble. At her high-heeled feet, Louie growled warning. No chattering silver metal beast was going to intimidate him, not even after a dose of something as civilizing as "shots."

"A beauty, isn't it?" Electra demanded.

"If you like cold steel."

"Hot steel, honey."

"It will be if you leave it parked in this noonday sun for long."

"Oh, no! This baby will shelter in the shade of the gardening shed at the back."

"Has it always been kept there?"

Electra's open glance shifted. "Not always. But it'll be coming out a lot more now. I just got my license today."

"Hey, that's wonderful!" Temple was always primed to applaud another person's self-improvement program. "It can't be easy to drive one of these monsters. But, Electra . . . why?"

The woman pulled off the sinister helmet, revealing a spiky crew cut of silver hair ending in a long pigtail in back. On most late-middle-aged women such a hairdo would seem a pathetic attempt at kicky youth; on Electra it looked funky and even elegant.

Electra's head tilted until her ear cuffs chimed. She eyed the silver motorcycle and tried, "Because it was there?"

"But *why* was it there?" Temple persisted with the determination of an ex–TV reporter. "You never mentioned having one. I've never seen—or even more to the point, *heard* it before."

Electra's hand patted the leather seat as if stroking the flank of a favorite steed. "It was Max's."

"Max's?" Temple hadn't meant to sound sharp, or shocked, but she did. Both.

Electra's silver-metal boot toe kicked the asphalt. "A cycle's real practical with all the traffic jams in Vegas. And it *is* a beauty."

Temple stared at the thing as if it had landed from Mars. "I had no idea that Max liked— had —a motorcycle."

"Hey, he used it as the down payment on the condo."

Temple eyed her landlady incredulously. She was getting tired of learning things about Max after he was gone—long gone. Four months gone without a goodbye, with no explanation.

"Speaking of the condo," Temple began uncomfortably, "I had to take Louie to the vet and it cost a fortune. I might be a little late with the monthly maintenance money, but not the mortgage."

"Don't worry about it, dear." Electra's waving hand ignited a shower of glints from the many rings mailing her fingers. "I know it's tough when suddenly one person is paying on a place instead of two. Besides, according to folks who know their motorcycles, this baby is worth major moola. It's a classic."

"How classic can a motorcycle get?"

"Plenty. It's a Hesketh Vampire."

"No wonder it gave me the shivers when I heard it coming. Why on earth is it called a vampire?"

"Maybe because it sounds dangerous. It howls in prime gear when the wind whistles by."

Temple shook her head. "Hesketh Vampire," she repeated numbly. "Any relation to a Sopwith Camel?"

"Well, it is British-made." Electra proudly circled her

new toy, ticking off its assets. "A full-liter engine, one thousand cee-cees. Nickel-plated and overbuilt to go literally millions of miles."

Temple followed Electra around the massive machine, eyeing the steeply raked windshield, the fluid silver front casing—not shiny like chrome but matte-soft, classy—and the emblem of a crown surmounted by an angry rooster head above the Cyclopean front headlight.

"*Max* had this, really?"

"Yup." Electra's finger stroked the word "Hesketh" under the regal but surly rooster. "The famous Hesketh flying chicken. Now it's chicken à la queen." She chuckled and lifted her emblazoned helmet.

Temple just shook her head. "I don't know much about motorcycles—and apparently knew even less about Max—but this is a humongous machine, Electra. Is it safe to drive?"

"Ride," Electra corrected quickly. "Driving is for sissies."

"Can a woman handle it safely?"

"Safety is not the idea with a superbike, dear," Electra explained sweetly.

"But a woman your age—"

"A woman my age can use a little excitement. They say women are horse-crazy, but those ninnies are living in the last century. This thing rides like a rocket. Besides, it's a good way to meet men, if you're so inclined. I found me some guys who knew something about cycles and they taught me the ropes."

"Where'd you find bikers?"

"They're not bikers, just some older guys who tinker a bit. Wild Blue works mostly on vintage planes, but Eightball has played with a bike or two."

"Eightball? Not Eightball O'Rourke?"

"Yeah, how'd you know him?"

"He's the private detective I hired to tail the ABA catnapper."

Electra looked bemused. "No kidding? Until not too long ago, he and his pals were fugitives."

"Fugitives? Eightball claimed he had a security background."

Electra nodded sagely. "And so he does; nobody around Las Vegas has been as secure as Eightball all these years. He and the Glory Hole Gang hid out in the desert looking for some silver dollars they hijacked during World War Two and hid so good they couldn't find them again themselves. Buried treasure. The statute of limitations had run out by the time anyone found out about them, and now they run Glory Hole as a tourist ghost town; it's in that string of abandoned towns off of Highway 95. I think Eightball got so used to looking for that lost treasure that he decided to get into the business of looking into this and that. Hooked on hunting, if you know what I mean."

"But he had a license, he said he'd been employed in detection for years!"

"What would you say if you had a dicey background and were trying something new at age seventy or so?"

"I can't believe you know these people, Electra."

Electra eyed Temple for a long moment. "I'm not responsible for what my friends or acquaintances do or did, but these are sweet old guys. Helped me out a lot, for nothing. They even had to chop the seat padding down so my legs could reach the ground." She slapped the black leather again, and Temple winced. "Hated to do it, but face it, Max isn't coming back. No sense letting a primo machine rot."

"Right," Temple murmured fervently.

"Heck," Electra added, "I bet even you could ride my new baby with the seat this low. Come on, hop on. I'll take you for a spin around the block."

"No, thanks." Temple turned to inspect her own "baby" in his vetmobile. "Louie needs to get his breakfast just as soon as I can tote in the twenty-pound bag in the trunk. I'll pass."

"Chicken?" Electra grinned wickedly, donning her helmet.

Temple didn't honor that with a direct answer. "I've got a lot of work to get out on my computer before the WICA meeting at five-thirty. Sorry. Some other time," she added with rare insincerity.

Electra's platinum-gray eyebrows lofted nearly to the helmet's brim. "Wicca? I didn't know you were interested in witchcraft."

"I'm not. It's Women in Communications, Associated. Great for networking, and digging up freelance clients in the recession is more like doing black magic than white witchcraft."

"I wouldn't joke about the dark arts, dearie," Electra said with a shudder, flipping her sinister visor down.

Despite needing to hustle, Temple couldn't resist waiting to watch the landlady mount, expertly kick away the support, start the engine and chatter off in low gear to the shed around back.

Then she glumly lugged Louie through the gate, shut it and headed across the area bordering the pool, relieved that Matt Devine wasn't in sight.

She couldn't believe that Max had never mentioned that thing, much less using it for a down payment on the condo. . . . He had glossed over that issue when he'd put the place in both their names. Electra was financing it, so it was simple—if not monetarily easy—for Temple to take over the payments after Max skedaddled. And here Temple had hoped buying instead of renting had indicated that Max was as serious about permanent relationships as she was . . . hah!

While these thoughts festered, her autopilot had called the elevator, punched the proper floor and gotten her off before the doors sliced together on her or Louie's carrier.

She walked down the semicircular hall to her door, unlocked it and sat Louie's carrier on the entry-hall parquet. When she opened the grille, he sulked inside, reduced to a resentful glare of electric green eyes.

"Sorry, boy. I'll feed you as soon as I drag the bag back from the car."

She was back in minutes, staggering, to find the carrier empty and Louie nowhere in sight. Temple sighed, slung the huge brown-paper bag to the kitchen countertop and proceeded to exercise her nails on trying to puncture the stitched-shut top. She finally fetched the kitchen shears and took several ill-tempered stabs at the tough paper until she worried a ragged hole in one corner.

Then she hefted the heavy bag and squatted to pour its contents into Louie's empty banana split dish. Green-brown pellets plugged the hole, then burped out in a dirty hail, scattering like run-amok marbles on the black and white tiles.

"Oh, holy horseradish! This feline health food is gonna break my back. Louie! Come and get it."

He refused to show, so Temple stomped into her bedroom to look under the bed. Nothing animal there but dust bunnies. The louvered closet doors were shut, but she jerked one open just the same. Jerk. Speaking of which, there was Max, face-to-face.

She studied the glossy, oversized poster she knew like the markings on her mauve snakeskin J. Renees. By now, Max, the most mobile of men both mentally and physically, had become frozen into this single, hype-ridden image: black turtleneck, black unruly hair, green stare. The Mystifying Max, vanished magician, former roommate, lost lover. Was he ever.

And now his past recycled: a massive silver Vampire on wheelies. It must have meant something to him, owning a classic. He must have ridden it at one time; left it behind when his act toured distant cities like Minneapolis. He must have figured a Heckwith, or whatever, Vampire wasn't Temple's speed, or he'd have kept it, shown it to her. Said, Hop on, I'll take you for a ride. He hadn't needed a motorcycle for that.

Temple sat suddenly on the bed, still staring at the poster. She wasn't a motorcycle moll. She couldn't see herself roaring along the never-ending white centerline on two narrow tires and a bloated black belly of steel. Maybe Max couldn't see that either. Maybe that's why he'd left; she was too conventional, took herself too seriously. Maybe she would have liked it, plastering herself behind Max, wrapped up in gear with a dark crystal ball for a crown and the wind rushing at them, the road running away behind them and speed thrumming with exultation between their conjoined thighs. . . .

Temple rose, then used her long, lacquered nails to peel the tape very carefully from the four corners of the poster. She folded the excess tape down on the back before rolling the heavy paper into one long white cylinder. Then she stuffed it down in the far dark back corner of the closet where the last of Max's clothes hung waiting to be taken to the Goodwill someday.

Chapter 2

A Crummy
Encounter

"I can't believe the nerve of that man." The tall blonde drowned her complaint in a swallow of white wine spritzer, the PR woman's national drink.

"Who?" Temple, looking around sharply with news-hound instincts, saw only women gathered in cocktail-party knots.

The blonde's name tag said she was Sunny Cadeaux. She turned away from the two other women in her schmoozing circle to spit out two loathsomely familiar words: "Crawford Buchanan."

"Oh." Temple quickly sipped her Virgin Mary while trying to dodge the leafy stick of celery afloat in the blood-colored beverage. "Awful Crawford. What's he done now?"

"You must have come in the back way," Sunny suggested.

Temple nodded. "I was late, and I wanted to talk to the hotel manager."

"Why? Are you on the arrangements committee? If so, I must say that we love meeting at the Crystal Phoenix, but I wish you'd rearrange Crawford Buchanan permanently."

"Sorry, I'm not on that committee or any other one." Temple finally decided to remove the bobbing stalk and eat it. She couldn't get near the buffet table anyway, she concluded, eyeing the horde of feasting PR types swarming it. All queens, not a drone in the bunch.

"What were you talking to Van von Rhine about?" Sunny persisted. PR people were insatiably curious for the story behind the story.

"About a pussycat."

"Pussycat?" parroted a lady in Sally Jesse Raphael-red glasses, leaning around Sunny.

"Well, more of a tomcat," Temple admitted. "Midnight Louie was the house cat here until he wandered to my neck of the woods. I just wanted Van to know that he was all right. She and her husband Nicky Fontana took an interest in him." Temple frowned. "At least I think he's all right. He wouldn't touch his Free-to-be-Feline all afternoon."

"Midnight Louie. Is that the ABA killer cat?"

Temple couldn't quite read the woman's name tag from where she stood. She often skipped wearing her glasses at social events; that meant that she got potluck from menus and met a lot of Petsys and Cerals, not to mention Jams and Retes at coed affairs. This lady appeared to be named "Nike."

"Midnight Louie got the publicity for finding the body," Temple explained. "He didn't kill a thing at the ABA but time."

"I wish he was here and would do away with Crawford Buchanan," Sunny suggested between her teeth in a tone that did not live up to her name.

"What has he done that's so horrible now?" Temple wondered.

"Check out the ballroom entrance foyer. There ought to be a law."

"Crawford's nature is to be awful," Temple quipped, "not lawful, but I can't resist seeing what God's gift to PR women is up to."

She set down her untouched Virgin Mary, sans celery, and glided through the crowd with the agile expertise of one whose business is going places fast without ruffling anyone.

En route she couldn't help but wish that she *had* been on the arrangements committee. The ballroom was papered with a gilt-stamped motif of either Oriental phoenixes or fireworks—without glasses she couldn't quite be sure which—that shone softly in the dazzle from the overhead chandeliers. The lavish picture-frame paneling painted the color of vanilla ice reminded Temple of a French chateau. Taste. Elegance. Refinement. In a Las Vegas world overdosed on shallow glitter, the Crystal Phoenix stood alone, an island of restraint afloat in a blitz of glitz and crass commercialism.

Speaking of which . . . Temple passed through the double ballroom doors, stopping so fast and hard that her Christian Dior black satin spikes threatened to drive through the carpet backing.

Crawford Buchanan sat at a table draped in peach linen and piled with the black-and-white proof of his journalism credentials, the latest edition of the *Las Vegas Scoop*. A silver candelabra flickered at one elbow, its light playing over the matching silver of his hair—no longer frizzed into a permanent Brillo pad, but worn long and slicked back with mousse until it ended with a froth of trendy curls at his jacket collar.

"Ugh," Temple muttered.

"If you don't like the spokesman, wait'll you see the product." The woman who had materialized beside her smiled grimly. This one she recognized: Sylvia Cummins, WICA vice president, ran PR for the Crystal Phoenix.

"What's he doing here?"

"Cutting into our pie," Sylvia said. "You notice the sign?"

"No—oh, pinned to the tablecloth. Uh. 'Cooties We Cherish'?"

"Better dig out the glasses, Temple, you don't want to miss this one," Sylvia advised sotto voce as she brushed past to return to the ballroom.

Temple pawed in her gold evening tote bag until she felt the soft padded form of her glasses case. By the time she donned them, the last arrivals had dispersed. Only she and Crawford occupied the foyer.

Total tastelessness. Vulgarity. Crudity. It all sat enthroned in Buchanan's little corner of the world. Temple walked over, glaring as she deciphered the offending sign. COOKIES WITH CRAWFORD, it read. Might as well advertise TEA WITH RASPUTIN.

"Have you sunk to crashing WICA meetings now?" she greeted him.

"Hey, it's a free foyer."

She studied his handout flyers advertising Crawford Buchanan & Associates Public Relations. "I didn't know you had any associates but fleas."

"Temper, temper, T.B.," he cautioned, unruffled. That was the most annoying thing about Crawford, he was uninsultable.

"Women in Communications, Associated, means just that. I haven't noticed you having any sex-change operation lately. I should ask Van von Rhine to toss you out."

He smirked. "At least you noticed. And try to eject me. I'll sue WICA for being a female-chauvinist organization quashing free enterprise by the opposite sex."

"The only thing worth tossing at your table is the cookies." She eyed the large brown circles, whose pink icing clashed with the peach tablecloth. "How can you do an objective job of public relations for anybody when you're writing a column for the *Las Vegas Poop?* That's gilt-edged conflict of interest. You've got a lot of nerve."

"Thanks. That's what you PR girls are missing out on. All your hen parties won't make up for some self-interested enterprise. This column"—he picked up the inky tabloid, his thumb under a front-page column titled "Buchanan's Broadside"—"gets me a lot of attention and more business. Got the stripper competition at the Goliath because of it. That's worth a lot of money and contacts."

"I've got news for you. They asked me to handle it first. I turned it down."

"Why the hell would you do that, T.B.?" Buchanan seemed genuinely shocked, his big melting brown eyes wet as fresh-baked chocolate chips. "That's self-employment suicide! Broads, glitter, bodies—a baby could get A-one news coverage on an event like that without dampening a diaper."

Temple sighed. "If the word 'ethics' doesn't mean anything to you, I don't imagine the word 'exploitation' would either."

"These stripper babes aren't exploited. They love the attention, take it from me. The stripper guys may be a little bent, and I'm not too crazy about spending time around them, but—"

"Crawford, you are too Neanderthal for words. Your attitudes toward women and gays are going to get you tarred and feathered someday."

"You sound like those hatchet-faced dames picketing the competition."

"Have you checked their signs? Maybe they're just picketing you."

Before he could answer with his usual amused calm, Temple turned on her heel, literally, and marched away. She stopped inside the ballroom doors, unsoothed by the civilized surroundings, briefly regretting the lucrative assignment Crawford was handling with all the sensitivity of a number fifteen sandpaper. She could have used the money even before Midnight Louie had turned up in her life.

But money wasn't everything, Temple told herself, or she'd be a high-paid stripper and someone else could be a struggling PR free-lancer. Maybe that was why she had a headache. She sipped her Virgin Mary down to the melting ice cubes, and left.

Chapter 3

Dial "M" for Matt

"Hello."

"Brother John?"

"Yes."

"It's Sister Sue."

"I recognized your voice."

"Me, too, I guess. Only I had to make sure. You never know."

"How are things going?"

"Not . . . good. I don't know how much longer I can take it sometimes. Sometimes I just wanta freak, you know?"

"I know. But you shouldn't have to take it at all."

"Easy for you to say."

"Once it wasn't. You know why you call?"

"Because I need help. I want out. But . . ."

" 'But's are excuses, not answers."

"I know. I hate myself sometimes—"

"Worse than him?"

"Sometimes. Sometimes I think all the things he says are right."

"You know they're not. You could leave tonight. The women's shelter—"

"Shit! I can't hide somewhere. My business is going great. That's my ticket out of here, not running away, hiding out. Not yet. I've got this big chance, in my business. Maybe that's why he's so mad."

"Is it worse?"

"It always gets worse. You know that. But . . . I can make it. Just another few days. If I get lucky next weekend, I'll have the money to drop out for a while. Take the kids. A week from today."

"Then why are you calling tonight? And gambling is no real way out. Sister Sue? Don't hang up—"

"I'd never hang up on you, Brother. Unless he came in and made me."

"I'd call the police then."

"God, no! Not the police. He just gets madder, badder, and he's always out so soon. Bigger, badder. He . . . smashed up the living room, hit me in ways it won't show. He's so good about that, so smart when he's crazy. And little Ria—"

"He's hitting the kids now, too? You've got to get out. You can't wait for a week from today."

"I know, I know! Just a week. Help me hang on for a week. If I didn't have this number, have you to call, someone who knows . . ."

"My knowing can't help you until you help yourself. Until you leave."

"A week from Friday. Honest. If you only knew what a chance I've got, how hard I've worked for it. I've made my plans, my escape plan, I've kept it secret. Not even his fists can pry it out of me. Only a few more days. I can make it. I can take it. Just a little bit longer."

"Don't take that risk; he'll only escalate. Don't—Sister Sue, are you there? Answer me!"

". . . I gotta go now. Baby's crying. Baby's always crying. Maybe baby will cry until Saturday, sweet Saturday. Bye, Brother John. God bless."

"Wait—don't hang up. Wait. . . ."

Chapter 4

Crawford Sees Red

Temple hated Mondays. Her normally creative brain always marked time until past noon. It had been true on the job, and it was equally true when she was her own boss, working at home. She made a face at her personal-computer screen, then got up from the glass-topped desk in the spare bedroom and wandered to the row of French doors in the living room, cosseting a condensation-dewed glass of Crystal Light clad in a terry-cloth sleeve.

Opening a door, she stepped barefoot onto the warm stones of the tricorn-shaped patio, keeping under the shade of the generous eaves.

The sole palm tree on Electra's property scrubbed the cloudless sky a brighter blue with its weathered green fronds. Oleanders hoarded a lingering bright red bloom among their spiky leaves. The pool's lucid blue looked cooler than an ad for Aquavit.

Something moved below, vague enough to make Temple clutch her glass and agitate the last floating islands of ice. A white shadow shifted in the ground-level shade two floors below.

Her breath eased out when a smooth blond poll blazed as a figure stepped into full sunlight: Matt Devine, night-shift man, up at high noon and ready to exploit his off-hours.

She watched him with idle detachment, through a frozen, lazy pool of thought and emotion. He wore the white, loose-fitting martial-arts outfit she always thought of as pajamas. Barefoot, barehanded, bareheaded, he began pantomiming the graceful motions of some Oriental discipline. T'ai chi maybe, or preliminary warm-ups for something more lethal, judo or tae kwon do.

Matt melted from one subtle movement into another, a butterscotch-topped Dairy Queen in motion, a small, remote figure on a painted parchment backdrop of cool blue water and hot white concrete edged with softly swaying green. God, he was good-looking, in an impersonal, almost artful way, she mused. Or was she only moon-struck by him?

Temple turned from contemplation, leaving Matt Devine to his more arduous ritual, and ambled back into her apartment. Her own bare feet polished the walnut parquet, scratching her insteps on the occasional raised cracks.

In the black-and-white kitchen, Louie's banana split bowl overflowed with brown-green pellets. Free-to-be-Feline was costing a pretty penny as fodder for the garbage disposal.

The cat was off on errands of his own, no doubt scrounging garbage cans for unhealthy but toothsome grub. Temple perused the open refrigerator while mulling a snappy lead for a press release on the Button Collectors of West Las Vegas. Yogurt would be smooth and chill, but she craved something sweeter. Maybe green grapes. She opened the fruit drawer. She had no green grapes. She had only a half-wilted fan of romaine lettuce, ruffled edges curled like ostrich plumes. And a deformed grapefruit. Grapefruit was not grapes.

And her press-release lead wasn't coming. She should take an invigorating walk. All right, a hot, drying walk. She should exercise, like Matt, who even now might be stroking smoothly through the aquavit water. Join him. Eeek. Did she want to be seen in last year's neon tanksuit? The sun planted instant freckles on her shoulders. Definitely not sexy. What to eat?

A knock at the door saved her from freezing in the refrigerated air while making up her mind. She glanced quickly at her knit shorts and top while hurrying to answer it. Uninspired but clean. Maybe Matt—

"Oh, hi, Electra. What's up?"

"Not the rent, don't worry," the landlady answered with a grin. "I come bearing what the paperboy dumped in the azaleas this noon. The whole building's supply ended up as lizard carpet. Thought you might have missed it."

"I didn't," Temple admitted. "Been fighting the button collectors all morning. While you were out beating the bushes for news, did you happen to spot Midnight Louie?"

"No. That scamp gone AWOL again?"

Temple nodded as she took the *Las Vegas Review-Journal* Electra offered. She stepped back to reveal the pyramid of untouched Free-to-be-Feline. "He's not eating his low-ash, low-fat, low-magnesium, high-fiber, high-protein food fresh from the vet's."

"I don't know as I blame him." Electra frowned at the brown pellets in the banana split dish, then turned to the expression on Temple's face. "You look kind of peaked, dear. Are you sure you're eating right?"

"I'd eat everything in sight if I'd let myself. You want some Crystal Light?"

"No, but a beer would be nice."

Temple explored her refrigerator and discovered one

lone Coors Light necklaced in plastic trailing an empty
string of five matching rings, probably dating to the last
days of Max.

"Does beer spoil?" she asked, wrenching the cold can
free of its plastic collar.

"Only if it's open." Electra accepted the beer and
headed for the French door Temple had left ajar. "Maybe
your rogue tomcat is basking on the patio."

"No, I looked—" Temple began, too late to head off
Electra's singled-minded course.

When Temple caught up with her outside, Electra was
by the retaining wall smacking her lips and enjoying the
scenery. "I forgot your unit had a pool view. Matt has
added a lot to the Circle Ritz's ambience since he came."

"Really?" Temple sat on the cushioned lounge chair.

Electra plunked down on the matching ottoman. "Really. How are things going between you two?"

"What things? You make us sound like an item."

"Well, you did go out with him a time or two after the
ABA hullabaloo."

"He was just being nice."

"Hmm. He's good at that."

"He is. He's the most genuinely nice man I've ever
met."

"Why do you sound so disappointed then?"

"I don't know." Temple sipped her poisonously sweet
low-calorie drink. "Nice is great if it's an opening curtain.
If it's the whole show—"

"No spice." Electra nodded sagely. "Like my second
husband. Perfectly nice, kind to widows and wackos. Boring."

"Matt's not boring, just reserved."

"You're just spoiled by the ex-Max."

"What's spoiling about someone who can walk out on
you without a word?"

"It's not boring."

Temple sat back, remembered Max. "No."

Electra leaned forward to pat her knee, her armful of

silver bracelets jingling like the spurs of song and story. "Don't fret, dear; men are always more interesting at a distance, or when they've just come or just gone. It's a trait of the breed. Take my ex-husbands, but then I really couldn't wish them on anyone."

Temple laughed. "Thanks for the paper, Electra. And the pep talk. I think."

The landlady winked, rose with her beer and let herself out.

Temple remained in the lounge chair, listening to the faint, rhythmic plash of water as Matt swam laps below. She sighed and unfolded the newspaper.

"No kidding!" She seldom spoke to herself, but had been doing it more since Louie's arrival disguised it as pet talk.

Her eyes whipped back and forth along the short lines of front-page type like a Singer sewing machine set on zigzag. Words leaped out: dead . . . Goliath . . . stripper . . . suspected murder.

Temple leaped up in unholy shock. "Good grief; a thief! Murder at the strippers' convention. And it's in Awful Crawford's own damn lap! I can't believe it."

Below her, the water stilled. Matt was standing in the shallow end, a shading hand to his eyes, looking up at her balcony.

"I'm okay," she shouted down. "I just learned that my worst enemy, who was boasting about snagging the strippers' convention away from me, has landed in the middle of a juicy murder. Not me this time, him!"

"Are you jubilant," Matt shouted back, glistening golden in the sun, "or jealous?"

Temple sobered. A woman was dead and Crawford Buchanan wasn't equipped to do anything about it but wring his pale white hands. She sat down and considered Matt's question again, seriously. Then she rose, leaned over the patio wall and invited him over for supper.

* * *

"Supper," she iterated when she opened the door to Matt's prompt ring at five o'clock. "Not dinner. I don't do dinner."

"What's the difference?" He presented her with a chilled matte black bottle of Freixenet. He was wearing a champagne linen short-sleeved shirt that made his tan and his brown eyes sing like the Song of Solomon.

"This says dinner." Temple hefted the wine bottle before depositing it on the table. "But it can stay for supper anyway. Supper is a little deli this, a little leftover that. For supper you can overgarlic the bread and burn the beans. For dinner you have to be perfect. For supper you can have your wine in a supermarket glass. For dinner"— she went up on tiptoe in her high-heeled Anne Klein emerald leather sandals, opened the shallow cabinet high over the stove hood and batted at the long-stemmed glasses just out of reach.

Matt came over and took down two of the hand-blown cobalt goblets.

Temple settled back to earth with a relieved sigh. "For dinner you drink out of craftware."

"Very nice." Matt set the princely glasses at the colorful Fiestaware places already set in the dining room. "I'm glad I brought dinner."

"And heeeere's supper." Temple swooped the plates of deli breads, homemade crab salad, cold baked beans and artistically arranged fresh veggies from the refrigerator.

They settled down to the food without a lot of small talk or fanfare, which she liked, although she belatedly realized that the large, handmade wineglasses would hold a lot of sparkling bubbles.

"I hope you don't think I'm too much of a ghoul after my outburst this morning," she said as soon as the main dishes had made the rounds.

"You do seem to have a certain detachment about murder."

"Well, the first time, it created a crisis on my job. It's

hard to empathize with a fly in the ointment, especially when he's as widely loathed as the late Chester Royal turned out to be."

"What's the story on this murder at the Goliath? Why are you so . . .?"

"Excited by it? Simple. You see, I could have had that strippers' convention PR job, only I turned it down. Not Crawford Buchanan. He's too greedy to reject any sure thing. So it could have been me and not Crawford Buchanan who's up to his neck in a murderous mess. If I'd stumbled onto a body a second time, you can bet that Lieutenant Molina would have put me in thumbscrews."

"He sounds like a terror, or a throwback to the days of brass knuckles."

Temple chewed crab salad and her impulses, then forbore telling Matt that her bête noir of the law was female. Somehow it made her look less in need of sympathy.

"Why did you turn the convention down?" he asked.

"This is one of the few times when I can grandly say, 'principle.' All that flesh on parade makes me uneasy, the notion of teasing a bunch of paying customers. Even regular working women are sometimes tempted into acting or looking like bimbos to get male attention."

"Aren't there men strippers now, too?"

"Oh, sure, but it's the same thing. Besides, they're all overblown plastic musclemen, about as attractive as steroid robots."

"Then you don't like them because you don't find their type attractive?"

"And stripping seems demeaning. On the other hand, I guess they make a lot of money doing it, so who can blame them?"

"You can. You blame Crawford Buchanan for being greedy."

"Don't make me sound like a prude or a pauper. What upsets me is that I came closer than I want to think about to getting tangled in another murder. Which explains my unholy glee."

"You had a hand in solving the last one; what's wrong with that?"

"That's not my job. My job is getting good publicity for my clients. I hate messes, and murder makes a mess you wouldn't believe. But this time it's in Crawford's lap, not mine."

"I'll drink to that." Matt lifted his glass. "What's the story on this Crawford guy?"

"The bane of my life since I got to Las Vegas. Goes everywhere. Writes a sleazy woman-chasing column about the nightlife for the *Las Vegas Scoop*. Has no sense of shame or ethics. Would steal a client from the Pope."

Matt choked on his wine at her heated description.

"Really! He's the most slimy, sexist, smug, smarmy . . . PR person to pollute a press club." Temple settled back for a sip of her own wine. "I shouldn't let him get to me."

"Is *he* getting to you, or the murder?"

"You keep asking these pointed questions."

Matt smiled. "That's my job."

"You're good at it. I always seem to need to explain my motives to you."

"That's not the idea. My questions are supposed to help you explain your motives to yourself."

"You're a model counselor," she admitted more seriously before rising to dash into the kitchen for the crème de menthe chocolate mousse that would crown their plain supper. Temple was adept with desserts if nothing else edible. "A lot of people wouldn't understand why Buchanan infuriates me," she said when she came back and sat down after placing the dessert dishes.

Matt nodded. "It's the injustice of it all, of Buchanan's golden survival while he breaks every rule. In a way, you envy him."

"I do not!" Temple meditated over her particolored mousse, dipping tiny spoonfuls from the deep narrow dessert glass and then letting them melt on her tongue. "Maybe I do envy his chutzpah."

"We all envy the insensitive people of the world; they suffer less."

"True." Temple had noticed Matt's wry tone on the last comment. "You must talk to a lot of suffering people."

"You mean in my job?"

"You're saying the sufferers are all around us. They *are* us." He ate his mousse as methodically as she, in silence. "The ones who call you, though, must be doubly desperate."

"They don't call me. They call the hot line. They call a distant, nonjudgmental voice. Someone who can't see them, find them, accuse them. A disembodied conscience or savior."

"Doesn't it ever get to you? Dealing with all that misery?"

He shrugged almost imperceptibly. "Sometimes you help."

"You can never know how much, though. Some callers you've given up on may have saved themselves. Some you're sure will make it, won't."

The wine bottle tilted in Matt's hand as it bowed deeply to Temple's glass. That's when she realized that they had drunk a lot, that her cheeks were flushed even as she felt suddenly sober, unbuoyed by bubbles, thinking about life and death. He was slow to answer.

"No, you can never really know what happens to the voices on the line when they hang up. Some you hear from again after a long silence. Some just vanish."

Temple swallowed hard. "Not knowing must be the worst thing on earth," she said fiercely.

Matt's warm brown eyes met hers, broke the polite barrier they always erected, penetrated hers like burning swords. "No. The worst thing is knowing."

Chapter 5

Sick to Death

Temple sat alone on her patio as the sun weltered slowly in the west behind the Circle Ritz. A grillwork of anonymous, elongated shadows overlay the pool area. In the distance, the Mirage Hotel's artificial volcano belched its preprogrammed flames with a roar that mimicked the uncivil growls of distant wild beasts.

Matt had left early, by seven-thirty, to go to his night shift at the hot line. Temple was musing on her glimpse of a hidden intensity in Matt Devine, one that pulsed behind his air of amused neutrality at her own energetic opinions.

Footsteps scraped the concrete below, so she rose to inspect the grounds. A darker shadow stirred in the pooled shade of tree and building.

"Louie!" The rebuking tone couldn't quite conceal her relief.

The cat, hunched over something, didn't look up.

While she frowned down at this mystery, a man's figure stepped from the palm shadow. "It's hard to see from all this far, but you wouldn't be Miss Temple Barr?"

From this height, the speaker looked like an out-of-focus Charlie Chaplin.

"Who's asking?" Temple returned.

The man squatted beside Louie, but continued to look up at Temple. "No one famous. Just Nostradamus."

For a moment she was speechless, then recovered herself. "Excuse me, but Nostradamus was a pretty famous fellow a few centuries ago."

"I'm a namesake forsaken," he said. "No offense taken." He laid something from his pocket before Louie, who gobbled it with catlike concentration.

"What are you feeding him?"

"Just some bits of leftover lunch meat. He acts as if he's had nothing to eat."

" 'Acts' is right. That scoundrel has ignored bowls full of the best catfood money can buy: Free-to-be-Feline."

"It wouldn't take a good detective," Nostradamus said with a sage nod, "to figure out why he's so selective."

"Stale lunch meat can't be good for him. Stop feeding him that junk and I'll be down to collect him."

She didn't wait for an answer but headed downstairs, barefoot.

When she arrived, both cat and man were in the same position, doing the same thing: Nostradamus feeding, Louie eating.

"Corned beef!" Temple identified the dry flakes in Nostradamus's hand at a glance even in the waning light. "Riddled with fat and sodium! I wouldn't feed that stuff even to a human."

"All right, lady, I'll heed your wishes." The man rose, stuffing the white butcher paper back into his pocket. "Louie really favors goldfishes."

"The only thing fishy here is you," Temple said sharply. "Why are you slinking around the grounds?"

"So help me it's true: I'm just looking for you. A mutual friend in trouble told me to find you on the double."

"Who would I have in common with you?"

"You'll find your man in Crawford Buchanan."

"Oh, he's common, all right." Temple bent to hoist Louie. A twenty-four-hour absence had not impaired his heft. "Come into the lobby air-conditioning, such as it is, and tell me about it."

Once she had Louie firmly indoors, she pulled the side door closed and turned to examine the so-called Nostradamus in the lurid light of the outdated ceiling fixture high above.

She inspected a narrow, small man of indeterminate age dressed in a green plaid short-sleeved shirt with a yellow bow tie at his stringy throat.

"You're a friend of Crawford Buchanan's?" She sounded a bit more incredulous than she intended.

The man sighed mightily. "That's not exactly the whole cookie. I'm really, actually just his . . . bookie."

"Oh. Well, what's the message?"

"Crawford's sick, and gettin' sicker."

"He sent you here to tell me he's got the flu?"

"Not flu. A faulty ticker." Nostradamus pounded his concave chest and looked in danger of pushing himself over.

"Heart trouble? I didn't know Crawford had one."

"He wants you to visit room eight-oh-three—"

"Visit him? Me?"

"In the medical center of the university."

"Gee," said Temple, waffling. "Is it serious?"

"His heart or his request?"

"Both, I guess."

"Neither one is any jest." Nostradamus tipped his battered straw fedora with the paisley band, opened the door, and ebbed into the now-opaque darkness.

A large puddle of interior darkness—Louie—hunched uncooperatively on the pale, ice-cold marble floor and gazed at Temple with accusing green eyes.

"All right! I might have some low-fat turkey slices in the

refrigerator. Come on up and you can take a vacation from Free-to-be-Feline."

He rose, stretched until his hindquarters and tail pointed ceilingward, then ambled down the hallway to the elevator.

Once Temple had let them both into her apartment and plied Louie with Louis Rich turkey slices (which she broke into pieces over the untouched Free-to-be-Feline), she called the medical center. Crawford Buchanan was indeed out of intensive care and occupying room 803. He could have visitors until 9 P.M. She should let the stinker stew in his own IVs.

Temple checked her watch—just eight—then went to make herself presentable for a visit to a sick enemy.

Chapter 6

No Love Lost

Alone at last! No sooner has Miss Temple Barr torn out of the apartment on an errand of mercy to a sick friend than I take the opportunity of eating the sliced turkey off the top of my tasteless pile of pet food, a veritable Everest of rabbit pellets.

My next task is to find a suitable spot for intense cogitation. After exploring the familiar terrain, I find that my hasty roommate has left an emerald silk dress flung across the bed in her flurry to find attire appropriate to the hospital.

First I pat it into the proper formation with my mitts, a task I manage without much resorting to my crudely clipped nails. Then I turn around on it precisely six times. Those of my particular breed are superstitious about numbers. Perhaps it comes of having nine lives, but we tend to do things in multiples of three.

Once the garment is nicely crumpled so the night-light reflects faintly off its subtle shades of green (the virtual twin to my own eye color), I allow my footsore nineteen-plus pounds to press the material into its new, nestlike shape.

Now I can think. And I have much to contemplate. While Miss Temple Barr's obnoxious new cuisine is most off-putting, it alone is not enough to drive a dude to a binge away from home. I am long used to feeding myself quite well without the intervention of a can opener, however convenient such a labor-saving device may be. When it comes to handouts, Midnight Louie is no slouch.

Monday morning, even before Miss Temple Barr arises, I return to cruising the streets. I am not afraid of work if it is amiable. Within my first hour away from home I collect a sixth of a Big Mac, a melted Dairy Queen in a plastic lid and four olives.

It is while wandering from way station to way station that I pass the Thrill 'n' Quill Bookstore, its windows thronging with murderous tomes and one sleeping tom of my acquaintance.

By stretching full length I can tap the plate glass right where Ingram's pale pink nose is pressing. He starts awake as if bee-stung, ears askew and rabies tags clashing at his collarline. When he recognizes me, he shows his teeth in a less than cordial welcome.

This cuts no ice with Miss Maeveleen Pearl, proprietress of the Thrill 'n' Quill. She bustles over to let the poor sot out. "Oh, Ingram," I hear her croon as the door opens. (Miss Maeveleen Pearl never speaks but in a syrupy tone that would glue most people's lips together.) "Your little friend has come calling again. Isn't that sweet? Besides, I wanted to arrange Baker and Taylor in that window anyway. There you go."

Ingram, out the door in a jiffy, is still growling when I approach him. He sits on the concrete stoop and angrily boxes his muzzle with his mitts. This ritual of keeping his nose clean seems more along the lines of slapping some sense into himself, which he could use, in my opinion.

He is in no mood to thank me for his sudden furlough, but watches the display window sourly as Miss Maeveleen Pearl sets about arranging a pair of stuffed Scottish fold–type felines amongst the books.

Her devotion to these inert bozos, Ingram tells me, borders on the psychotic.

"A human must have her hobby," I reply, reaching out to give

50

PUSSYFOOT

Ingram's rabies tags a jingle. "Now quit whining and tell me what is happening in this town of late."

Ingram is the scholarly sort who thinks nothing of drifting off over the entertainment section of the *Las Vegas Review-Journal*. It is amazing what he can commit to memory without even trying.

Well, he says, spreading his toes so as to count off on his six digits (Ingram's forebears are prone to quirky genetic modifications), the Cat's Meow across from the Sands has quite a few layabouts on the premises, but the word is the proprietor is a kind of Carrie Nation.

This is bad news. While I have no time for Scottish folds, in the flesh or the fabric, I am partial to a touch of scotch in my milk now and again.

"What kind of Carrie Nation is she?" I inquire. There is a cute kitten or two at the Cat's Meow I have my eye on.

She is a crusader, and not the rabbit kind, Ingram replies. Certain dudes of an uninhibited nature have been disappearing from the alley behind the Cat's Meow and when they show up again, they are singing soprano. Not, Ingram adds snootily, that there is anything wrong with a higher register.

He is one to talk, having long since sacrificed his masculine prowess to the joys of being a kept cat.

"Dudes are being swept off the street and returned minus their operative parts?" I demand in horror and something of a falsetto.

Ingram nods sagely, his old-gold eyes glimmering. It is true, he says, so help him, Havana Brown. The atrocities, he goes on to say, are part of a pet population control program.

"If they want to control the pet population," I growl, "why do they not stick to pets, instead of snatching innocent dudes from off the street and abstracting their oysters? Have you any news that will not turn my stomach?"

Kitty City, says he, is offering a new revue of naked talent.

I report that I am not interested in transfeline entertainment.

Too bad, says he. Then you will not be interested in the fact that the Goliath Hotel is hosting a competition of striptease artists of all sexes including questionable.

"Why should I be?" I reply.

Here Ingram looks unbearably sly and runs his barbed pink tongue over his scanty whiskers. He hears, he goes on, that Miss Savannah Ashleigh, the film star, will help judge the action at the striptease competition. Is not this the same Savannah Ashleigh who visited my old stomping grounds, the Crystal Phoenix Hotel and Casino, in palmier days, along with her companion, a foxy number of the female persuasion named Yvette?

I stare at Ingram as if seeing him for the first time. The name "Yvette" hits my ears like a bouncer's fists. Yvette. The Divine Yvette. I hear again her subtle throaty voice, see the infinitely changing kaleidoscope of her baby blue-greens, feel sable-tipped silver fur brushing against my broad shoulders. . . .

The Divine Yvette is back in town.

Wait, Ingram yodels in his scratchy voice as I rocket down the street, headed for the Goliath Hotel, do you not wish to learn about the exotic goldfish display at the Mirage—?

I pay no mind. If there is any force on earth that can distract me from the pursuit of food, it is the Divine Yvette.

In fact, even thinking of her in retrospect as I lounge here in silken comfort in the lap of Miss Temple Barr's luxury almost makes me forget the shocking events of the past twelve hours, in which I have slipped the gentle bonds of my little doll's attentions. I doze off, dreaming of crystal ashtrays brimming with champagne, catnip caviar and a world-class lady friend with whom to share them.

The Cookie Crumbles

Overhead fluorescent lights lent Crawford Buchanan's normally pasty complexion a sallow tinge. The breath-mint-green hospital gown did nothing for him, either, except to tinge his silver hair yellow. Temple rebelled at expressing false sentiments, so her "Gosh, Crawford, you look . . . tired" avoided coming out "awful" only by a hair.

He lay in the industrial-strength hospital bed, looking puny and pathetic. Temple unconsciously lowered her voice to a genuinely solicitous level. "How are you feeling? Is it . . . serious?"

"The heart attack? I'll live." His voice was still a surprisingly deep basso he played like a cello. "The murder? If they nail me for it, I may not live," he added gloomily.

"You? A murderer?" Temple hovered on the brink of laughter. "Victim, maybe, but perpetrator—"

"Listen, T.B., you've been where I'm sitting, or lying, rather. I found the goddam body! You know how that looks."

"PR people may kill stories, but they don't kill people. Nobody could seriously suspect you."

"How about Lieutenant Too-tall Molina?"

"She *is* the suspicious sort," Temple conceded.

"Listen. I want you to take over for me."

"No way! I turned the job down, remember? Why should I take it now that it's a hot potato? Besides, Molina doesn't like me, either."

Even in a hospital bed Buchanan managed to preen. He rolled his big, cow-brown eyes. "Oh, she likes me, all right. She just suspects me, too."

Temple strangled a groan in view of the surroundings. "Why? Lieutenant Molina may have a suspicious nature by profession, but what would make her think you particularly would kill a stripper? And how was it done, anyway?"

He paled, if that was possible. The pallor emphasized his dark, thick eyebrows and the languid-lashed eyes as melting as a panda's. His hand clenched the slack sheet over his chest.

"She was in the dressing room. Alone. Very alone. I took her for a costume at first . . . only the lights around one mirror were on and all the costumes glitter so you can't tell what's real from what's unreal. She was hanging—"

He stopped, shut his eyes, the lashes resting on the puckered bags beneath them. Temple kept quiet, moved despite her dislike of Buchanan, recalling the moment a few weeks before when she had found herself sprawled across the corpse of Chester Royal in the Las Vegas Convention Center booth.

"How . . . how was she hanging?" Temple made herself ask.

His eyes opened slowly, but the words came out staccato. "G-string. Rhinestone. G-string."

"How? From . . . what did it hang?"

"I don't know! You think I looked that close? I'd gone nearer to see what was wrong, what—it—was that was turning there silently like a becalmed wind chime. Feathers fluttering, rhinestones twinkling. Looked like a damn Mardi Gras figure on a float. An animated costume. But it wasn't—animate or a costume."

Temple sat down on the varnished wooden seat of the tasteful Swedish modern visitor's chair, the shape and surface so conspiratorially slick that she thought she might slide right off it onto the floor. She'd seen a lot of dressing rooms at the Guthrie Theater and, before that, in amateur theatrical playhouses. She understood the dramatic quiet of an empty dressing room and its eerie occupation of hanging costumes. But this costume was empty only by virtue of death. She realized she was shaking a little, like a hanging costume in the stuffy, backstage air.

"Who was she?" she asked.

"Just a stripper." Buchanan's answer shocked Temple out of her newfound empathy. "One of the girls."

"Why should Molina suspect you of doing it, even though you found her?"

His languid eyes eeled away from her direct gaze. "I . . . might have . . . asked her out."

"Asked her out? Or picked her out? Did you walk up and ask her out, or did you sidle by and play with her hair, the edges of her feathered costume, then glide away before she could object? Did you hang around, annoy her, make a nuisance of yourself? Get noticed by everyone else?"

"What are you trying to do? Turn a few friendly overtures into a sexual harassment case?"

"Listen, C.B., your idea of friendly overtures to the opposite sex falls somewhere between a boa constrictor's and a caveman's."

The heavy hospital door hushed open. Temple whirled, hoping a nurse hadn't caught her being unsympathetic with a sick man.

The overhead florescent pulled the features of the dish-water-brunette who entered into a lugubrious mask, but she was no nurse. A teenage girl with a sullen, pimple-dotted face shadowed her.

The two advanced to Buchanan's bedside.

"Merle," he introduced the woman, as if her first name were all that was necessary.

"We'd gone to the cafeteria for a bite," Merle apologized to Temple. "I came straight from work and never stopped at home." She glanced with quick concern to Buchanan. "What about your fish? When should I feed them?"

"Tonight when you get home will be fine," he said shortly.

The silence stretched out like a patient anesthetized upon a table. Temple studied the mousy woman across the white sheets. A pleasant, unstriking face. Little makeup. Why did downtrodden women always have pale eyelashes, so their sad eyes floated in a flesh-colored aspic that emphasized their bland passivity?

The young girl, the woman's daughter by every other feature, on the other hand, burned. Burning, Blackboard Jungle teenage eyes missed nothing and judged everything. Everyone.

The pitiful twosome should have strengthened Temple's resolve to keep out of Buchanan's business. Instead they sealed her fate.

"Okay," she told the man in the bed linens. "I'll go on with the show. It's being held at the Goliath, isn't it?"

He nodded.

"My favorite hotel," Temple added darkly. The Mystifying Max had just finished an engagement at the Goliath when he disappeared.

She tried to edge inconspicuously out of the room, but Merle and daughter followed her out into the hall.

"He says he'll be all right," Temple repeated dutifully.

Merle nodded, her wan features slack with worry. "The heart attack was minor, although it'll be an adjustment. The notoriety—"

"He loves it," the teenager put in.

Temple searched discreetly for a wedding ring on Merle's left hand and found none. The daughter's ears dangled an intriguing array of silver scorpions, spiders and peace symbols. Her features were still blurred in her pale, blotched skin, but Temple discerned some fine bones and a future beauty peeking past the studied disdain that drew her youthful lips and eyes dolefully down.

"Quincey—!" Merle admonished her daughter. "C.B. has had some terrible shocks. Can't you forget your everlasting wrangles even in the face of illness?"

The girl looked down at her thin arms folded over her barely there breasts. She gave no answer except the unspoken "Oh, Mother . . ." screaming from her stance and expression.

Sweet sixteen, and stuck with Crawford Buchanan for a stepfather of sorts, Temple guessed, for this gangly, tall girl could never be his natural issue.

"Thank you, Miss Barr." Merle ignored her daughter's disregard. "C.B.'s spoken of you so frequently. I knew we could count on you."

"No trouble," Temple assured her insincerely. She glanced once more at Quincey, who was leaning against the wan wall making Kim Basinger lips, then left on the echoing click of her high heels.

A live-in girlfriend, she mused in disgust, but that didn't prevent him making bachelor noises. Maybe this murder would scare Crawford Buchanan straight and make him stick closer to home. Not that Quincey would appreciate that. Temple considered. There was something worse than having Crawford Buchanan for a quasiprofessional colleague. Oh, to be in the Terrible Teens and have Crawford Buchanan for a stepfather!

Chapter 8

Dance of Death

I have drifted off again, at which I am most adept, until I am unduly awakened by Miss Temple Barr's impetuous return.

"Oh, Louie!" my little doll cries upon finding me ensconced on her queen-sized bed in a dark lit only by the night-light.

It is not the greeting of joy and affection it should be, although she promptly sweeps me into her arms.

"My Hanae Mori silk dress!" she wails, as little dolls will when they are irked for no good reason.

I am deposited upon a cold, uncrumpled portion of the comforter while she snatches my warm, comfy resting place from the bed. She waltzes around the room holding it at arm's length—first to the light switch, which she flicks on, the better to shrink my wide-open irises into thin, light-bedazzled slits.

While I am blinking in confusion she is brushing at the garment in question and interrogating the air. "*Why* did he have to lie right there? Why did he have to paw it into a ball?"

PUSSYFOOT

Miss Temple Barr may have her strong points, but an understanding of the masculine feline mind is not among them.

She hangs the injured dress in the closet and takes off her high heels as if sinking three inches in height mirrors an inner droop. "I know it was not intentional, Louie," she announces with a sigh, "any more than Crawford Bloody Buchanan meant to find a body and have a heart attack. But it is aggravatingly inconvenient."

Having expressed herself, she proceeds to disrobe while I take a gentlemanly clue and turn myself to face in another direction. Miss Temple Barr's dramatic return, and dislodging of myself, has reminded me of my own trauma of the morning.

I picture my discreet arrival at the Goliath via the rear service entrance. The approach is the most delicate maneuver. My sable silhouette shows up to great advantage against the pale, sun-washed exterior. I pause in the shadow of a Dumpster and watch the door with narrowed eyes. Legs come and go, and finally one pair comes out followed closely by a linen trolley. Before you can say "Nostradamus," I am darting past the racket of the wheels and merging into the interior shade.

My feet have pounded most of the Strip's hardest and hottest pavements, but they are not too jaded to appreciate a cool expanse of vinyl tile. I pussyfoot down the hall, my nose for news leading me past the clattering hotel kitchens and into the guest areas. Here my already silent steps are buffered by plush, well-padded carpeting in a pattern I can only describe as "Hairball Revisited" or "Goliath Buffet Regurgitated." It is a good thing that my breed is not fussy about colors (except in the instance of choosing flattering backgrounds), or I would be seasick and add to the psychedelic ambience underfoot.

No one notices my presence. I am a past master at darting into the dark side of a cigarette stand, into the shadowy underside of a potted palm, around the nearest corner.

The unmistakable blurt of an audio tape and stop-and-go chatter of human voices leads me to a ballroom filled with scattered folding chairs, enough tangled industrial-strength electric cords to give Indiana Jones a snake attack and more long bare female legs of the human sort than have been seen since Busby Berkeley choreographed thirties musicals. Most of these unappealingly hairless gams are upheld by shoes of such skyscraper ambitions that my little doll's collection looks like London flats.

I dart from the safety of chair to chair, pausing only to sniff the smoke and sweat-perfumed air for a scent I will never forget: the faintly powdered pheromones unique to the Divine Yvette.

And still the high heels come and go, talking of feathers and furbelows. Then, while crouching nonchalantly underneath a camera tripod (nobody faced with a camera ever looks *down*), I find my heart doing a double axel. A piquant feline face haloed in rhinestones is nose-to-nose and toe-to-toe with yours truly. One inhalation and I know that fraud is afoot. This vision exudes an odor of well-worn Dr. Scholl's instep liners. I see that the shining eyes and sleek body, the tail so cunningly curling up like smoke, add up to a mere satin doll. Like the faux Baker and Taylor, my nearby vixen is a dummy: a shoe masquerading as a fabulous feline. It turns in its sassy tracks and minces on.

I proceed to make my weary way around the crowded room. By now the many scents pleasant and not-so have merged into one overpowering human stink. I retreat in my staccato way, from chair to chair, avoiding the sudden roll of equipment over any of my extremities. One chair proves my undoing when it becomes the center of a flurry of activity.

"Here," booms a deep male voice, picking up my shelter.

I run along under it and just miss having my rear foot punctured when the chair is suddenly slammed to carpet again. I hunch beneath its shelter, ears and eyes alert for any other sudden dislocations.

"You can sit here, Miss Ashleigh," the same loathsome voice announces.

Ashleigh? What a sweet sound. A swirl of floral fabric tents me with blessed concealment. A pair of pearl-embedded Lucite wedgies come to a prim stop before my nose.

"Thank you, luv," a purring contralto voice says. "Where is my margarita—?"

"Here," a female voice answers with a quick, oncoming shuffle of ballet-slipper flats.

PUSSYFOOT

Feet dance attendance on the occupant of my chair, Savannah Ashleigh herself.

I contain my own purr of satisfaction.

"Ah," Miss Savannah Ashleigh allows. The retinue holds a respectful silence.

"These are, of course," says the loudspeaker man, "tech rehearsals to familiarize the crews with the routines."

A camera dollies over like a hungry mechanical mongrel. I sense Miss Savannah Ashleigh sitting up straighter, even as her voice burbles on.

"Tech rehearsals are the best time to get the feel of a show," she pronounces. "Some of my directors say I do my best work at the rehearsals." Laughter hearty, hers. Laughter polite, her attendants. Laughter silent and unconvinced, mine. "Do you want me to turn left? Right?" Her feet swivel so fast that one translucent heel nearly kicks me in the kisser. "Three-quarters is my best angle."

I hear the murmur of some camera jockey.

"My—what? Hat. Oh, cat! Of course, my Darling Yvette. Yes, I still travel with her."

I hunch forward, all ears.

"Not here. She was sleeping. I left her carrying case in the dressing room. I could send someone for her—" Said hopefully, even as the camera dollies back and away. "Rats!" Miss Savannah Ashleigh hisses to herself, and inadvertently to me.

Or rather, to my decamping posterior. I, too, am dollying away, slinking among the oblivious feet and chair legs, heading for the dressing room and my own particular Sleeping Beauty. I am a habitué of the chorus girls' dressing rooms at every hotel in town. Nobody is as generous as a hoofer, especially to a dude who has to pound the pavement day in and day out with four feet instead of two.

So I am down the back stairs before you can say "Stage door Louie." No guard is on duty yet: the show doesn't start until seven P.M. Since everybody else is beating their feet on the ballroom floor, the windowless depths beneath the stage are dark and deserted, except for muslin-shrouded costume racks lining the concrete corridors. I stick my puss in a few dressing rooms and encounter—more shoes, these in a scattered, un- paired condition; more chairs askew; the poignant twinkle of sequin and rhinestone on abandoned headdresses; the tremu- lous nod of ostrich feathers dyed a color no self-respecting ostrich would claim.

At last a sound draws my alert ears to another dressing room. I hear a shoe scrape across the bare floor—no sense carpeting a room where spilled cosmetics will soon make it a twin to the deliberately nauseous carpet upstairs. I also hear the apparent gargling of a parrot—ugly birds with uglier beaks and claws.

I dart inside the door and shelter under a row of identical magenta sequined Flamenco gowns with turkey-feather ruffles. A feather tangles in my eyelash, then tickles my nose. I am about to sneeze when I spot a pink canvas bag under the opposite chair. In emblazoned silver letters, I read the name "Yvette." Behind the pink mesh side lies a dim form.

I control my impending sneeze. No princess wishes to be awakened by an asthmatic prince.

Then the idiotic parrot squawks again and a scuffle erupts in the dressing room's far corner. How dare a scaly, foul-mouthed bird disturb the Divine Yvette's rest? I turn with a swallowed snarl to the site of the disturbance to see two pair of human legs, dancing. They are doing what is known as an Apache dance in chicer circles than I move in, for the black-clad legs are moving purposefully, with vigor. Her naked gams, however, hang mostly limp, kicking idly at the black-garbed shins.

Then I look up, through an undergrowth of fuchsia feathers and past the constellation of sequins. They are not dancing. I glimpse the woman's face, painted into a slightly iridescent mask of beauty that Miss Savannah Ashleigh might envy. Her head is at an odd angle and her apparent partner has lifted her high in his arms, as if she were a ballerina. She seems to be hanging from a necklace of stars with a sad, forlorn tilt to her motionless mask of a face.

Her partner—only a vague back and black legs—scrabbles away, yet she hangs there, swings slowly, idly from an invisible hook. I smell not only the faint, sleeping fragrance of the Divine Yvette but the slow heavy odor of fear. And death.

I duck back under the feathers, Black Legs scissoring past me so fast that a black sneaker as silent as the Grim Reaper stubs its toe on a chair leg. The chair screeches across the concrete, like chalk on a blackboard. Black Legs curses softly, lurches toward the pale pink ark in which slumbers the Divine Yvette, then kicks—kicks!—the Divine Yvette's sanctuary into the wall and runs from the dressing room.

I am across the floor in one mighty leap, pawing the pink canvas away from the wall. I hear a plaintive, sleepy cry from within. Had the Divine Yvette not been curled up in utter relaxation, such a blow could have been devastating.

The dim light reflects from a dawning glimmer of opening eyes. A cool pink triangle of naked skin presses against the barrier mesh. We inhale deeply, knowing each other in an instant.

The Divine Yvette calls my name in a dazed, bewildered voice. . . .

I can resist no longer. I must sneeze. Being the gentleman that I am, I turn my head—and look up to see the dancing woman suspended above me, her melancholy, tilted face looking down on the reunion of Midnight Louie and the Divine Yvette with the open, empty eyes of a forsaken puppet.

The puppetmaster who abandoned her will rue the moment he meddled with the Divine Yvette, or my name is not Midnight Louie.

Chapter 9

Perfect Recall

"Brother John, I'm scared."

"So am I. You've got to leave."

"Five more days. If I can just make it for five more days! I'm trying to be so quiet, so perfect, but sometimes that makes him worse."

"You can't win with him, whatever you do. Except by leaving."

"Yeah, but I've held on this long. Thirty-five-years-old last April. You'd think I would have learned something by now."

"You have. You've got an economic way out now. All you have to do is take it."

"They hang on, though, just like the last one. They treat you like scum, call you a slut, but the minute you try to leave, you're suddenly too good to let go of."

"He's sick. He needs you to be sick, too."

"But I'm not gonna let him drag me down, not anymore. Damn man. He's not nice like you. He doesn't listen, just . . . slam, bang, pow."

"I'm paid to listen."

"That's not why you do it, though, is it? That's all right, don't answer. We're supposed to be talkin' about me, not you. Me and my 'problem.' It'd be nice to meet you, though, someday when I'm outa here, Brother John. Maybe I'll call you up and we can have lunch and talk about the bad old days."

"I don't think—"

"Probably rules against it. Maybe it's better. I've told you things that make me ashamed."

"You don't have to feel ashamed for what someone else does."

"No, and it's him, isn't it? Always him. Always mean, always running me down. They always seem like Prince Charming at first, and then, Godzilla. Maybe Godzilla's too nice. He's been real quiet lately. He hates what I'm doing Saturday. He wants to stop me. I can see it building up; he's yelling about the country going to hell and no chance for white men and women are nothing but whores—why does he hate so much?"

"He's afraid some of what he hates might be inside him."

"Him? Afraid? Excuse me for laughing. But yeah, maybe laughing will help. He's pathetic, really, big son of a gun with nothing better to do than beat up on some little woman. He's scum. Guess you can't comment on that. I'm not going to be afraid of him anymore. I won't!"

"The best thing would be to leave now. Tonight."

"Oh, not tonight. Not tomorrow night, or tomorrow night, or tomorrow night. But a couple nights after that, yeah. Whether I win or not. Yeah, I'm gone. Thanks. I feel less . . . nervous now. If I didn't have you to call, and be silly and scared to, I don't know what I'd do."

"I'm here to help."

"You do, you do. You help me not be afraid all the time."

Chapter 10

Vamp of
Savannah

First thing Tuesday morning, the aqua Storm idled silently at the driveway leading to the Goliath Hotel, the engine struck with what Temple imagined was automotive awe.

Against the bright blue sky loomed the silhouette of a man straddling the road and sidewalk—a giant three stories tall. Between his braced legs must pass pedestrian and passenger alike. Temple gazed through the deep-tinted windshield at gargantuan thighs vanishing into the shadow of what charitably could be called a kilt, though it more resembled a sumo wrestler's diaper.

Lines about "that colossal wreck," Shelley's fallen statue of Ozymandias in the poem of the same title, filled her head. The actual inspiration for this overblown anthropomorphic archway was the Colossus of Rhodes, a lost wonder of the ancient world. Beyond the huge figure sprawled the garish bulk of the Goliath Hotel, a Theme Park from Hyperbole dedicated to the purging of any iota of good taste impertinent enough to rear its modest head within view of the Goliath's blissfully gauche patrons.

Temple tapped the Storm's gas pedal. The sleek little car whisked under the colossus and up the sweeping drive (hotel drives in Las Vegas are compelled by law to sweep). It stopped under an entry canopy lined with yawning ribs of mirrored copper that reminded Temple of the whale in *Pinocchio* about to devour the unwary. This was as apt an image for the entryway to a Las Vegas hotel-casino as any.

Eight A.M. sharp, read her Big Ben–size watch face.

"I'll be getting a ramp pass from hotel PR," she told the uniformed valet who leaped to open the Storm's door.

"Uniformed" was overdoing it. Valets at the Goliath wore gilt sandals, white linen Egyptian-style pleated kilts and short blond Bo Derek–dreadlock wigs. Tens, unfortunately, they were not.

Temple pushed the seat all the way back to wrestle her overloaded tote bag out of the car, then waited to see how the valet would maneuver that getup into the diminutive Storm. His efforts showed almost as much hairy leg as the colossus, but Temple was more interested in making sure his brass wristbands didn't scratch the dashboard. She still had forty-three months left to pay on the car.

Although the Goliath Hotel was one of Las Vegas's many landmarks, she hadn't visited it since Max had performed here. She strode briskly through the glittering carousel of copper-framed revolving doors. Their glass panels showed outsiders a mirrored face, but gave insiders a see-through view. The click of her heels on the marble floor sounded reassuringly confident, as it always did.

Unlike most hotels, Las Vegas hostelries feature discreetly hidden registration desks. What welcomes guests is not the bellman, but ringing ranks of slot machines and the chime of quarters washing down durable but greedy stainless-steel throats.

Temple blinked and took off her dark glasses while her

eyes adjusted to the deliberately dim interior. Gambling meccas cultivate an eternal three A.M. atmosphere, the better to lure visiting Goldilocks into trying to find the "just right" slot or craps table. "If you don't succeed, try, try again" was truly the house motto.

She crossed the carpet—burgundy imprinted with camel-colored . . . er, camels—aware of massive chandeliers glimmering above her, of slot machines spitting out a silver lava of coins here and there for lucky players.

The dim and smoky cocktail area lay beyond the first circle of slot machines. Veiled waitresses shimmied among low divans and gilt camel-saddle cocktail tables. Beyond them tiny, gleaming fairy lights trimmed the bare trees that bordered the Goliath's most infamous feature.

Temple paused beside it—a twelve-foot-wide waterway meandering through a cocktail lounge. At a velvet-roped landing, visitors could embark on an automated ride in miniature red-velvet-lined gondolas. For a few titillating seconds, the gondola route wound through an artificial cave with glow-in-the-dark stars dimpling a Styrofoam-rock ceiling. The attraction was called "The Love Moat."

"Corny," Temple pronounced under her breath with wistful disdain. Max had thought so, too. It hadn't stopped either of them from embarking on a glide into the manufactured dark and a stolen kiss under cover of same.

She sighed and moved on, past a flight of plush-carpeted stairs kept off limits for now by showy red-velvet ropes—the entrance to the Sultan's Palace Theater, where Max had performed. Finally she turned down a nondescript hallway, slipping with relief into the hotel's functional areas. Her goal was the offices of Brad Mitchellson, head PR honcho.

The outer office sported the usual chaos: piles of printed matter occupied every flat surface, including vast portions of the floor and all chair seats.

"You here to see Brad?" the receptionist asked crisply. The only tip-off that this was Las Vegas were her false eyelashes and dagger-length faux fingernails.

Temple's nod resulted in a quick buzz. Mitchellson soon burst through the ajar inner-office door like a warm puppy.

"Temple! Come in. Glad to have you working on this. Great of you to substitute on such short notice. We're in a mess," he finished, leading her into his only slightly less well-papered office. He whisked a stack of brochures from a chair seat so she could sit.

"By 'mess' do you mean the usual"—she gestured at the surroundings as she gratefully slung her tote bag to the floor—"or the killing?"

"Oh, God." He sat.

Like most PR types, his personality was genial and attractive, but today his tie looked like it had never been decently knotted and his short brown razor cut showed the rumpling of harried fingers. He gestured at the green squiggles on his personal-computer screen.

"Trying to outline a new strategy: Life After Death, so to speak. Here's the week's schedule."

Temple took it, glad to have hard data in hand. "So Monday's killing occurred well before the weekend competition?"

"Monday was the first day we had acts scheduled to come in, to start rehearsing and cueing the tech staff. We were starting to line up media exposure, too, ahead of time. Only we got more than we wanted."

"But the choreographed PR isn't needed until the weekend—Friday through Sunday?"

"Right. And we attracted a lot of early interest before Crawford Buchanan even got the job."

"I can imagine," Temple murmured, paging through eight-by-ten black-and-whites—a stunning array of the bare and the beautiful of both sexes. "Quite a variety of acts here."

"This began as a female-only stripper's get-together and contest, but times have changed. Now we have a small men's competition and some novelty categories, including Loving Couples, a thing named Over-Sexty, as we call it, even Bods of a Feather, to cover animal acts."

Temple studied a photograph of an excessively long snake enhancing the anatomically impossible position of a female stripper. "Does the SPCA sanction that?"

Brad smiled as she flashed the photo, looking relaxed for the first time. "No problem. Our only protesters are the usual Holy Rollers and feminists. We welcome them. You know how calling something sin gets the press out in droves."

"Indeedy. God's gift to the struggling PR person. What about the murder, Brad?"

He shrugged beige-shirted shoulders. "You know the routine better than I do, after the ABA thing. Cops underfoot. Mucho interviewing. The strippers are shocked, of course, and they were all nervous to begin with. Winning a Rhinestone G-string means something in this business. Some contestants have rehearsed for months. These people put everything they have into coming up with a mind-boggling act."

"So I see," Temple commented, "but I didn't think it was minds strippers were out to boggle."

"You still have problems with the ambience?"

"Call it a middle-class hang-up. What's the difference between a bare-breasted show girl wearing a G-string and most of an ostrich—and a stripper? Why do I feel that the subtle sexual tease of a nightclub show is classier than the frank titillation of a strip joint?" Temple's hands hit the top of his desk in concert. "I'm going to use this assignment to find out. I'll interview the competitors, work up some angles on how normal they are, where they come from—geographically and mentally."

Brad eyed her cautiously from under an appealingly dislodged lock of brown hair. "You going to ask about the murder?"

Temple shook her head. "Only if they want to bring it up. It's none of my business. We're all better off putting this behind us."

"I hope you can convince the local media of that." Brad swooped a fan of papers into one pile. "The murder made

the wire services, too. Here are the releases I'd hammered
out before the competition people hit town. Buchanan
didn't have a chance to put anything in writing. How's his
heart, by the way?"

"Hard as ever," Temple muttered before giving her
public statement on that topic. "He seems to be recovering well," she told Brad.

Mitchellson chuckled as he showed her out. "Probably
better than you will be by next Sunday. It should be an
interesting week. Ask for Lindy when you get to the ballroom area. It's off the Sultan's Palace."

"I know." Temple stuck the fat sheaf of papers in her
ever-present tote bag and headed down the hall. Did she
ever.

Lindy. Sounded breezy, minty, girl-next-doorsy.

"Hi," said the person answering to that name once
Temple was inside the ballroom. "I'm coordinator for
WHOOPE, a strippers association."

"WHOOPE? How did you come up with that
acronym?"

Lindy made a wry face. "The same way we have to do
our jobs; really had to bust our butts, and bump and grind
it out. WHOOPE stands for—are you ready?—We Have
an Organization Of Professional Ecdysiasts."

"It should really be WHAOOPE," Temple had to
point it, "but who's going to argue?"

"Right. And the WHOOPEs are all glad you're doing
this after all. We liked your Guthrie Theater background.
It lends class to our annual endeavor. This"—she gestured
at the roomful of leotard-clad women playing with exotic
bits of costuming, props and their own spinal alignment—
"is theater."

Lindy shot sleek, airheaded stripper stereotypes from
hell to Sheboygan. Her cigarette-roughened voice emitted
from a buxom brunette frame clad in an oversized Vir-
ginia Slims sweatshirt and black stirrup leggings that disappeared into dirty white jogging shoes of no particularly
chic manufacture; in a word, Ked tennies. She gestured

with strong, corded hands that ended in unvarnished fingernails clipped to sickle-moon tips.

Temple eyed the assemblage, and the scurrying, blue-
jeaned tech men brushing unconcernedly past straining
flank and fanny.

"Theater," she repeated obediently. That was how Max
had always described magic shows. Just theater.

"Would you like to meet one of our celebrity judges?"

"Doesn't the competition begin Saturday night?"

"Yeah, but this judge hit town early. She's making a
movie about a stripper, and the film crew is getting canned
background shots while she soaks up 'atmosphere.' "

Temple gingerly threaded her way over the thick cables
veining the floor; at least they obscured the vomitous
pattern of the carpeting.

Metal folding chairs sat at odd angles all around the
room. Some were faced together so long-stemmed dancers
could put up their warmer-wrapped legs. Only one chair
was a zebra-pattern upholstered bastard Egyptian number
dragged in from the lobby.

On the clashing zigzags of black and beige posed a
woman with air-whipped, ash blond hair and a pert little
Barbie face on a long, slender neck. Temple rapidly took
in her outfit: an off-the-shoulder cowl-collared pink angora top and white leather miniskirt that lived up to its
name more than any patch of hide she had ever seen.
Then, omigod, pink pearlized patent leather ankle boots
with four-inch heels that could only have come from a
fifties-vintage Frederick's of Hollywood catalog!

"Savannah Ashleigh, of course," Lindy's Bogart growl
announced behind Temple. "This is our new PR person,
Temple Barr."

Savannah Ashleigh was a woman after Temple's heart.
Her first glance went to the feet. Temple's high-summer
white sandals with the three-inch magenta patent heels and
the electric blue, magenta and emerald pompon on the toe
caused not a ripple of envy on that gorgeously static face.

"Hello," said Savannah Ashleigh. She spoke in an absolute monotone. It was not easy to convey such lethargic diction in two syllables. "I don't want too much publicity early in the week; save it for the competition finale. I have the most divine wardrobe, and my hairdresser doesn't arrive until Thursday. He was most tiresome about doing some visiting royalty."

"Perhaps I could ask you some questions now to save time later?"

Savannah's shrug drew the eye to firm, smooth shoulders dusted with pearlescent powder.

Temple dragged a metal folding chair over a small clot of cables and plunked it down just far enough from the actress so she wouldn't be asphyxiated by fumes from her least-favorite scent, Emeraude.

"What kind of atmosphere are you hoping to gather for your new film?" Temple began gamely, notepad in lap and no. 2 pencil poised in hand.

Savannah Ashleigh rolled the fingers of her right hand as if balancing an invisible ball upon them. "Um, mood stuff, you know what I mean?"

"You're . . . ah, a . . . method actress, Miss Ashleigh?"

"Uh-huh."

"Sure sounds like it," Temple added.

"And right now my mood is not good." She paused after this pronouncement, as if expecting somebody to offer to make up for it. Alas, everybody in the room was busy about his or her business. Temple was Savannah's only audience. Her heavy lashes, invisibly implemented, lowered in frustration. "I'm not getting it. The Vibrations. The Ambience. The Core Experience."

"What kind of movie are you doing involving strippers?"

"Film," Savannah corrected with more articulation and energy than she'd shown thus far, so much that the word came out, "fil-mah."

"And my subject is an exotic dancer, not a stripper," she went on. Her hands, the only animated portion of her anatomy at the moment, planted themselves delicately on her bare collarbones. "A wonderful script. So . . . moving. I am trying to find the spiritual center of . . . of all this."

Temple took another look at the prerehearsal chaos and just nodded. "What makes a girl become a stripper?" she asked.

Savannah Ashleigh leaned closer without altering the taut blandness of her expression. Emeraude emitted a powdery, choking scarf of scent that tightened around Temple's throat.

"Some," the actress said in a stage whisper, "are failed dancers. Some are failed women. Most do not look well naked unless they are moving. I, of course, am portraying an exceptional exotic dancer."

"Oh?" Temple searched the computer in her head for the right references. "Mata Hari? Sally Rand? Blaze Starr? Tempest Storm? Come to think of it, I've got a car called that."

"I can't say," Savannah said. "The script is secret. Really, I can't talk." Temple was tempted to agree. "I'm so upset after yesterday."

"Yesterday? You mean—"

"Oh, that awful incident."

"The . . . murder?"

"Yes, we are most upset by it."

"We?"

"My Darling and I. My Darling was in the dressing room when it happened."

"Your . . . darling was a witness? What did he see?"

"*She*," Savannah Ashleigh corrected with as much sternness as a face that resembled a Franklin Mint porcelain of a Southern belle could muster.

"She." Temple considered and found no comeback to that one.

Savannah Ashleigh bent, again from the waist, as if that were the only joint in her lithe but lifeless body, and lifted a rectangular, pale pink canvas bag from the floor beside her chair as Exhibit A.

"They think," she confided in her strange pulsing whisper, "that the miscreant left his footprint on the side. So they dusted my Darling's home-away-from-home."

"Footprint. Dusted. Darling." Temple knew she was babbling, but Savannah Ashleigh didn't seem to notice.

The actress unzipped the top and withdrew a limp handful of silver-gray fur. She arrayed it on her lap, which was mostly lace-patterned white pantyhose.

"Oh, the darling!" Temple exclaimed, understanding.

Savannah's pale blue eyes lit up for the first time. "My Darling Yvette was alone with that monster! She witnessed the entire . . . act. And it was hideous. He . . . hit the poor girl first." Savannah's hand pantomimed a sudden karate chop. "Then he . . . hoisted her unconscious body." Her exquisitely expressive hands mimed lifting an offering to a god. "Then he wrapped a rhinestone G-string around her neck and hung her from a costume hook high"—here the deliberately dusky voice went small and wee, like a little girl's—"on . . . the . . . wall."

She sank back against her upholstered chair back, exhausted. "Yvette saw it all, heard it all. I cannot even begin to guess what trauma this has caused, but I can tell you this: my Darling has not been herself since yesterday morning!" Narrowed eyes and heavy emphasis had Temple retreating even as Emeraude advanced.

Temple lowered her head to examine the downcast darling. For all the fur, Yvette seemed petite. Temple found a calm but breathtakingly wistful face with round aqua eyes outlined in black mascara, and a rose-colored nose emphasized by the same natural accent line.

"She's gorgeous!" Temple admitted with more sincerity than she had managed to muster for Savannah Ashleigh so far. "I have a jet black cat, but he's just a stray."

"Yvette has not a stray hair on her body. She is a purebred shaded silver Persian. Her full name is Diamond Bleu Moon Sirena Yvette."

"Is she . . . adult? She's so small."

"Yvette is two," Savannah said, "and she always travels with Momsy."

"Louie—my cat—is much bigger. He weighs over nineteen pounds."

"Yvette weighs six-point-eight pounds," Savannah said with satisfaction. "She is not designed to be subjected to rude shocks. If I come across the miserable man who murdered that poor girl and apparently kicked my Darling Yvette, I will string him up myself. Personally."

Savannah Ashleigh's long fingernails convulsed on the darling Yvette's coat, but luckily it was thick enough to buffer the owner from its mistress's fury on her behalf.

"The police are sure the killer was a man, then?"

"Who else would kill a woman like that—hang her from her own G-string? Nasty sort of thing a man would do. And I know few women who would kick at a cat."

"But Yvette was in her carrier. He might not have noticed what his foot hit—"

"Not have noticed? Her name is written plain to see right on the top. Y-v-e-t-t-e."

Temple examined the writing in question, a tortured silver script that looked more like "Gavotte" to her. "He might have been in a hurry."

"That is no excuse." Savannah hoisted the limp feline in one hand and draped her into the carrier as if dropping a chiffon scarf into a drawer. "I see that I dare not leave my Darling out of my sight in a common dressing room. My private dressing room was not yet assigned, since the competition has booked the penthouse suite for me. Some of these hotel buffoons tried to hint that I didn't require a downstairs dressing room! Idiots. A moment's carelessness and look what happened. Yvette has not eaten her Free-to-be-Feline since yesterday morning."

"Oh, really," said Temple, interested for the first time. "Have you tried putting some deli turkey over the top?"

"Not even Alaskan salmon will work, although I might have better results with Cajun shrimp. Yvette has a most piquant palette."

"No kidding." Temple leaned nearer for a consultation

across the noxious moat of Emeraude. Feline eating hab-
its—or the lack of them—drove human companions
to desperate measures. "Have you ever thought of
trying . . .?"

Chapter 11

The Naked and the Dead

Temple had learned in her TV reporting days that the best way to sniff out a new environment was to follow her nose for novelty. The born newshound's tenacious curiosity often leads down offbeat byways that no one else would bother investigating; she'd snagged some of her best news stories that way. If she followed her instincts, she'd have a handle on the stripper competition by noon.

Not that Temple really wanted a handle on the dizzying array of activities erupting all over the ballroom. A rapid glance around showed a circus of firm flesh on the half-shell, most wearing little more than a thong-style G-string: Samsons with bulging muscles and oiled tans and long hair tickling their shoulder blades; Delilahs with thin thighs and flat stomachs and breasts that were anything but. The current robust, hirsute view made the trendiest health-club exercise floor seem populated by dull and flaccid duds.

All of these beautiful people in motion were understudying Narcissus, gazing raptly into perimeter mirrors as they stretched muscles and studied costumes under the overhead spotlights. Taken together, they seemed larger than life, not just because they all conveyed a kind of in-person, airbrushed comeliness, but because even most of the women were model-tall.

Temple felt like Pinocchio at the fair, an undersized stranger out of her depth and in danger of succumbing to something, even if it was only amazement. Her gaze inventoried the huge ballroom while she decided who to approach first: the Amazonian miss with Raggedy Ann red hair who was affixing helium-filled balloons to her skimpy bikini, or the apparently naked, tattooed muscleman emerging from the bottom half of a gorilla suit.

"Barr, is it?" a male voice behind her said, gruffly.

She turned, expecting Billy Goat himself in person. She was relieved to face one of the few fully clothed men in the room. However, a peach knit shirt under a Madras plaid sport jacket paired with black trousers was no advertisement for the post-Eden advantages of clothing. Once past the color clash, she saw a man in his thirties: good-looking in an aggressive, humorless blue-collar way.

"Ike Wetzel," he introduced himself. "Lindy said you were good at your job, but I might as well tell you I woulda got along with Buchanan better. I see enough of broads all day in my work."

"What is your work?" Temple asked, knowing that a self-directed question turneth away wrath, or at least sour preconceptions.

"I run Kitty City."

She looked blank.

"On Paradise Road."

"Oh, the topless place. You've got the sign showing cats in anatomically incorrect positions."

"Right." His muddy brown eyes flicked her up and down, an unconscious gesture designed either to take in what she was wearing, or to mentally take it off. "I'm cosponsoring this competition thing. A lot of my girls have their hopes pinned on it. I don't want this murder messing up their chances."

"It sounds to me like the only person this murder has messed up so far is the victim."

"Let's keep it that way," Wetzel suggested. He frowned, an expression that came easy to the permanent furrow between his dark brows even when he was trying to look genial, which he wasn't at the moment. "It's bad enough that we got cops all over the premises. Your job is to get the attention off the corpse and back on the corpuscles—on what every red-blooded guy wants to know about the greatest strippers in the world."

"I understand," Temple said, "but aren't men competing, too?"

"Yeah, a few." Wetzel snorted his opinion of that trend. "Separately, though. Concentrate on the gals; they draw the real dough. Male strippers are a passing fancy, except in the gay clubs. And even in the straight clubs, broads don't tip as good as guys do."

"Maybe women don't get the same service," Temple answered coolly, recognizing a moment too late that she had let herself in for any number of double entendres.

Not to worry. Ike Wetzel wouldn't recognize an opening for a double entendre if it parlay-vouzed Francais with a Milwaukee accent and asked him to dance. Down-the-middle-of-the-bowling-lane kind of guys don't notice linguistic detours.

"Women's hearts just aren't in it," he commented disdainfully. "Watching guys strip is good for a giggle when they're out in a gaggle, but they're not connoisseurs of the art." He pronounced it "con-no-sirs." "So lay off the guys and the old dames; stick to the foxy chicks."

"Any other advice?" Temple's temper simmered behind her most professional facade. Ike Wetzel seemed as impervious to veiled indignation as he was to treading on professional toes.

"Well—" He no doubt intended his knowing smirk to be a confidential grin. "Off the record, put your time in on my girls. They do real well at these things. If you're nice to me, I might even be able to tip you off early who's gonna win."

"Mr. Wetzel, if my job included being nice to everybody, I wouldn't get anything done."

"Just letting you in on who's who around here. Buchanan knew the score."

"Exactly what did Buchanan know?" a new voice asked sharply. The voice was low, an excellent thing in a woman, but hardly soft and gentle, and that was an even more excellent thing in a Las Vegas Metropolitan Police Department homicide lieutenant.

Wetzel turned, his eye whites widening as he found C. R. Molina regarding him with an expression even more perfectly deadpan than his own.

"Buchanan knew—knows—the clubs, the scene," he sputtered. "You know what I mean, Lieutenant."

"I hope so." Lieutenant Molina turned deliberately to Temple, her blue eyes narrowing. "You homesick for the ABA, or what?"

" 'Scuse me," Wetzel said, eager to be off. "I gotta take care of some things."

The two women watched him leave in mutual silence, then returned to the business of fencing each other. Molina hadn't changed a bit, Temple saw. She was wearing one of her nondescript neutral-tone poplin suits, even in July—navy, this time. She hadn't shrunk by so much as one of her imposing five-foot-ten inches; she hadn't loosened her by-the-book manner one tiny turn of the screw; and she hadn't plucked one forceful hair from her luxurious black eyebrows.

"I'm filling in for Crawford Buchanan on publicity," Temple told the policewoman, finally answering her ABA jibe.

"Since when does Barr race to the rescue of Buchanan?"

Temple wished that high heels elevated her to more than a scant five-foot-four. "He's had a heart attack," she said with high dignity.

"I'm aware of that. It happened during my interrogation. I repeat: since when do you run to Buchanan's rescue?"

"I know he's a creep, but . . ."

Molina raised her formidable eyebrows, obviously not about to be convinced by the quality of mercy.

Temple shifted her weight to her other heel, and her defense to fiscal issues everybody understands, presumably even police personnel. "The job pays well," she said in steely tones.

"Make up your mind, are you here in the cause of guilt or greed?"

"Maybe I just know how it feels to stumble over a dead body when you're the one who's supposed to keep things running smoothly."

Molina abruptly changed the subject. "Buchanan was badly shaken, though he probably didn't admit it to you. Not a pretty murder."

"Not . . . a suicide?"

Molina's long, disconcerting silence forced Temple to fall into her trap and babble on, giving information instead of getting it. "Hanging seems a cumbersome way of killing someone, but I guess the victim had taken a blow to the head first, so it can't be suicide."

"Why not? The victim could have banged her head while mounting the dressing room chair to position herself by the hook. And how did you know about the head wound?"

"Someone told me."

"Who?"

Temple hated revealing a source, especially a ludicrous one. "Savannah Ashleigh."

"Savannah Ashleigh—? You do get around. How long have you been here?"

"About an . . . hour."

Molina sighed and reached into her side jacket pocket. Temple had never seen the lieutenant carry a purse. What little makeup she wore, and any necessities, must be crammed into her pockets along with a badge and a gun, presumably.

Temple studied the plain-Jane card Molina's fishing expedition produced for her perusal.

"Call me if you hear anything that you think that I don't know," Molina said. "This is another cast-of-thousands murder scene, and I can't afford to ignore rumors. But keep your nose out of the murder investigation." Molina turned to go.

"Wait, Lieutenant! What *do* you know, so that I know what you don't know, and don't try to tell you what you already do know?"

"That's one of those Temple Barr tortuous tunnels of illogic, isn't it? Anyone ever tell you that you were terminally nosy?"

"Nope."

"Then let me be the first. All right, the facts will be in the papers, many of them. You might as well get the proper information from the horse's mouth so you don't go blundering into trouble."

"Could we sit?" Temple asked.

Lieutenant Molina glanced down at Temple's baby-doll shoes and shook her head. "Those things can kill you." But she pulled a vacant folding chair over and sat.

Temple sank onto the abandoned chair behind her. Even sitting, Molina loomed, but at least Temple didn't feel like a tourist overshadowed by the Statue of Liberty freshly togged out in navy poplin.

"I just skimmed the news story last night," Temple admitted. "Who was the victim?"

Molina pulled a narrow-lined notepad from her roomy jacket pocket and flipped through. "Went by the stage name of Glinda North. Real name: Dorothy Horvath. The other strippers say she had a face that would stop even a dead man in his tracks; the manner of death took that

83

away along with her life. Born March 4, 1963, in Tucson, Arizona. Claimed to be twenty-six; birth certificate says thirty. Not much traceable family, schooling, employment record. There rarely is for these women. The clubs, the road, they're home for strippers, a big, extended family."

"And do they have family quarrels?"

Molina smiled tightly and shut her notebook. "Funny you should ask. Most definitely. Over men, over billing, over acts, over costumes. That rhinestone G-string she was found hanging from—"

"How is that possible, Lieutenant? A G-string is pretty skimpy. Is there enough of it to hang from?"

"Men in jail cells have hung themselves from shoelaces. There's plenty of play in a G-string, and most stage G-strings are pretty strong. They're tip-money clips, after all. Plus, the strippers lose that thin thread of decency, and they're violating some state's obscenity laws. That's a jailable offense."

Temple smiled her agreement. "I remember from my Guthrie Theater days in Minneapolis. No matter how delicate they look, stage costumes are made industrial-strength to hold up to repeated wearings. And rhinestones would have to be stitched to some powerful backing, like flesh-colored horsehair netting."

The lieutenant nodded without comment, which told Temple that Molina had investigated her background thoroughly enough to know that Temple had worked PR in regional theater.

"This wasn't just any rhinestone G-string," Molina added.

"There's a difference? You *have* been taking a crash course in burlesque, Lieutenant!"

"A definite difference here. Glinda North won the G-string that killed her two years ago in this same competition. She was making a comeback. The other strippers thought she stood a good chance of winning a second Rhinestone G-string."

PUSSYFOOT

"Like family," Temple repeated slowly, "and like family quarrels. Sibling rivalry. One of the other strippers might have wanted to keep Glinda from competing."

"Just don't forget that when you're tripping through the tulips here in Pastie Land. Keep out of what you don't understand." Molina stood and moved her chair back to its former place, as if anyone would care amid that orchestrated chaos. Maybe Molina did.

Temple frowned, biting her lip, as she imagined what a strangled face would look like: swollen, distorted, discolored? No wonder Crawford had keeled over, especially after seeing someone he had hoped to date—the two-timing rat!—in that condition.

"You don't really think Crawford might have done it?" Temple asked Molina's already retreating navy blue back.

The tall lieutenant turned and paused a few feet away. "Anybody might have done it."

"Not me," Temple couldn't resist pointing out. "This time I didn't find the body."

"But Buchanan did. Rivalry, remember? Maybe you wanted his job. You got it, didn't you?"

"Hey!" Temple was on her feet, indignant. "I turned this puppy down. I was offered it first and refused."

"You did?" Lieutenant Molina stalked back to stare down at Temple. "Why?"

"I find the ambience a little cheap, all right?"

"True, pasties aren't as highbrow as books."

"And I'm not sure women would do this for a living if they weren't exploited."

"What about the men?"

"I don't know," Temple confessed. "I hope to find out."

"Stick to your amateur sociology," Molina advised, amusement seeping through her stoic facade. "Keep out of amateur crime-solving."

"Yes, sir."

Molina no longer looked amused. She turned on her sensible heel—Temple had checked her footwear out:

85

navy-blue, low-heeled matron-issue for fallen arches, ick!—and left Temple teetering atop a coil of heavy cable.

She picked her way among the cables, trying not to let the bulky tote bag overbalance her.

Where to start in such a wonderland of overexposed flesh? Despite Temple's theatrical background, which inured her to casual states of undress backstage, she found this single-minded focus on presenting the naked flesh disconcerting.

She'd have to get over that. Anything Crawford Buchanan could do, she could do better.

In the next hour she met and quizzed a confusing array of acts. Bambi and Thumper, a rare man-woman stripping team, explained that some local ordinances decreed women-only and men-only stripping nights to skirt the X-rated area of live sex shows.

Wholesome and smiling like insurance sellers, the couple sported matching glossy brown tans and bright lime thong-style bottoms. Bambi had submitted to donning a tight, cutoff T-top for the rehearsal, but the thin material left nothing to the imagination but the placement of any identifying marks.

Near the stage, an arresting pair of gilt-haired twins in gold lamé bikinis were mirroring each other's moves through and around the prop of an empty-looking glass frame.

"Bikinis?" Temple asked. She didn't consider beachwear imaginative enough for a stripping costume, despite the fact that some current bathing suits seemed designed to give local decency codes a workout.

The twins immediately posed as if modeling the swimwear, stomachs taut, rears firm, and bosoms high, wide and handsome.

"I'm Gypsy," said one.

"June," trilled the other in the exact same vocal tone.

"Wait'll you see our act," Gypsy added.

"Gold body paint from head to toe," said June.

"And we don't wear the bikini top for our act." Gypsy.

"Just darling little golden cones." June.

"With gold chain tassels." Gypsy.

"Gold paint?" Temple interrupted their informative duet. "Isn't that stuff dangerous? Didn't a body double die from it in *Goldfinger*?"

"We're a body double and we're not dead," June resumed in turn.

"Say," said Gypsy, flashing perfect teeth. "That's cute: Body Double. Maybe we should have named our act that."

"Our name is cute, too," June insisted, executing an eerily identical smile.

Temple tumbled. "What is it?"

"The Gold Dust Twins," they declaimed together, turning cartwheels in opposite directions, so spokes of bare brown legs flashed by.

They finished and came together, clonelike.

"How did you get into stripping?" Temple asked.

"Easy," said Gypsy.

"As pie," June added.

"We did dance and gymnastics together," Gypsy said.

"And cheerleading and modeling." June.

"And our bodies were great." The modest Gypsy.

"And the money is great." The practical June.

"How much?" asked the curious Temple.

The twins regarded each other and shrugged in tune.

"Depends on the quality of the clubs, but five hundred a night," Gypsy said.

"Special dates, up to fifteen hundred." June.

"One thing is sure." Gypsy.

"Beats Doublemint commercials. Have you seen those yucky green maillots the latest models were wearing?" June's expression grew pained.

"Vile," Gypsy agreed, also wincing. "Like fifties girdles."

Temple nodded, too. "You're right. Gold's the only way to go, onstage and off."

She moved on, unable to resist computing what five to

fifteen hundred a night added up to in comparison to her off-again, on-again free-lancer's income. Maybe she could do a Munchkin act. But before she got carried away, there were more mysteries to conquer in the art of the strip-tease.

An earnestly bouncy young woman in a pearl-dotted fuchsia spandex cummerbund that somehow had been stretched to cover the essentials, however barely, top and bottom, answered Temple's question as to how she got started.

"Majorette," said the girl who performed by the name of Racy. "And I played golf and tennis in high school."

She bent over from the waist, hands to the floor, without flexing her knees. Spandex boldly left where spandex had been before, exposing cleavage north and south.

"So you're basically an athlete," Temple hazarded.

Racy stretched her lean ectomorph form into a backward shimmy. "Yeah, I guess you could say so."

Temple left her there, defying gravity, and gingerly approached an Amazon with Cher-black hair tumbling down her lean bare back. Black was her color: thigh-high patent leather boots and a silver-studded wet-look G-string/teddy combination topped with a velvet garter belt. Open-knuckled wrist-length leather gloves and an understated leather crop completed the outfit.

She posed in the mirror, jutting hips in turn, cocking out first one knee, then another, analyzing her looks and movement with concentrated objectivity.

"May I ask your stage name?" Temple said a bit diffidently.

The woman flicked a glance to Temple's notebook. "What are you writing down?"

"Just some notes to myself. I'm doing PR for the competition, but got in late—"

"Oh, you replaced that Buchanan creep."

"Right."

"Well." Shoulders shrugging, the woman returned her

eyes to her image in the mirror and took a straddling stance while flinging her whip-hand behind her head.

This was a big-boned, plain woman, despite her aggressively erotic attire. Temple wondered how much she appealed to men on the town, with her lanky body, bony shoulders and stingy breasts.

"Switch Bitch." The woman threw the words sharply over her shoulder at Temple, like a whip lash.

"I beg your pardon?" Temple responded, bridling. Was the creature inviting her to trade places?

The long, serious face peered past the false fall of lusterless curls. "My stage name," she repeated patiently. "Switch Bitch."

"Oh." Temple nodded and wrote it down, desperately wondering how she could work that into a family-rated press release. Maybe she should stick to mentioning the straight acts, like Randy Candy, Lacy Lavender, or the ever-tasteful Otto Erotica.

She wandered on, clutching her notepad amid a mob carrying far more lethal props, beginning to feel that she was overdressed.

She didn't have to worry about approaching one of the he-men stalking to and fro with musclebound gait: a veritable Hercules stomped into her path, pectoral muscles twitching on his bare and hairless bronzed chest. Hadn't any of these people heard about overexposure to UVs?

"Hi" was his ancient yet unoriginal gambit. "You're new here."

"Yup."

"Don't be shy, little lady. Find a spot and get to work."

"I am. I'm doing PR for the competition, so I'm going around getting a feel for—er, a grip on . . . I'm learning about the contestants."

"Great." He grinned down at her in utter self-satisfaction, blocking her way with his inescapable nudity as well as his formidable physique. As a stray riff from another stripper's nearby boom box surged to a climax, he circled his hips and ground a pelvic bump in her direction.

Temple gazed on massive thigh muscles oiled to mahogany perfection, and a commendably flat groin clothed only in a glossy gold G-string and apparently housing a croquet ball. She was not impressed. She had heard about rock stars and their socks in the crotch trick.

"Ah, very nice," she said, taking advantage of his frozen pose to skitter around and past her human obstacle.

"Hey, don't you want my name?"

The man actually sounded hurt, so Temple stopped a safe distance away, turned and held her pen at the ready.

"Ken," he said, flashing teeth, charm and smoldering eyes. "I'm with Newd Dudes. N-e-w-d. We're the hottest group on the Coast."

"Newd Dudes," Temple repeated. "Shrewd. See ya."

And she clattered away so fast she bumped into someone.

"Oh. Sorry!" Temple recognized the T-shirt. "Lindy, isn't it?"

The woman nodded, glanced back at the still idiotically grinning Newd Dude, then jerked her head toward the ballroom doors. "Listen. I could use a smoke in peace. Come on down to the dressing rooms, and I'll fill you in on more stuff about the contest."

Temple hesitated. She wasn't crazy about cigarette smoke, but she could use a break from so much blatant skin. Not being used to it, she didn't know where to look. She felt like a nun in a nudist camp.

"Shell shock," Lindy said with a grin that revealed she could read Temple's mind. "Civilians always get it the first few hours. Come on, there'll be fewer girls down in the dressing rooms and you can get some straight dope. Strippers don't screw around with half-assed answers."

"No, they don't. I can see that," Temple agreed as Lindy propelled her past an agile miss engaged in bending from the waist and sliding to the floor by doing the splits.

"Isn't the dressing-room area where the murder occurred?"

Lindy was making top time in her battered sneakers, but she stopped on a dime at Temple's question.

"Yeah. It's hard for the girls to use that room now. Dorothy was a sweet girl. But that Savannah Ashleigh bitch wouldn't keep the room after the killing—claimed it upset Yvette, her cat—so the regular working girls got it."

"That's right." Temple followed Lindy into the relative normalcy of the hall outside the ballroom. "Savannah Ashleigh's cat was in the dressing room during the murder. If only cats could talk." She considered how much Midnight Louie had witnessed of her life and times. "On the other hand, thank God they can't."

Chapter 12

WOE vs. WHOOPE

No matter how ritzy or glitzy the hotel, its understage dressing rooms are as welcoming as a warehouse basement. Temple knew that. What point was there to installing such luxuries as wall-to-wall carpeting, upholstered chairs and decorative countertops in the theatrical equivalents of Grand Central terminal? Too many itinerant bodies come and go, spilling lurid makeup, burning out the bare bulbs that surround the inevitably smeared mirrors and dropping sequins from slowly disintegrating costumes like gaudy tears shed at their passing.

Yet Temple found herself standing hushed in the cavernous dressing room beneath the Goliath's glittering superstructure to which Lindy had led her. She was spellbound as usual by the tawdry glamour of these cold, hard-surfaced places where people transform themselves and emerge to perform wonders in the way of song, dance, and in miming emotion or magic.

One of these human butterflies had not emerged from the cocoon beneath the stage to spread her performer's wings in the spotlights, Temple reminded herself.

"Where—?" she began.

Before she could finish her question, Lindy pointed to a row of gorgeously feathered capes hanging about six feet from the floor. The single crooked finger of one empty wrought-iron hook beckoned, as might the ghost of Dorothy Horvath.

Everything about the room reverberated with absence, rather than presence. The flimsy wooden seating common to dressing rooms—battered, round-seated ice-cream chairs with splayed legs—sat askew to parallel gray Formica countertops. A dressing room, even empty, always held its breath in expectation of a chatty, frantic throng of invaders.

Lindy's lighter scratched in the silence, conjuring flame, then the faint perfumes of fluid and sulfur—presto, a lit cigarette made a dramatic entrance into the dormant setting.

The mundane sound and scent of smoking banished the spell of recent death. Temple stared at the opposite wall and mentally counted cloaks. "What happened to the sixth cape that should have been on the empty hook?"

Lindy's first drag on the cigarette ended with a smoky "I don't know." Her voice creaked like a scratched LP record. "Don't know what happened to Dorothy's prize G-string, either. The cops probably have 'em both."

Temple approached an abandoned chair, curled her fingers around the curved wooden seat back and gently shook it. Its feet screeched against the floor as it rocked to and fro.

"Tippy," she pronounced. "These chairs always are. Doesn't help the suicide theory, the victim having to balance on a tippy chair to reach that hook."

"Hey, strippers are used to high heels." Lindy leaned against the countertop, inhaling with the true nicotine addict's slowness. "Wouldn't a murderer have to climb a chair to hoist poor Dorothy up, too? A tippy chair would be twice as hard on him.''

"The police say it's a him?"

"Well . . . a mostly naked woman strangled with a G-string. Who else? Besides, strippers always have man trouble.''

"They're not the only ones," Temple muttered as she strolled through the space, getting its feel, trying to impress the fact of a murder on her fond memories of a dozen dressing rooms exactly like this one, including Max's upscale private dressing room just down the hall.

A mostly eaten birthday cake frosted with turquoise and pink rosettes sat on a cardboard tray atop the counter. All that remained of the sweet, icing sentiments, also turquoise, were the looped terminal y's of "Happy," "Birthday," and the birthday girl's name. Was it Missy? Cindy? Lindy? Or Dorothy?

The room was filled with discards. Powder dusted the worn countertop, snaring a lone bobby pin in its tinted toils, while an abandoned false eyelash lurked in a corner like a curled spider. The scents of a dozen cheap perfumes melded into olfactory goulash. A two-inch-long pencil with no lead lay on the floor. The same corner that harbored the eyelash also held a bit of paper flotsam.

Temple picked up the crumpled shape: beige and orange, with black printing on flimsy card stock. Some kind of ticket—? A clue?

"Food stamp," Lindy's down-to-earth voice said flatly.

Temple dropped it as if she had been caught stealing. Or was she just guilty that she hadn't recognized it? No matter how dicey her cash flow got, she could afford food, even Free-to-be-Feline.

Lindy ambled around the place, too, pausing before a mirror. Six of its framing makeup bulbs had gone gray and cold instead of pouring out the usual white-hot glare. Her fingers touched an eight-by-ten glossy photo stuck into the mirror frame's lower right corner.

"Someone must have put this here," Lindy rumbled pensively, and coughed.

Temple came to join her in staring at the portrait: pale hair and features scribed by a classic oval, posed at a flattering Hollywood tilt, caught in stark theatrical tones of black, white and shades of gray.

Even without a hint of coloring, the face was gorgeous. Perhaps a makeup artist could analyze the proportions, features and their balance, could explain why the face was so mesmerizing. Temple wouldn't want that. The face spoke for itself, radiated an inner expectation that enhanced the outer loveliness.

"Dorothy Horvath?" she asked.

Lindy nodded, tears turning her dark eyes into slick, black marbles. "She was a beautiful kid, a drop-dead knockout. She would start her act in an organdy pinafore that went electric blue-white under the overhead ultraviolets. Called it her 'Dorothy act,' 'cuz she came from Kansas, she said. Funny, quiet kid with a face to die for." Lindy realized how apt that expression was, and winced before dragging deeply on the cigarette.

" 'Glinda North,' " Temple said. "I understand her stage name now; it's after the good witch of the north in *The Wizard of Oz*. Maybe Dorothy wished for a fairy godmother like Glinda. What about the men in her life?"

Lindy shrugged. "Same old story, and, anyway, who knows?"

Temple studied the photograph. "Beautiful women often complain that no one relates to the real person inside."

"I wouldn't know," Lindy said with another shrug.

"Hey, you've got a great face."

"Maybe." Lindy's quirky smile wanted to, but didn't quite, believe Temple. "Once you're past thirty in this game, you can either be an old stripper trying to keep up with the young stuff, or an old ex-stripper."

"Don't say that!" Temple gave a mock shudder. "I just

95

turned thirty myself. Now I learn another career choice is kaput. I'll have to keep slinging press releases."

Lindy waved a dismissing hand. "You don't look a day over twenty-two."

"Don't say that, either. That's the story of my life." Temple shook her head at Glinda North's glamorous photo face. "I wish I knew the story of hers."

"Come back later, when the other girls are here. Maybe you can put the pieces together. We all know a little bit about each other. Can't help it in such close quarters."

"But no one had an obvious motive to kill her, not even a jealous rival?"

Lindy shook her lusterless black-dyed hair. "No way. We all looked out for Dorothy. That girl couldn't string two safety pins together without losing one."

Temple eyed Lindy's world-weary features. "Is your age the only reason you don't strip anymore?"

"No. I manage a club. The money in stripping's good, but you get tired of that eight-hour bump-and-grind." She looked at Temple, then puffed on her cigarette. "You ever see strippers work?"

"The . . . topless hotel shows."

"No, not those hoity-toity, touch-me-not walking department store dummies loaded down with eighty pounds of feathers and rhinestones. I mean real working strippers, who get down and get dirty with the guys in the front row. That would help you understand the life more than bumbling around upstairs. Come on, I'll take you."

"Where to?"

"Where else? Kitty City, my alma mater."

While Temple contemplated objecting to the word "bumbling," Lindy crushed her cigarette in the discarded lid of a makeup tin. She strode from the room with such surety that Temple clicked along in her silent wake, her high heels echoing eerily on the concrete floor.

In no time the pair was jostling through the stream of incoming crowds until they hit broad daylight outside the Goliath. Shocking. Lindy and Temple stood blinking in the bright, blazing heat that drenched them the moment they left the entrance canopy's shade. The Goliath's massive desert white exterior trimmed with scarlet and gold almost outdazzled the sun.

Temple paused to don her prescription sunglasses. "My car's in the ramp way out back. We'll have to take a cab."

"Fine. We'll put it on Ike's tab."

"Ike?"

"Didn't I mention it? I manage Kitty City for Ike Wetzel."

"And run the show over here, too? The Kitty City crowd has a lot invested in the competition."

Lindy squinted down the sidewalk and made a face. "It's our job. Look. Now, there's somebody who really should take a walk on the wild side."

Temple followed Lindy's gaze to a sign-carrying figure pacing in the hot sun twenty feet away. She could read this block-letter message better than Crawford's: RESPECT NOT RHINESTONES: STOP STRIPPING WOMEN OF DIGNITY AND CUSTOMERS OF MONEY. The letters "W.O.E." underlined the sentiment.

"Ouch," Temple said. " 'Politically correct' protesters could use the murder to justify their position, and draw the press's attention *to* it, rather than distracting the media from it. Are many picketing the competition?"

"Only one at a time, so far, but the signs suck."

As if overhearing Lindy's pronouncement, the protester's measured walk brought her within speaking distance.

"You don't know what you're complaining about," Lindy yelled in a disgusted tone.

The woman came nearer. She embodied everything that gave feminists a rap as ugly man-haters: minimal makeup; short, serviceable brown hair; thin gold hoop earrings; unexciting clothes. Only the fact that she was pretty despite, and perhaps because of, her pared-down style ruined the stereotype.

"Do you know what I'm complaining about?" she asked Lindy quietly.

"You bet I do, kiddo." Lindy threw Temple a knowing glance. "Say, I was heading over to a strip place to give this PR lady the grand tour. Want to come along and see what you're stalking around mad about?"

"Degradation doesn't require a microscope."

"Degradation! What about the degradation of working a minimum-wage dead-end job and supporting hungry kids? What about being too beat to have any kind of life but drudgery? Hell, strippers aren't downtrodden; they're doing the trodding down for a change."

"To make money from men, for men."

"And for themselves! More than they'd make waiting on some Snob City bitches in a restaurant."

The protester blinked at Lindy's fury, but visibly counted to a commendable ten before she tried replying.

Temple leaped into the opening. "Lindy used to be a stripper, but I know from zip about it. Why don't you join us and see for yourself?"

The woman hefted her sign uncertainly.

"By the way, what does WOE stand for?" Temple asked.

"Women Opposing Exploitation."

Lindy hooted. "Why oppose it? Why not *use* it?"

"Then that would be WUE," Temple said promptly. "Women Using Exploitation."

"That's ridiculous," the protester retorted.

"Sometimes that's the way it is," Lindy said. "What's the matter, don't you want to see the truth? Chicken?"

The protester twisted her poster stick, looking around for rescue.

Temple remembered her own reluctance to ride the Hesketh Vampire. Visiting a strip joint wasn't as dangerous, but might seem just as intimidating.

"Leave the sign with the parking valet," Temple suggested with such certitude that the protester did as she said.

The parking attendant graciously accepted the sign and a tip, but leaned the sentiment facedown against the Goliath's white stucco side. The protester cast an unhappy look back at her abandoned principles as the trio stepped forward while the bellman whistled up a cab.

In two minutes flat the three women were crammed black leggings to pale pantyhose to blue jeans in the backseat of a white Whittlesea Blue cab, headed for Kitty City.

Temple, of course, sat in the peacemaker's middle— blessed are they—and eased tensions by asking questions. The protester's name was Ruth Morris. She was thirty-something, and a paralegal for a divorce lawyer. Lindy's last name was Lukas and she had been divorced three times. Neither Temple nor Ruth admitted to having seen a stripper do her stuff except on television.

"I see enough gyrating seminaked women in the background every time a TV or movie private eye goes into a bar," Ruth said darkly.

"I've seen some seminaked gyrating *men* on the talk shows," Temple admitted, "and women. But those acts must be cleaned up for Oprah and Phil and Sally."

Lindy didn't comment, so a short silence lengthened into a lull. Garish La Vegas daylight flitted past the taxi's closed windows as the air-conditioning hummed. On the far horizon the hazy blue mountains snagged a crown of clouds.

"Will there be women in the audience?" Ruth asked finally, sounding less enthusiastic about the expedition by the minute.

"Sure," Lindy answered. "It's now an in thing for women to go to strip joints with their dates."

Ruth's unstyled hair shook with her head. "That's putting a stamp of approval on their own sex's subjugation."

"What's subjugated about making a hundred to two hundred and fifty bucks a night?" Lindy demanded.

"Too many women are well paid for doing things that harm themselves—making porno movies, prostitution. The pay wouldn't be so good if the work weren't demeaning."

"Wait a minute!" Lindy sounded righteously indignant. "Only a few strippers moonlight in that other stuff. Most are strippers, period."

Temple jumped in before she got caught in the cross fire. "What exactly are most strippers, period?"

"Dancers," Lindy answered. "Erotic entertainers who work hard for a living. Some are also ex-cheerleaders, good-time girlfriends, girls you went to high school with—"

"And abuse victims." Ruth leaned past Temple to address Lindy. "Physical and/or sexual abuse victims with damaged self-esteem who have a sexually unhealthy need for the distance and control the stage gives them."

Lindy's eyes darkened, but she didn't respond with her usual hair-trigger answer.

"Is that always true?" Temple asked Ruth.

"Pretty much so. A lot of girls are runaways from abusive fathers. If sexual abuse was involved, they've confused intimacy with exhibitionism and self-display, and sometimes even pleasure with pain."

The scratch of Lindy's lighter sounded like a derisive *tsk-tsk*. She defiantly lit a cigarette and puffed a stream of smoke into the crowded cab. "Big words for someone who's never seen the real thing in the flesh."

The cab made a lurching turn, then the driver, a chubby guy in his forties with a black mustache and a baseball cap, turned around.

"You wanta go to Kitty City or a debating society? We're hee-eere."

Chapter 13

The Naked Nose

I am strictly the monogamous sort: one at a time.

Therefore, it is not surprising that I do not keep a wide-open eye on the doings of Miss Temple Barr once I have discovered that the Divine Yvette is back in town.

Not that Miss Temple Barr's attractions have diminished in any respect. If anything, they have improved with age—i.e., during the five weeks that I have consented to room with her. It is true that she was a party to my odious outing to the veterinary clinic, but she meant well. As for the unappetizing pellets with which she has mounded my plate of late, I can overlook that, and that is all I do with them. I do not need to rely on foreign food or home cooking. I have always depended on the kindness of strangers for my better meals, and must say that I have fared quite well.

No, my infatuation for the Divine Yvette predates the entrance of Miss Temple Barr into my life. And, face it, this petite fur-person with a penchant for silver fox is exactly my type. One cannot argue with a match made in cat heaven.

Luckily, the Divine Yvette is as taken with me as vice versa. This is not always the case in the mean streets and the real world. Some unrequited dudes are forced to howl their hearts out, singing the I-Found-My-Baby-but-She-Ain't-Looking-for-Me blues in the night.

Even more luckily, the Celestial Jewel of my heart and other, less fashionably mentionable parts takes me for a hero. To hear her tell it, I attacked the fleeing murderer and was rewarded with a boot in the backside for my trouble. Yet I was still able to leap ten feet across the room and prevent her canvas ark from smashing into the wall.

The lady was asleep at the time, and far be it from me to present myself in a less noble light.

Yet misfortune did enter the scene of Love's Young Dream. First came the perplexing human pantomime. After calming Yvette, if not myself, I amble over to the wall, loft atop a conveniently close chair seat and cautiously sniff as much of the suspended lady as I can reach. Until my nose for news has registered its impression, I believe nothing of what I see, and even less of what I hear. Once satisfied that the poor little doll is dead and in no need of further attentions, I return mine to the contents of the pink carrier. No sooner have the Divine Yvette and I settled down for some romantic trans-mesh smooching, when I hear a sneaky step in the hall.

The newcomer is none other than the miserable dude with whom I tangled a time or two at the ABA. Naturally, he does not look down, so he fails to notice Yvette and myself—mostly myself, for Yvette is as well veiled as a novice in a convent in her carrier, and I am hard to miss unless you are not looking for me, which this Puke-cannon person is definitely not doing.

"Glinda—" he calls softly. "It's Crawford. The others said you never went upstairs. I know you stayed behind because you wanted a private rendezvous. Glinda—" Hearing him makes me want to reconsider my romantic notions, permanently.

And is this guy blind, or what? First he pokes his nose into the hanging costumes. Then he sniffs out the various makeups that litter the countertop, although he is massively deficient in the sniffer, like all of his breed. Even a perfumed Pomeranian would have noticed by now the distinctive odor of death in the room.

But Crawfish Puke-cannon, may his tribe get rabies, bumbles through looking—not high and low, where he would at least spy the dangling damsel on the far wall, or yours truly huddled beneath the counter—but right in front of his prying nose, which instead is investigating one of the absent stripper's canvas bags.

I hiss a disgusted warning, but he is too deaf to hear it over the grind of the air-conditioning system. He pauses to taste a finger-ful of frosting he scoops from a lurid wreck of cake on the counter, then moves on. He has almost reached the wall before he notices the suspended bare legs. Had Miss Temple Barr stumbled onto this murder scene, she would have fixed on those magenta satin spikes from the doorway, and have followed them up to their logical conclusion, or, rather, the dead woman's conclusion.

Now Puke-cannon's basset-hound brown eyes are widening to display their bloodshot whites, as unappetizing a sight as squid-eyeball sushi. He looks up, and up, and up to the dead dancer's sad, tilted face. He whitens, stumbles backward into a series of chairs, which he pushes aside. Then, right by me he pauses and turns.

One last look at the far wall and its macabre decoration, and he is out of there faster than an Irish Setter on No Doz.

Then things commence to get hectic. In no time flat, a couple of brave souls peek in to verify the Puke-cannon claims. They retreat. I am forced to bid my Lost One a long goodbye (which has certain compensations). I no sooner desert the dressing room for a bird's-eye view atop a costume cabinet in the hall than I hear the hysterical approach of little pink feet: the extremi-ties of the Divine One's so-called owner (a convention my kind accepts only to lull human companions into the proper state of ignorance as to who really has the upper mitt in such arrange-ments).

Miss Savannah Ashleigh proceeds to wail in the hall and demand that someone enter the dressing room and extract "her

Darling" from the awful place. Cooler heads point out that the police will want to see the scene untouched.

She does not care, Miss Ashleigh declares, pacing back and forth, what the police want to see. Her Darling must not be subjected to such stress. She clutches her throat, a gesture I find tasteless given the likely means of the deceased's death, but then I find Miss Savannah Ashleigh is talented enough to give even tastelessness a bad name.

At length another old friend from the ABA strides onto the scene. I could jump down on her head from here, and contemplate it, seeing the bad time Lieutenant C. R. Molina saw fit to give the delightful Miss Temple Barr in that instance.

Instead I eavesdrop, yawning. The sound of yammering, excited humans is hard on the ears. Eventually I drop into a meditative state, repeating a soothing mantra, "tuuu-nah . . . tuuu-nah . . . tuuu-nah." (Carp is a personal favorite of mine, but its short, sharp name does not lend itself to musing upon.) With such a password to psychic peace, I could snooze at a dogfight, and often have.

I stay only long enough to see the Divine Yvette borne from the room at the hands of Lieutenant Molina herself.

"The carrier has to stay until our technicians are done with it," she tells Miss Savannah Ashleigh, who is draping her right shoulder with Yvette's languid length and making much over her. (Meanwhile, Yvette is making blue-green goo-goo eyes at me atop the cabinet.)

"Oh, thank you, Lieutenant," babbles Miss Savannah. "See how the Poor Baby is purring with joy at reuniting with Momsy! Please tell me what you think happened to My Darling in that awful room. We will be in the private dressing room next door."

Once Yvette is safe in the silicone bosom of her family, I see no point in sticking around like a used Band-Aid. No one will listen to me even if I should deign to offer my eyewitness testimony. I will be taken no more seriously than Miss Savannah Ashleigh, which is a dreadful state of affairs.

I retreat like the shadow I so much resemble and repair to the Circle Ritz to think things over. One thing needs no thinking: the

PUSSYFOOT

Divine Yvette is still too close for comfort to the murder scene, and likely, to the murderer, as yet unknown.

This is why a day later I find myself in another dressing room occupied by little dolls in the business of dressing down. I have long made a habit of visiting the chorus girls' backstage digs to pick up a nugget of good gossip (much tastier and more nourishing than this Free-to-be-Feline stuff, believe me), get some strokes and lots of female admiration with no strings attached.

My favorite hangout is the Crystal Phoenix, but I have graced similar scenes in such establishments as Bally's, the Flamingo, the Sands, Dunes, et cetera. I avoid the Mirage on principle, despite its many piscatorial attractions, including a shark tank. Some heavy muscle of the feline variety prowls that turf. These individuals wear black and white prison-striped suits, which is appropriate: their kind has often been kept behind bars, for good reason. They all answer to the name of "Tiger," being associates of Seigfried and Roy, the magicians, and outweigh me by several hundred pounds.

I may be feisty, but I am not witless.

However, in all my rambles, which include the Lust 'n' Lace downtown, I have never touched pad to the dressing room of Kitty City, for reasons other than the odiously inaccurate name of said establishment. Besides not having a single specimen of the advertised sort inside, Kitty City's little stripper dolls are always rushing from one club to another and have little time for exchanging pleasantries with a dude of my sort. Plus they live on Mars bars and diet soda, a regimen only slightly less appealing than Free-to-be-Foolish.

I am not surprised to find that the Kitty City dressing rooms are even less nicely appointed than others of my experience. Nor do I advertise my presence. I arrive in the late morning, the better to establish myself in a snooping spot before the first wave of lovelies hits in time for the lunchtime show. The deserted dressing room is barer than Mother Hubbard's cupboard and equipped with rows of mirrors that could betray my position of concealment, could I find one.

So I boldly leap atop one long countertop and inspect the

place, not even pausing to admire my handsome reflections in the facing mirrors. The bruised Formica bears the residue of many long nights and a merry-go-round of dolls coming and going, most of it not visible to the naked eye. However, it is cat's play to my naked nose.

Amid the bouquet of scents—body makeup, cheap perfumes, and (ugh!) coconut oil—I detect a faint odor of almonds. There is not the bitter overtone to the scent that would indicate poison, but it is an unusual smell that I have encountered twice before in the dressing rooms of the Goliath Hotel. Common scent is not what the riddle-solving investigator needs. Still, one of the three sources of this particular perfume is . . . none other than the Divine Yvette. I see a yet-unplumbed link between the murder at the Goliath, the stripper's competition and Kitty City.

Girlish voices echo in the unadorned hall. While I debate playing musical cubicles in the adjoining rest room, the sound of oncoming footsteps forces me to dash for the only cover: an open metal locker currently occupied by a teal nylon gym bag. I dive into a tangle of jungle-print G-strings, feeling right at home with all those spots and stripes, and tunnel under the bag's limp folds. There is a lot of me to hide and not much bag. I freeze, sensing the arrival of intruders not two feet away.

"God." One contralto voice replays a classic line. "What a dump."

"What's this?" trills a soprano.

I can do nothing but shut my eyes as I await discovery and its traumatic consequences. At the least I will get kicked out. At the worst, I might be carried off on another visit to another veterinary clinic, which are no more than legalized shooting galleries, in my opinion.

"Can't anybody even shut a damn locker door?" this high-pitched voice asks.

The locker door bangs shut, leaving me in the dark lit only by the luminous strips of the locker vent. Talk about a slammer. The latch is on the outside, and three feet up. Discovery, I decide, is no longer my Waterloo, but my salvation.

Chapter 14

Kitty City
Nitty-Gritty

Temple looked out the open cab window at a windowless, bunkerlike cinderblock building whose only reason for existence seemed to be supporting the massive neon sign frame above it. Nothing was less glamorous than an unlit neon sign by daylight. The curved white-glass tubes that spelled out KITTY CITY looked dingy, and the cat shapes cavorting beside the name resembled ferrets.

Lindy wanted to pay the cabdriver, but Ruth wouldn't hear of it. They spent a couple of minutes dividing the tab three ways, and Temple needed a receipt. The cabdriver was shaking his head and counting change by the time he watched them pussyfoot toward Kitty City.

Only a few vehicles dotted the asphalt parking lot—pickup trucks, a van or two, older coupes with their vinyl tops sun-blistered to a leprous peeling skin the color of a rusted orange.

Even from outside, Temple heard the brutal bass thump-thump-thump of a sound system at full throttle.

A canvas awning over the door featured a cat's-eye graphic up front. The leering, green-eyed black feline face had none of Midnight Louie's dignified intelligence, Temple thought somewhat smugly.

In the awning's shade, Lindy pulled open a heavy, coffered door and moved into a blast of icy darkness throbbing with ear-piercing rock music.

Temple and Ruth followed, then stopped in the disorienting dimness, glimpsing clumped tables, the silver sheen of the obligatory slot machines and the glitter of a bar.

"It's midday," Lindy shouted. "Not too many customers. Come on."

Leaning into the chill interior dusk and the wave of noise as if facing a north wind, Temple and Ruth followed Lindy to the relative haven of a table and chairs.

Temple exchanged her sunglasses for her regular glasses. As her vision adapted, she began to make out slim pale figures moving rhythmically in the darkness. One pranced on a low stage some twenty-five feet away, shadowed by her reflection in a semicircle of mirror behind her. Another was writhing around a chrome pole on the bar; yet another danced on an empty table in the middle of the large room.

The scene reminded Temple of an Old Master's evocation of a Renaissance Hell, especially when she inhaled and drew in the scent of stale smoke.

Gradually the room and its few inhabitants came into focus: men seated alone or in pairs at the scattered tables, and a glass-enclosed DJ's booth above and left of the main, mirrored stage. True to the emblazoned but pallid TOPLESS! on the exterior sign, bare-breasted maidens writhed to the mind-numbing music on the various stages while a Big Mama of a giant-screen TV flickered images from a Western at the main stage's right side.

A waitress wearing a long-sleeved French-cut black leotard whose bottom barely covered hers appeared from the dimness. A perky pair of cat—bat?—ears topped her brown shoulder-length hair. She had the fresh-faced appeal of a girl in a Clearasil TV ad after the medication had worked.

"Anything for you ladies to drink?"

Lindy ordered a screwdriver, Ruth passed, and Temple asked for a white wine spritzer, hoping that a wine buzz would help drown out the high-decibel rock music, not that one drink would do the job.

The dancers undulated in their own little worlds, cocooned in overpowering music. Some wore—shades of the long-gone sixties—white patent-leather boots; others black high heels. Their G-strings were glitzy versions of thong-back bikini bottoms.

Temple didn't know what your average red-blooded male mused upon when viewing this skimpy item of undress; she always wondered what kind of depilatory aid such scraps required, and how often. Did the women wax, pluck, shave, or simply napalm any offending body hair away?

After the waitress returned with the drinks, Temple insisted on paying for hers—and nearly choked to find out it cost six dollars. The wages of sinning, she guessed.

She was beginning to recognize patterns in the women's movements—not the tried-and-true burlesque bump-and-grind announced by an emphatic drumroll, but a fluid undulation half belly dance and half sexual pantomime. Pelvises swiveled clockwise and counterclockwise; arms lifted to show off torsos doing likewise; bare breasts, less imposing than she had expected, pulsed like gentle molds of Jell-O to the motions.

It didn't do a thing for her. She checked out the men at the other tables. It didn't seem to be doing much for them either. They sipped long-neck beers and lowballs, watching quietly. God knows that there was no point in talking against the pounding music.

Then the big front door opened, splashing in an oblong of blinding sunlight and a bristle of silhouettes. Five new paying customers felt their way into the dark.

These guys headed straight for the stage and sat down. Temple saw now that the stage was ringed with a slightly raised lip and chairs, and that the room's other small dancing areas were merely tables with the centerpiece of a living, dancing doll.

On the main stage, the dancer had turned to offer her audience a rear view while she dreamily watched her mirror image brush the back of one hand over forehead and hair, run the other down her breast and hip. An air-conditioning vent in the floor lifted the hair at her nape, fluttered the flimsy scraps of fabric covering her G-string.

Next to Temple, Ruth stirred uneasily.

As the dancer exited without turning through a shaggy curtain of aluminum fringe, the DJ's voice—a big, booming, carnival-barker kind of voice—blared out over the slightly muted music.

"Now, gentlemen and ladies"—Ruth and Temple cringed in tandem to realize that their table hosted the only ladies in the place beside the strippers—"a special treat. Please welcome the delectable Dulcey!"

As his words died the recorded music revved up to eardrum-bursting intensity. "Wild Thing."

A thin red beam of light lanced the entrance area, while the silver streamers shimmied as if shaken by an irresistible force; then a woman sashayed through. She wore thigh-high black leather boots and a black-and-white zebra-striped spandex dress cut low across the shoulders, high across the derriere, and sparkling with random rhinestones. Her hair was a bleached platinum fountain exploding from a clip at the crown of her head. Black-and-white zigzags of opalescent and black glitter shadowed her eyes.

The lights shifted, painting the white stripes an unearthly blue-white. Temple glanced above the stage to a black-painted ceiling mounted with fluorescent light fixtures holding bright purple bulbs—the ultraviolet lights that painted what was already exotic with another layer of intensified artifice.

This lady moved; no languid, sensual wiggles for her. She strutted, she swung her assets fore and aft, she ground her shoulders and her hips in every direction on the compass, each movement threatening to dislodge the dress's tenuous cling to her torso.

Ultimately, however, she actually had to shimmy out of it, which she accomplished by turning her back and peeling it off inch by inch, facing the audience only when some great revelation had been accomplished. Given the shortness of the garment, this didn't take long.

The zebra-dress crumpled to the floor, ignored, while she strutted around the perimeter in her rhinestone-strewn white thong-back bikini bottom, jumping up on the foot-wide serving area, then pouncing back on the stage and casting herself on the dark floor in contortionist positions.

Temple heard an old-time barker's singsong spiel unwinding in her head: Ladies and gentlemen, she slinks, she shimmies, she crawls upon her belly like a snake; she bends like a bow and thrusts back her head and her leg until one black spike heel meets her white-lightning hair. She does the splits six ways from Sunday and ways that wouldn't be legal the other six days of the week, either. She—

But she wasn't the main performer now. A man at the stageside seats jumped up and lay grinning on his back atop the stage rim. A small cylinder protruded from his mouth like a periscope.

Ruth leaned closer until she could shout into Temple's ear. "Is that a cigarette?"

Temple pushed her glasses' bridge tight to her nose. About as long as a cigarette, about as thick as a cigarette, but . . .

The smiling dancer noticed the man, came over, straddled his head with her Wicked Wanda boots. She began gyrating her hips and twisting downward.

"No," Temple shouted back. "It's a rolled-up bill."

"A what?" Ruth screamed.

The dancer's bending knees brought her pelvis lower and lower, bit by bit.

"A bill. Money," Temple screamed back.

"That's disgusting!" Ruth shrieked in turn.

Temple watched, running various possibilities through her head. She was relieved when the dancer dropped to the floor behind the man and slowly extracted the bill from his mouth with her teeth.

"Not sanitary," Temple agreed at the top of her lungs.

Ruth gave her an incredulous look.

The dancer tucked the rolled-up bill in the side of her G-string, then repeated the performance with another man who had cast himself faceup on the stage, smoking a greenback. Temple contemplated the likely denomination of those bills—ones? Too cheap. Fives, maybe. Tens, twenties? Irrelevant curiosity often distracted her from maintaining a strong moral posture at all times.

As for taking strong postures, period, the dancer had faced the mirrors, dropped down on her hands and stretched out her legs to demonstrate an exercise that Temple had viewed intimately many times in aerobics class. The men seemed to find it vastly more interesting than she did, especially when it was performed without benefit of leotard or tights. A man from an outlying table had come quietly to stand before the stage. Temple didn't notice him until the dancer did; she must have been watching something else.

Smiling, the dancer moved to his position, pulled up her pale hair with both hands, and began to gyrate her significant parts in a sort of presentation package. Since the stage was only at table level, her athletic ability to move up and down gave the expression "in your face" a whole new dimension.

Then the dancer dropped down to sit on the stage rim, putting her arms around her one-man audience's shoulders, whispering in his ear, lifting the G-string over her hip almost coyly, allowing him to place a rolled-up bill in its elasticized safekeeping.

"Garters," Temple said sagely to no one who could hear her, "have come a long way, baby."

Beside her, Ruth Morris just shook her head.

By the time Miss "Wild Thing" left the stage, bending provocatively to retrieve her bit of elasticized dress, her G-string sides bristled with bills, which added a piquant savagery to her costume.

Within a minute, a successor was announced, and then another. Some performers' names sounded like a yuppie parent's dream: Berkeley, Madison, Tracy. Others fancied liquor names: Champagne, Brandy, Tequila. Temple was struck by how many adopted place-names—Miami, Phoenix, Wichita—established both anonymity and a stage persona tied to place, to a possible home. Nobody picked Tampa, probably because it sounded too much like "tampon."

Each act lasted only the four or five minutes of a song. Then the main stage performer rotated to bartop or tabletop, writhing for the solitary men who occupied the stools and seats. After several acts, Ruth indicated she was decamping. Temple rose to accompany her, and Lindy followed.

Instead of leading them to the big front door, Lindy threaded a path through the tables occupied by a sprinkling of men. Ruth was as nervous as Temple about their passage blocking the audience's view of their entertainment. They scurried after Lindy like ducklings not about to abandon Mama, and dove in relief through an open doorway to the right of the main stage.

They found themselves in a ladies' room so unglamorous that the phrase "ladies' john," however oxymoronic, best described it: graffiti-tattooed, generic cubicles; a single sink; a mirror above a powder-strewn shelf. On one cubicle door, the words "Theda's Throne" were picked out in transfer letters and adorned with the iridescent metallic decals so popular among teenage girls.

Besides the standard wall-hung tampon dispenser, this john offered a wall-hung perfume dispenser, mute testimony to how hard a girl had to labor to make disrobing look easy.

The irregularly shaped room, obviously chopped from whatever space was available, also served as a hallway. Lindy passed through to a long narrow room equipped with lockers on one end, and with the stock mirrors and makeup lights lining both long sides.

Only a couple of chairs occupied the space, abandoned far from the mirrors. This was not a dressing room where one sat and applied makeup with leisurely care.

Three or four slim, small-breasted dancers in a state of stage undress stood before the mirrors fussing with their getups. Nylon gym bags gaped open on the countertops before them, disgorging hair spray, makeup and pins.

Female visitors were immediately drafted as dorm sisters.

"What do you think?" a blonde with Madonna-black roots asked the newcomers, ankling over on high heels. A purple satin garter belt frosted with black lace was all the coverage her thong-back G-string got, and was the only thing holding up her black lace stockings.

She turned. The garters were absent from the back set of black satin streamers. "Can I get away with tucking these suckers up?"

While she demonstrated what she had in mind, Temple wondered how long the energetic pelvic motions required on stage would keep anything tucked up, including the presumably private portions of her anatomy.

"Looks stupid," said a towering redhead wearing a Day-Glo G-string-plus-suspenders outfit. It mimicked a teddy that had been left in the rain too long and had shrunk beyond belief. "Pin the ribbons to the stockings."

"No pins!" the first woman wailed.

"Let me check." The redhead rooted through her huge bag, but despite unearthing a vast quantity of makeup and costume fragments, dredged up not a single safety pin.

The blonde turned to regard her bare, unbestreamered rear in the mirror. "I need the stockings held up in back," she decided. "Besides, it looks better."

In the name of full coverage, such as it was, Temple dropped her tote bag to a chair and began rummaging. From her fat paisley cosmetic bag she took the big-mama safety pin with all the little baby safety pins hanging on it that she always carried.

She flourished this find like an enemy scalp. "Voilà."

Blondie ambled over, loose garter streamers swaying pertly aft like a show horse's tail.

"Great, thanks." She accepted the pins that Temple detached, then twisted her agile torso to fasten the garter streamers to her stocking backs, and straightened. "How do I look?"

"Uh, terrific," Temple said.

Ruth said nothing, apparently being in a state of shock.

"Okay, babies," a new, full-bodied voice announced, "Mama's here with a brand new bag."

A plain-faced, heavyset, middle-aged woman wearing loose black knit slacks and matching top swung into the room on an invisible raft of energy and good humor. She slung her camouflage-colored bag to an empty countertop and pulled over a chair, into which she plopped.

Blondie and Scarlet hustled over.

Lindy remained leaning against a banged-up locker, smoking. For a moment, Temple thought she had heard a muted thump from within it, but Lindy remained unmoved. Temple decided she was imagining things, which was better than standing like Ruth in the middle of the floor, her purse clutched in both hands, as if she feared contamination from the cheerfully tacky surroundings.

Temple was as curious as the next woman, and possibly more than most. She approached the newcomer, who had whisked a chrome belt-ring bigger around than a bowling ball from her bag. Dangling from the ring was a glittery, colorful, lacy array of thong-back G-strings sewn from spandex pieces the size of Band-Aids. A young black dancer arrived wearing an elongated forties-patterned jacket that served as a dress, and was also swept into the whirlpool of interest eddying around the Baglady.

"Oh, Wilma, those are so cute," thin, tall Scarlet cooed. "Have you got any bigger ones? The last T-back I bought almost made Kitty City live up to its name."

Wilma thumbed through her supply before pulling a green flocked-velvet number off the ring.

Scarlet dropped everything to wiggle into the equivalent of a slingshot. She adjusted the skimpy elastic over her narrow hips.

While Scarlet considered, beautiful Blondie of the impeccable makeup was paging through the selection with bitten-off fingernails decorated with chipped fuchsia polish.

"This will go with a gauze float I have." She snatched at a lurid lime green leopard-print T-back that Temple wouldn't have tried to sell to a desperate chameleon.

Off the ring the item came. Going, going, gone—for twenty-five dollars. Scarlet paid thirty-five bucks for hers, which fit just right, not that Temple could tell. Ebony stripped off her street jacket on the spot, and nearly everything else, to model a metallic-spangled copper-colored G-string-cum-straps that she bought for fifty flat. The trio scattered to separate mirrors with their booty.

Wilma didn't need to be a hard-sell artist. She glanced at Temple from under unruly gray brows. "Anything for you?"

"Huh? Me? Oh, no . . . just browsing."

"That's okay; look all you want. Say, kids, I got some hot new cosmetics, too."

The ducklings came clucking back to look at glitter-embedded body gels, metallic powders, at transfer tattoos and jet black lipstick, and at nail polish in every color from green and purple to pale pink. Temple hoped that Blondie would buy some lacquer to disguise her tattered nails, but she seemed oblivious to this telling chink in her beautiful body armor.

Besides, Blondie was apparently new to the club. She was more interested in frantically filling out a form so the disc jockey could personalize her introduction.

"Favorite actor," she fussed, reading the line. "Who was the guy in *Roadhouse?*"

"I didn't see it," Temple answered, "but Patrick Swayze."

"P-a-t-r-i-k. How do you spell 'Swayze'? Quick! Anybody."

Silence.

"S-w-a-y-z-e," Temple said. A PR person couldn't stop herself from giving out information on any occasion.

Blondie jiggled on her high heels. Showtime was coming. "Actress, actress, actress—who's big?"

"Uh, Sharon Stone," suggested Temple, coming to the rescue again. She hadn't seen *Basic Instinct*, either. Now she wondered if a man-stabbing lesbian made a suitable role model for a stripper, but it was too late to backtrack.

"Favorite fantasy," Blondie prompted again, looking expectantly at Temple.

"Don't *you* have one?"

Blondie tilted her head at the questionnaire and pouted her lips indecisively. "Beating the shit out of my old man." She laughed, her eyes uneasy.

Temple caught her breath at the unspoken volumes behind those few words.

Blondie shrugged, as if dismissing herself, her notions, her past. "Being tied between two horses and ripped apart." She laughed again.

Temple remained speechless, more shocked by these words than she had been by anything she'd glimpsed yet in the world of sex entertainment. Classic clues to abuse and battered self-esteem had come tumbling out; she didn't have to be a professional counselor like Matt Devine to know that.

"Say," said Wilma's deep, motherly voice. "Why not write down Lady Godiva? You know, on the horse."

"Oh, right." Blondie was happily diverted, her problem

solved. "I can do something with that. Um, 'To ride a horse naked through Caesars Palace.' There. Done. Can you drop it at the DJ's booth on the way out?" She thrust the flimsy paper at Temple. "I gotta finish getting ready."

Temple nodded automatically, and glanced at the sheet with its childish block printing. In her haste, Blondie had to cross out several transposed words and letters.

"Let's go," Ruth said uncomfortably between her teeth.

In the silence Temple heard another suspicious thump, but Scarlet turned on her hair dryer and began fingering mousse through her kinky curls.

Lindy crushed her cigarette out on the painted concrete floor next to a crumpled food stamp—Temple hadn't noticed ashtrays anywhere—pushed away so hard that the locker door twanged like a drum, and led them back through the ladies' john.

Temple regretted her mission for Blondie. It forced her to slip backstage behind the waiting performers. Then she had to do an elaborate pantomime to get DJ Johnny's attention. She finally wended out between the seminude bodies crowded backstage.

Ruth and Lindy waited for her near the door next to the stage. They wove their way through the tables again just as the DJ was announcing a fresh new talent, Little Sheba— Blondie in stage persona.

Finally the trio stood on the sidewalk outside, adjusting to the shower of daylight.

"Well?" Lindy demanded.

"Sad," Ruth said. "The false names, the faux glamour can't hide the fact that they think so little of themselves that they have to display their bodies before men for money."

"Oh, come on!" Lindy's fists clapped to her hips. "Who do you think gets rich off of those evil, exploitive men? The clubs and the performers. Those poor jerks put a lot of good money down those G-strings, and down their gullets in an afternoon or evening of drinking. The strippers control *them*, not the other way around. You saw that, didn't you, Temple?"

Temple looked from one to another, thinking. "I saw what you both saw, and something else. Strippers are performers who put their hearts and souls into their acts. Maybe it's a neurotic need to manipulate the men who abused them when they were too young to fight back. It still adds up to a performance with personal significance. And that's what all artists do."

"We don't want to be called artists! We just don't want to be called tarts!" Lindy said.

"You can't excuse what they're encouraged to do by calling low self-esteem a royal road to self-expression!" Ruth argued just as forcibly.

They were united in disagreeing with her. Temple stood between the two women feeling like the cat that ate the canary and followed it with a sparrow chaser.

"You know what I'd like to do? Book you two on some local talk radio shows. Pro and Con. And then I'd like to hear what the strippers say when they call in, and I bet they will, in droves. Are you game?"

The two women regarded each other suspiciously, and then Temple, with dawning excitement.

"Talk radio would really get the word out on the competition next weekend," Lindy said first.

"Radio is an excellent forum for WOE," Ruth added, "and would be a lot less hot than stomping the pavement all day."

"Don't bet on that." Temple, who had heard her share of talk radio shows on controversial subjects, felt obligated to warn Ruth. "But it would bring some interesting issues out into the open."

"The interesting issues are already out in the open," Ruth pointed out as the door to Kitty City exploded open and a miniskirted stripper dashed out.

Temple turned to watch the Zebra lady stride down the street on long, tan, bare legs. "Don't count on it," she advised, wondering exactly how much might come out if the strippers got revved up enough to speak for themselves—how much about their always-titillating profession, and how much about the murderer among them. The horrible death of Dorothy Horvath was not a debatable issue.

As she watched, and just before the door swung shut, a black cat with ruffled fur slipped out, gave her a furtive green glance over one shoulder and trotted around the corner of the building.

Temple opened her mouth, but the cat was gone.

"What's the matter?" asked Ruth, who had noticed Temple's expression.

"Nothing. I thought I recognized another Kitty City escapee."

Lindy and Ruth craned their necks to look around.

"There ain't nobody here," Ruth finally said with rueful humor, "but us chickens. So let's get out of here before somebody sees us and assumes the worst."

Chapter 15

Little Girl Lost

The three women debarked from their cab—they had hailed one on Paradise—amid a flurry of cordial good-byes. While Ruth headed for the Goliath valet stand to retrieve her sign, Lindy and Temple dashed inside.

The lines were drawn, Temple knew, but at least the combatants were willing to talk turkey on the live airwaves. Meanwhile, Lindy led Temple to the second-floor hotel suite that served as competition central.

Though the rooms were empty now, the normally neat furniture sat askew. End tables were littered with ashtrays, bowls of stale popcorn and paperwork. All Temple wanted was an empty chair and an unengaged telephone.

She plopped down, dropped her heavy tote bag beside her and dug out her straining personal organizer. Phone numbers took up half the bulk. Time to play radio-station roulette. She dialed one string of numbers after another,

quickly learning who was in, who was out, who was interested, who was too busy to talk. After forty minutes of
nonstop calling, Temple had lined up three talk shows in
the next four days and had four more shows scheduled to
call her back. Whether producer or interviewer, the radio
people she contacted loved the notion of strippers calling
in and baring their souls instead of their bodies for a
change. Las Vegas took its exotic entertainers for granted,
but with guests lined up to debate the issue, stripping
suddenly got a lot sexier, as far as radio ratings were
concerned. Nothing made for good media like a major
clash of opinions.

Satisfied but talked out, Temple restored her precious
sourcebook to the tote bag, then cruised the littered ta-
bletops for something nutritious. She was forced to settle
for seven stale pretzels and three green M&Ms.

All the competition personnel, she decided, must still
be down in the ballroom trying to whip lights, action and
cameras into shape for the big show on Saturday night.

Taking the elevator down, she found herself wondering
why the murderer had killed his victim so early into competition week. Only half the performers had arrived yet;
only half the chaos was available to confuse matters.

She charged through the teeming lobby, well aware that
all Las Vegas hotel lobbies resemble sets for *Airport*, with
tour groups booking in and booking out in long, luggage-
clogged lines; all Las Vegas hotels, that is, except for the
unfortunate few that aren't doing big-time business. Their
lobbies resemble deserted bowling alleys.

Pausing to glance into the ballroom, Temple viewed the
same controlled chaos she had penetrated before. She
hesitated, wondering if Ike Wetzel would make a good
sparring partner for Ruth on the talk shows. No, too
inarticulate; one of those maddening men who retreat to
smug, smirking silence in the face of female outrage, like
the ever-lovable Crawford Buchanan.

She didn't spot any reporters milling about, and sighed
her relief. The murder had already run its sensational

course in a town brimming with sensation and crime. All she had to do now was organize sufficient, sedate publicity and beat off any overeager news people.

In that case, she could go home and pound out her radio schedule so far, or . . . since she was here anyway, she could check out the dressing room again. Alone. She headed for the back stairs, her mind manufacturing ways to justify her nosiness if anyone—say Lieutenant Molina—caught her snooping.

She figured that the police had been over the dressing room with a forensic fine-tooth comb by now. She should have the place to herself, and, without Lindy present, something about the murder scene that nagged at her might become clear.

Her heels clattered in four-four time down the concrete stairs. No one had seen her, proving that the murderer hadn't needed to be clever, just lucky. The Goliath was a massive beast of a hotel whose functional underbelly was often deserted if you knew when to explore it.

In the nondescript corridor narrowed by racks of muslin-covered costumes Temple tried to muffle her ringing footsteps. Just because the place was deserted was no reason to announce herself to ghosts.

One ghost haunted a different dressing room. She paused, then pushed open a door she had entered many times before.

A glamorous wardrobe of glittering gowns occupied the costume niche where Max's deliberately subdued performance clothes had hung not many months before. Either a female impersonator occupied the room now, or some glamour-puss songstress.

Temple advanced to the mirror, saw herself looking perfectly respectable and as guilty as any trespasser. Cosmetics spewed across the glass-topped Formica counter, and none of these makeup bulbs showed the tattletale gray of burnout.

She almost expected to glance down and find Max looking back at her in the mirror. Funny how you conversed with a person's image when he was using a mirror, as if he really were on the other side of it . . . already. Was that where Max had gone? Behind the illusion of his own image?

Temple eyed the distinctly female cosmetics, an odd combination of expensive Borghese eyeshadows and inexpensive Maybelline products. Although the room's fixtures and furniture remained the same, it had been essentially transformed somehow. The magician had changed it into something else by making himself disappear. It held memories that smelled faintly stale.

Temple shook her head, at the room and at herself. She was about to back out, feeling like an intruder who had stumbled onto a stage set for a play she wasn't in. Then her mirror's-eye view spotted something odd atop the wicker sofa on the opposite wall. How often had she perched on its chintz upholstered arm after a show, waiting for Max's makeup to come off, ready to keep him company until he came down from the exuberant high of performing? Stop it! she ordered herself, and walked over to the sofa to inspect the anomaly.

A pink gym bag. That fit the overfeminine, slightly junky touches in the room. The mesh side insets, Temple thought, must help air out soggy exercise wear.

Something moved behind that pastel barrier.

She jumped back, her heart beating, the heavy tote bag swinging hard into her hip, once, twice.

"Ow."

The contents of the bag echoed her complaint. Only its cry of protest sounded more like "*me*-ow."

How had she forgotten the unforgettably feminine feline darling? Certainly she hadn't paid much attention to the cat carrier at the time. Temple crouched down until the mesh was on eye level and peered inward. Two gleaming round eyes gazed back. Long spidery silver hairs brushed the mesh.

"Aren't you the natural beauty! Of course. Yvette. Savannah Ashleigh's pampered baby cat." She could see the same unreadable silvery script embroidered across the bag's top. As Temple's forefinger scratched the mesh, Yvette's delicate pink nose outlined in flattering black tilted to sniff it.

"Well. I hope your mistress comes back soon. We don't want you all alone down here witnessing any more murders—like mine!"

Temple stood, aware of the deserted dressing rooms surrounding her, of the recent, nearby violent death lingering with a kind of half-life. Even if Max's strong personality had left no aura in this room, perhaps the dead dancer's brutal passing had managed to haunt the entire area.

Temple hurried out of the dressing room, embarrassed by the thought of explaining her presence to a suddenly returned Savannah Ashleigh. She wouldn't even want to explain it to herself.

Down the hall, the door to the murder scene stood ajar. Temple halted, even though she knew that doors are always ajar in deserted dressing rooms. The last thing weary, absconding performers want to deal with is closing doors behind them.

Still, she tiptoed closer, managing to keep her reverberating heels just off the floor. She eased inside without having to push the door further open. The cloak-shrouded end wall caught her eye instantly. Had the victim been posed there deliberately, she wondered, like dead meat on a hook? Cruel and crude, but then so was using the woman's own prize G-string for a hangman's noose.

Was there a message in the manner of death, the place of death? Temple thought so. Maybe if she stood very still and emptied her mind, an intuition would creep in.

A strangled whimper ruined her concentration.

Temple's eyes jerked from the wall of gaudy cloaks to the opposing rows of mirrors and chairs that lined the dressing room. Empty. She turned. Only lockers stood behind her, pushed up against the wall with some of the doors sprung, the shiny gray enamel paint chipped off like cheap fingernail polish.

No one could hide in a locker. Not a murderer then. Not even a figment of her imagination now.

Still, she had heard a noise, very near. She wasn't hallucinating. Temple looked around again, methodically: along the ceiling line, down the row of chairs. Last, she examined the hanging costumes—from the fuchsia turkey-feather numbers jammed together at the far end to the equally imaginative exotica imported by the visiting strippers, and the truly tasteless high heels and boots lined up under them.

A muffled hiccough. The last gown on the left, a scarlet-sequined bodice with a ruffled Flamenco skirt, trembled.

Temple looked down again, below the froth of glamorous hems. This time she spied a jazzy satin pair of spike heels with a rhinestone-framed cat face on the toe. They were inhabited by real feet and legs.

She strode over and pushed back the scarlet costume. The hanger screeched against the rod like a scalded cat, making Temple jump along with her discovery.

A petite, dark-haired woman huddled against the wall, hands over her face, shivering, as well she might in her black spangled T-back bikini bottom and strapless bra.

"I'm sorry," Temple apologized. Nothing was more embarrassing, for both parties, than finding a stranger crying.

The woman shook her head, too distraught to speak.

"Is there anything I can do—?" Expecting a negative answer to that inanely ineffective question, Temple retreated, prepared to tiptoe out again.

A hand left the face and then seized her wrist. "Is he still out there?" the woman asked. Her voice was strangely low and hoarse for such a small woman, choked with emotion and something else. Fear.

"He?" Temple repeated.

The hand tightened painfully on Temple's wristbone. "The man! A man. Any man. Is he out there?"

Temple shook her head. "No one was around but me. And a cat."

Relief allowed the woman's hunched shoulders to drop two inches, but she kept her face and body pressed to the wall. One hand still covered her eyes, as if to keep them from seeing something horrible.

"Hey," Temple said gently, "I sometimes look pretty awful in the mornings, but I'm really not a scary person. Come on out. It's just us two down here, honest."

The woman laughed tentatively, peeking at Temple through spread fingers, like a child. "You're not . . . with the show."

"I'm doing public relations for it."

"Why are you down here?"

"I came to check out the murder scene," Temple admitted sheepishly, her eyes flicking to the far wall. "I'm congenitally curious."

"Oh." The woman sighed instead of sobbed this time and turned around to put her back to the wall.

She may have been tiny, Temple noticed, but she had a dynamite hourglass figure. Her vivid coloring suggested the Hispanic, or Italian.

"What's your name?" Temple asked.

The woman's long dark lashes fanned up and down behind her hand as she studied Temple's linen suit, tote bag, high heels and, finally, her face.

"K-Katharine," she said in a subdued, shy tone.

"All right, Katharine, why don't you come out of there? Those ruffle sequins must scratch! I'll prove that there's no one here but me."

Katharine edged out like a child from a closet, a bizarre image when combined with her seminaked, fully female form.

"Those are downright awesome shoes," Temple said with sincere admiration. "I've got a cat with big green eyes almost as bright as those rhinestones."

"Thanks." Katharine turned one foot so Temple could admire the shoes fully—see how cleverly the shape mimicked a cat stretching: the high heel was its hindquarters raised in the air, the sole its ground-touching belly; the toe formed its extended front legs. A twining ankle strap mocked a tail.

"Darling!" Temple pronounced. "Did you think that up yourself?"

Katharine nodded solemnly. "You're sure no one's out there anymore?"

"Swear to God on Ginger Rogers's dancing shoes. Did—" Temple eyed the far wall, the suggestively empty hook. "—did remembering the murder scare you? Were you suddenly afraid that the murderer might still be around?"

Katharine shook her head of naturally wavy dark hair, as lush as Counselor Troi's Cretanesque hairpiece on the new "Star Trek." Temple wasn't often jealous, but this tiny, ultra-zorchy woman made her feel a pang: in junior high she would have traded all of her record-setting Girl Scout cookie sales for some blatant sex appeal like this any day. It wasn't fair: this brunette bombshell wasn't even tall.

"I didn't even remember that—the murder," Katharine was saying. "It happened so fast, but then it always does."

"What? What happened?" Temple demanded a bit impatiently.

Katharine's shoulders twitched hopelessly, then she lowered her hand from her face.

"Oh, my God." Temple saw reddened eyes of Swiss-chocolate brown, tear-smeared mascara, those Daddy Longlegs lashes, and natural, too! It had taken her a few more seconds to notice the incipient swelling of Katharine's cheekbones, the bruises beginning to congeal around her lovely eyes.

"Someone hit you! The man you were asking about. Who?"

Katharine shrugged. "Don't do no good to say. It's done. It did what he wanted. I—I can't compete, not looking like this."

"You don't know how you look—it's not so bad. . . ."

Brown eyes turned bitter black. "I know how I *will* look, like a three-D sunset by competition Saturday. He knows how I'll look, too. Like shit. Knows just how much to hit, and how hard."

"Ice! I'll get some from the machine down the hall—I saw it yesterday! We'll put ice on your face. Don't move, I'll be right back."

Temple sprinted away, grabbing her clutch purse from the tote and clawing out quarters in transit. The soft-drink machine stood only twenty-five feet away. She congratulated herself on remembering it while waiting for a paper cup to pop down, lopsided. She straightened the cup just before a mother lode of crushed ice crashed into it, then jerked it away, letting the clear liquid Sprite dribble down the drain.

Katharine was sitting at the counter staring disconsolately into the mirror when Temple returned. "Ice won't do no good—what's your name, anyway?"

"Temple. Here, I'll wrap the ice in this towel." She snatched a clean but rouge-stained one from the countertop. "Hold that there."

"Thanks," her patient said. "Still won't help the color."

"Makeup."

"You gotta look perfect for the judges. They'll see."

Temple hated hearing that anything was hopeless. She had a feeling that Katharine had been told that everything was hopeless for as long as she could remember. Temple's eyes roamed the dressing room, looking for inspiration. The cloaks—no, Katharine needed to hide her face, not her body. Hardly her body, that was the whole point. But . . . her face was not.

Temple pointed at the cat-faced shoe at their feet. "Cat cloak!" Katharine looked puzzled, rightfully. Temple's inspiration came so fast she stumbled over the words. "Mask. You'll make a cat mask to match the shoes!"

Brown eyes opened wide, then winced half-shut again. "Yeah. I could do that—maybe."

"Sure you can! Then how your face looks won't matter. What's your routine, the music?"

" 'Batman.' Only I play Catwoman."

"Perfect! It'll be even better than before. Trust me."

Katharine, dazed into docility, nodded while clasping the homemade ice bag over one eye.

"Will he . . . come back?" Temple asked next.

"No. He'd figure this took care of it."

"Why did he do it?"

She shrugged. "He likes to. And I'm gonna leave him. Soon. I got my own business, my card—" She patted around for a purse, then sank back into the chair in chagrin. "No room for cards on this costume. Upstairs in my purse. He wanted to talk, he said, alone, so we came down here. Anyway, I have this private stripping service, for parties, you know? Good clean fun. Gags. Go-go grandmas, guys in clown costumes, whatever fits the occasion. I win this contest and get the prize money, even if I don't, I'm outa stripping myself. But a win would help my business. Grin 'n' Bare It. That's the name of my business, spelled 'b-a-r-e.' Cute, huh? I got four people working for me part time. We do singing telegrams, 'birthday suit' strips, lots of things. I'm not just . . . a dumb stripper, you know. I'm an entrepreneur."

"Sounds great." Temple had noticed how Katharine's spine had straightened as she began talking about her business. "If you need a PR person, here's one of my cards." She squatted to dig through her tote bag.

Katharine's hand on her arm made her pause. The expression in her one visible brown eye was serious, a curious mixture of supplication and defiance. "I wasn't crying 'cuz it hurt, you know. Only 'cuz it ruined my chances."

"I . . . know."

Temple tried not to think how a woman had learned to take pride in not crying when it hurt.

Chapter 16

Crime and Punishment

Sobered by Katharine's sad predicament, Temple bustled out the back of the Goliath to the guest parking garage. Eager as she had been to get home and type up her radio schedules for Lindy and Ruth, the image of Katharine's battered face haunted her. In the elevator up to the ramp's fourth floor, that face seemed to float on the stainless-steel door, a distorted reflection of herself.

Her heels clicked across the concrete garage floor as she pawed through her tote's awesome collection of effluvia searching for her key ring. She hardly heard the footsteps approaching behind her.

They didn't stop, and they didn't overtake her. Just followed along. A woman who lives alone gets used to being wary, and her stint with Max had not been lengthy enough to blunt that self-defensive instinct.

Temple turned casually to see just who was behind her. Two men, who noticed her noticing them.

"Where do you think you're going?" one demanded with the voice of authority.

Temple speeded up. Was there some snafu about her guest parking status? They could discuss it once she was prudently locked inside the Storm, which was just down several vehicles. . . .

Steps pounded behind her, few and hard.

She glanced back, primed to run, and found the men sweeping past, sweeping her up between them, carrying her away in the irresistible current of their force.

Temple felt like a little kid being hustled away by two of the block's big-boy bullies. Mean preteens, they would whisk her tiny five-year-old self behind an empty garage and make her swear eternal silence— "Don't you ever blab, baby; hope to die and tell a lie"—about what they'd done to Mrs. Saletta's cat, or the secret location of their forbidden tree house or . . .

These real-time big boys—men—whisked her away, all right. Each grabbed an elbow; between them, Temple's high-heeled feet barely touched ground as they dragged her around a concrete pillar and pinned her against the wall behind it.

Temple fought to catch her breath, aware that she now occupied a dead-end notch in the parking ramp design, invisible to anyone who wasn't looking for people to be there.

As the men's grip on her upper arms relaxed a bit, she realized that their initial grab hadn't hurt only because it had clamped off the blood supply. Sensation screamed back into her veins, pulsing hotly around the impressions of their fingers in her flesh.

But, unlike childhood bullies, these goons didn't want her silence, quite the contrary.

"Where is he?" one demanded in a raw whisper.

"Who?"

"Your boyfriend," came the other's impatient rasp.

"I . . . I don't have a boyfriend. You must—"

Fingers tightened like wrenches. "Don't be funny. Your boyfriend the magician."

"Max? You want—?"

"Where is he?" the first man repeated, glancing nervously toward the main area as a car engine wheezed down the exit spiral.

Temple shook her head in confusion, in disbelief. "I don't know—"

She heard the oncoming car draw near, its tires peeling over the rough concrete like tape being pulled free, the cramped steering wheel squealing as it took the torturous exit curves.

The noise covered her yelp as the first man suddenly twisted her right arm behind her at a shoulder-wrenching angle.

Pain paralyzed her. The tote bag slid off her left arm, hitting the concrete with a solid clunk followed by the brittle shift of its contents.

"Where is he?" The second man's face leaned down to hers, so that his unwelcome breath warmed her cheeks, her eyes.

"I don't know," she began again, trying to figure out what they wanted her to say, why they wanted her to say anything.

She stopped when the second thug's big hand circled her throat and clamped it to the concrete wall. The dry, piercing pressure on her windpipe made her want to cough.

"We don't want to hear that," the first man whispered almost intimately in her right ear. His breath tickled, and smelled of radishes.

"The police don't even know!" she managed to gag out.

"We know that," the second man said. "That's why we're asking you. You'd better tell us. You were his girl-friend. They always know."

"No point in being a martyr," the first riffled into her ear.

Martyr? The man illustrated his remark an instant later. His fist jabbed into her side, jolting her against the concrete wall for a secondary buffeting.

Temple doubled over despite the grip on her throat, pain exploding in her midsection. Before she could absorb the incredible reality of the assault, another fist followed the first, even as the other man's meaty, salty hand clamped over her nose and mouth. Breathless, she felt pain rising like a sudden tide, pulling her down into the watery dark.

But the men wouldn't let her sink. Hands slapped her back to startled consciousness. "Where? Tell us. Where is he?"

Her arms pinioned, she began kicking frantically, fighting unconsciousness. Keep afloat, she told herself. Keep moving, don't let the sharks get a good grip on any part of you. . . . Temple felt her spike heels graze shins and bounce off bone. Her angry, frightened cries were muted by a palm slimed with her own saliva; she bit into the meager pleats of flesh her teeth could find.

Then her right wrist, elbow, shoulder seemed to be twisting off in another direction. The men hemmed her in, fists pummeling, just hurting her now, not asking anything. She heard their hard, exhausted breaths, glimpsed faces ugly with unreachable violence.

Brakes shrieked.

Someone yelled. A man. An angry man. In Temple's mind, her assailants had divided like amoebas, had multiplied and invaded the entire universe, inflicting pain, pain, pain in a kind of manic rain. . . . Blood gurgled in her mouth. At least at the dentist's they let you lean over into the white bowl and spit it out—no, not anymore, not for a long time; now they vacuumed it out.

"Goddammit!" a furious male voice exploded on the other side of the wall. "You nearly ran into me. I just had the goddam car waxed. Watch where you're going!"

"Listen, you barreled around that corner so fast it's lucky you didn't get a new buffing job all along the side."

"Fuck off!"

"Same to you, buddy!"

The voices, despite their anger, sounded distant and sleep-inducing, like the murmur of visiting relatives in the kitchen on a rainy Sunday morning.

Temple flailed to pull herself above the enveloping tide of dreamy dark water, away from the crimson stingers of the jellyfish and the bloody white teeth of the circling sharks.

When she finally reached up and her shoulder shouted with pain, she listened and let her arm fall back limply. Something was fading away. Shapes large and not quite seen. The quarreling drivers continued berating each other, their words growing clearer, though no more meaningful for Temple.

She looked around through the blur in her eyes—not tears, because she didn't think she was crying. She was too shocked to cry.

The world seemed vaguely askew. She took a cautious step forward, away from the wall, clammy despite the Las Vegas heat. The whole world jumped. She looked down, dizzy, and saw the contents of her tote bag scattered at her feet. Inching her back down the wall, her left hand touching it for balance, she finally crouched on the balls of her feet and began sweeping her things back into the bag one by one.

The men still shouted. Now one wanted the other to move his car out of the way. "Over my dead body!" the other vowed.

Their belligerent voices kept her anchored in reality. She leaned past her fallen personal effects and spit out the sour, tangy saltwater in her mouth.

A red blob blossomed on the gray pavement. Sidewalk spit revolted her, something only crude men did, but this was her own, an oddly disassociated lovely red phenomenon, like a blooming rose.

Her fingernails scraped the sandpaper-textured concrete as she shuffled papers, pencils, makeup bag, card case, keys back into her bag. No. Not keys. Would need keys. Her right hand clasped them, a gesture felt all the way to her shoulder.

She was about to rise when she saw something odd lying in front of her. About three inches long, tapered. And purple. Oh. Her heel. One of her heels had broken off.

Anger flared in Temple's anesthetized brain. Her favorite Liz Claibornes!

She scooped up the heel in the same hand that clutched the keys, and—again using the wall as a support—pushed herself slowly upright. Her lips, mouth and jaw were burning now. She knew she was hurt. What to do? The other men— But as she listened she realized that they were gone.

Her car. Must get to her car and lock the doors. But first she must unlock them. Keys in hand, she edged around the pillar, not sure what she would do if two tall men were waiting.

No one there. Only the noncommittal humps of parked cars. Her own wasn't far. She had almost reached it. A miss is as good as a mile, an inner voice mocked. Left. Facing the outside of the ramp. Aqua.

She limped along, carrying the tote bag in her left hand, because it freed the right hand to use the keys, because the arm hurt too much to carry more than a ring of keys and a broken heel. She had to brace herself on the trunks of cars she passed, hearing her car keys chime on metal, wincing and hoping she wasn't scratching the paint. Couldn't look. Couldn't stop. Need help. Find help. Find car!

The Storm's cheerful aqua hit her hot, blurred vision like a splash of cooling water. She staggered along the driver's side and slung the tote bag onto the hood while she fumbled with the keys. The heel kept getting in the way, but she had to hang on to it. For a moment she couldn't remember whether the key turned left or right, couldn't remember ever knowing that. And then instinct resurfaced. She wrenched it right—a sharp hot needle of pain jabbed all the way up to her collarbone. The door opened to her left hand. She was easing herself in when she remembered the tote bag, straightened and retrieved it. She paused for a minute, panting, before the open door. She needed to get in, to lock it. But how to get the heavy tote bag past her first, into the passenger seat?

Sighing, Temple swung it with her left arm, let its weight pull her arm back and then pull her arm inward. She loosened her grip. The tote plopped upright in the passenger seat like a bag of groceries.

Temple eased herself into the car seat, let her right foot reach in and her knees bend—that felt all right—let her torso bend—that didn't—and her head dip forward . . . oh. She was seated, gripping the steering wheel, watching its spoked circle whirl around and around in her gaze.

Her left leg still trailed out the open car door. She pulled in the foot with the heelless shoe; at least she didn't have to drive with it. Her left arm pulled the door shut. Such a nice sound. Solid and safe. Her forefinger hit the door locks, and they snapped to attention.

Safe in the car, alone in the car, Temple felt pain pool into one tidal wave of agony and almost swallow her.

Home. She had to get home. Safe at home. Keys in ignition. Yes. Taken-for-granted motions were returning. Her teeth suddenly started chattering, scaring her more than the pain, than the mental haze that still surrounded her. Shock. Shouldn't drive. Had to. They might come back. The engine purred obediently at the right movements with the key. She would have to shift with her right arm. Ow. Reverse. Back out. The pallid red reflections of her own taillights startled her into braking sharply for an instant. Then the car was backed up. She gritted her teeth and pushed the automatic gear into Drive. The Storm was idling along to the exit ramp, ready to circle down. No one coming. She entered the concrete corkscrew. Dizzy, oh God! She hit the brakes, then reconsidered. Had to circle out. Had to. Only way.

Every turn set the whole gray concrete world lurching, made her stomach do somersaults. She turned and turned and turned before finally seeing the straight stretch that led to the attendant's booth. Maybe here—?

But the sullen young man on duty barely glanced at the guest parking placard on her dashboard, and she was already beyond him, rolling toward a wall of blazing Nevada sunshine.

Sunglasses! Her right hand pawed for the familiar case in her disheveled tote. She must find her sunglasses before her bloodshot eyes hit blaring daylight. She had to see better to drive in traffic.

Her fingers played blindman's buff among a raft of displaced items—makeup bag, not glasses case!—while the Storm rolled toward a force field of sunlight as inevitable as a wall of fire. Then she clutched the padded vinyl case, clawed the glasses out, forced the bows open and clapped the glasses to her face just in time.

Masked, disguised, sheltered, she breathed again. She could see to drive. She could get home. Or should she drive downtown to the police station? No. Far. And she'd have to say why. They wouldn't believe her, or if they did, she'd get Max in more trouble. Apparently he was in enough already.

Las Vegas streets were clean, uncomplicated, pin-straight for the most part. The Storm virtually smelled the way home, the wheel canting right and left in a specific rhythm. Second nature took over. Even the occasional red light passed in a blur of gleaming, sun-baked auto bodies and the funny static buzz in Temple's head, funny because she didn't have the radio on.

And finally every tree looked familiar and the oleanders were massing in predictable clumps. The driveway into the Circle Ritz parking lot was one more right turn away, one more interminable pull on her bad right arm.

Someone had left the shady spot for her.

Temple struggled out of the car in the reverse order of her painful entrance. She teetered beside it for numb instants before she locked it, hating to leave her mobile safety zone. Maybe the men were waiting for her here. No. Too close to where she lived, not enough crowds around to disguise their purpose. Too many witnesses who might know her. No. Besides, they'd have to tangle with Midnight Louie, almost-twenty-pound watchcat, if they tried anything funny in her own place. Right.

She lurched forward, touching the ball of her left foot to the asphalt and keeping her heel in the air at the right height, so she barely limped. Like the wine, the properly aged instep remembers. She was amazed to find a rueful brand of humor resurfacing amid the shock and pain, like unsuspected flotsam from a shipwreck. Something she could hold on to. Just a few more steps to the gate. Once there, she struggled to open it, her key ring and the severed heel still keeping clumsy company in her right hand, her left arm captive to the heavy tote bag slung over the wrist.

The cumbersome stockade gate scraped across the concrete and pulled shut again as ungraciously, but at last it was latched. She could cross the searing cement to the nondescript side door that offered shade and safety in equally blessed doses.

Only a few more steps. This one. That one. Careful. Don't shake the shoulder, the head, the eyes. Step as daintily as a cat on a hot tin roof. Fire-walking.

She was halfway there when the voice came.

"Temple," it said.

She paused, swallowing. Her throat was as sore as if she had strep. Temple. She had to think about that one.

"Temple?"

Closer now, the voice. It was becoming a person. She didn't want to see a person. She didn't want a person to see her. She froze like a rabbit. A stupid, helpless rabbit on a moonlit lawn. Maybe you can't see me. Maybe you will just go away, or I will. Maybe—

"Temple, what happened?"

Shocked now, the voice, and too familiar to ignore. She

turned, looked through the comforting dark of her glasses to find Matt Devine approaching her in cautious disbelief, like a nosy neighbor in a TV commercial viewed through a distorting fish-eye lens. Go away! she wanted to scream, but her throat hurt too much to shout.

"Good God, Temple, what happened to you?" he demanded in the hushed, awestruck tones reserved for funerals and hospital rooms.

The words, the shock, did what she had feared. They released the logjam in her emotions, rejoined her physical and mental selves, forced her stability meter off the scale.

She opened her right hand, where the keys she'd clutched had impressed their cryptic profiles into her flesh, across her lifeline and headline and heartline. The severed heel lay there, too, a greater cipher to anyone but her.

She felt the tide coming, sensed the flash flood behind her eyes, heard the flux thickening her voice. "They . . . they broke it. They broke the heel off my shoe," she managed to explain, heartbroken as a child with a shattered toy, before she began sobbing.

Chapter 17

Official Abuse

"I hate this," Temple muttered, tears and a blood taste mingling on her lips.

She leaned against the welcome support of the faded chartreuse wall outside her condominium. Matt had set the tote at their feet and was frowning at her key ring in the dimly lit entryway.

He had reacted to her breakdown with swift, masculine action. He had taken the tote bag in one hand, then scooped her up and carried her in, up in the elevator, and to the door of her unit.

Not long ago she would have adored being swooped away in Matt Devine's strong, lightly tanned arms. Of course in her imagination she would have been perfectly coiffed, gowned and made up and they would have been heading for a devoutly mutual rendezvous somewhere high above the city; she had not yet decided where.

But now the ease with which he had swept her off her feet, however gallant and practical the intention, only reminded her how easily the two thugs had overcome her free will by the same expedient. Besides, now she felt like a child who'd been in a scrape at school—dirty, humiliated and in the wrong, somehow, for being hurt at all.

The right key finally clicked and Matt picked up her bag and took her elbow to guide her inside. Her right elbow. She cringed away, sucking in her breath.

His hand dropped as if he had touched a hot burner. Temple tottered in on her own power, through the hallway and into the living room, where she sat on the white-muslin-upholstered sofa.

Matt gingerly set the tote bag down on the cocktail table in front of her. "Can I get you anything?"

"Water."

He vanished, and Temple looked around cautiously, toting up her possessions, marking their unchanged presence, becoming thankful for that.

He returned with a lowball glass full; apparently he hadn't found the twelve-ounce tumblers in the next cabinet. She found it hard to swallow, and the liquid didn't help her stomach.

Matt sat on the edge of the cocktail table, a sturdy wood-framed square of thick glass, facing her. He laid the keys on the table, and the broken heel, then bent to gently pull her shoes off, the damaged one first, then the other.

Temple curled her toes into the zebra-print area rug under the cocktail table. At least *they* didn't hurt.

"Can you tell me now?" he asked.

"I must look awful."

He nodded gravely, and she almost rose to consult a mirror, but his fanned hand stopped her.

"How do you feel?" he asked in a kindly tone as impersonal as a doctor's.

The question, and the distance, set her at ease. "Awful," she admitted. She shrugged. "I suppose my clothes are ruined."

"Maybe not. Can you talk about it."

Temple sighed, sorry immediately afterward. The small inhalation hurt her shoulder. "Two men accosted me in the Goliath parking ramp. They got pretty physical."

"Robbers?" he asked incredulously. "Did you resist that much?"

"I couldn't resist at all, except kick a little. Until a couple of drivers had a near-brush and got into a loud argument. Then the men . . . melted away."

"What did they get?"

"Nothing."

Matt frowned again, which only emphasized his warm brown eyes under slanted sun-bleached brows. "What did they do to you?"

Her left hand lifted to pat her right shoulder. "Twisted my arm halfway around." The hand touched her cheek. "Slapped me for not keeping quiet. Everything happened so fast . . . so fierce. I hardly knew what hit me, or how I was hit—" Saying it was reliving it. She stopped, her teeth clattering together as uncontrollable shivers battered her aching frame. "It's like I've got a fever and chills."

"Shock." Matt confirmed her earlier instinct. He rose and went into the kitchen, ran some water, put something in the microwave. She could hear the high-pitched wheeze of the machine as it zapped whatever was inside. His face appeared around the kitchen wall. "Got a blanket somewhere?"

"Not out in summer," she murmured. "Left bedroom, in the bathroom linen closet."

He came back with a thick rose-colored wool blanket she'd forgotten about, and wrapped her in it. The microwave tinged and he vanished into the kitchen again. Cupboards banged. Matt returned with a hot cup of black coffee and a box of soda crackers.

"Coffee will help. And eat some crackers."

She sipped the bitter, steaming liquid, tried to gum down the cracker. Her jaws hurt. Her teeth hurt. The cracker paste oozed down her esophagus like rubber cement, but a little clarity was seeping into her foggy brain.

Matt came to sit beside her on the couch, to hold the cup between sips because she was still shaking. "Could you identify these guys?"

"I don't know. Can you identify a hurricane? Maybe."

"Did they say anything, have any reason for being so hard on you?"

Temple was silent. Matt took her reserve for weakness and brought the coffee cup to her lips. She sipped the strong brew gratefully. The heat was reaching a place inside her that had become very cold and indifferent. The excuse for not speaking allowed her to consider her answer. To tell the truth meant mentioning Max, whom she couldn't explain to herself, much less to Matt Devine. And the more people who knew about Max, perhaps the more danger they were in.

She finally looked at him and shook her head, trying to indicate that it was no use asking or answering such questions. He took the gesture for a no, and she let him.

"Let me see." He reached for her face.

She winced but held still.

"You cut the inside of your cheek on your teeth. Bleeds a lot but not serious. Looks like some swelling near the left eye. May swell more later."

The calm cataloging of her injuries made them seem remote, removed. Her chills were subsiding, but the pain was deepening.

"Why are you holding your arms like that?" Matt was asking.

"Like what?" She looked down where her hands clutched the blanket's satin-bound edges. She was sitting huddled over herself, as if cold, her arms crossed over her midriff, the left one cradling the right.

"They"—just mentioning it revived the feel of the blows—"punched me."

He gently lifted her right arm, supported the wrist. "Wrist isn't broken, or you'd be screaming." He pulled until her elbow straightened, and she hissed through her teeth. "A bad wrench, I'd guess. It could be sore for a while."

He shot her an apologetic glance for hurting her, then rotated the arm. The pain wasn't as intense as when she tried to do something with it. Matt was watching her arm and her face with that same distant consideration, like a doctor, or a personal trainer. Of course. He practiced the martial arts. He'd know about . . . combat injuries.

"Ice," he said.

"Huh?" How odd, not long before she had been urging ice on someone else.

"You'll need ice packs on it, to bring the swelling down. I've got some gel packs you can have."

He pulled the blanket away, releasing a hoarded store of body heat she immediately missed. "This side?"

She nodded as his fingers probed softly along her rib cage, and crossed her arms over her breasts to keep the precious heat in. The third rib up she felt a stab of pain and cried out before she could pretend to be a big person and ignore it. The next rib was no easier.

Matt's frown grew deep. "Looks like they did a real job on your ribs. They used their fists on you?"

Temple nodded. Matt's eyes went to her arms, again cradling each other. "That arm shouldn't be that painful if it's just a wrench. Think. Why are you holding your arms that way? Where does it hurt?"

She hadn't been able to differentiate the miasma of ache and pain besieging her body into specific zones, but Matt's words made her realize why she assumed her defensive posture.

"They didn't just punch me in the ribs," she remembered suddenly.

Matt's face whitened beneath the tan. He turned his head away, saying something curt she didn't hear, then put a hand to his eyes as if seeking inner control. When he turned back to her he was calm, but grim.

"Temple, you've got to go to a hospital, an emergency room." He read the reluctance in her eyes and went on.

145

"You could have serious internal injuries. What were these guys—gang punks? Did they try to rape you?"

She shook her head. Adult white males. Mean. Max's enemies. *Oh, God, Max, what were you into?*

"No, they didn't try to rape you, or no, you don't want to go to the hospital?"

His splayed fingers rested lightly on her ribs, a healing touch that made up for the trauma of assault. "No. No attempted rape. And no . . . hospital, please." She anticipated the objections forming on his face and said quickly, said lightly, "Couldn't we just stay here and play doctor? You seem awfully good at it."

His expression remained troubled, then he laughed wearily, but pulled his hand away. "Not good enough to substitute for the real thing. Don't be like one of my callers, Temple. Don't fight against your own good. I'll take you to the emergency room. Please let me."

He was right, darn his big brown honest eyes. She'd known she was hurt even during the adrenaline-anesthetized flurry of the attack.

"I hate this," she repeated.

"I know." Matt looked deep into her eyes. "It's scary and humiliating to be a victim. But the worst is over; I promise."

His tone was so reassuring, his eternally attractive expression so sincere. He was wrong, of course; the worst was still to come, when she had time to wonder what Max had been involved in—and with whom—and when someone would come for her again. But she couldn't tell Matt that. Couldn't tell anyone. The matter was too complicated, and now it looked like it might be too dangerous.

Temple also hated being a passenger in her own car. From the moment the two men had trapped her in the parking ramp, she had lost control of her life. Even the fact that it was Matt driving the Storm—he couldn't afford a car on his hotline salary, he told her apologetically—didn't lessen the insult of how much had been taken from her in a few, cataclysmic minutes. Besides, the Storm's stops and accelerations, its occasional turns, burdened a body no longer anesthetized by the shock of injury. Temple concentrated on not adding a chorus of moans to her unwanted progress to the hospital.

In the glow of an orange-purple sunset, Las Vegas was beginning to light up the sky with artificial candlepower. Strip traffic was thinning to a constantly moving stream of pallid headlights after the rush-hour logjam. Matt drove straight to the University Medical Center emergency room on Charleston, and helped her in. The moment the automatic door whooshed open to receive them, Temple felt a cold stone in the pit of her stomach that said that this was a mistake.

Glaring overhead fluorescents. Functional walls and plain, tiled floor. The inevitable plastic chairs lining the wall, some filled with waiting people whose harshly shadowed faces never looked up. A ballpoint pen chained to a clipboard. A lined form demanding that Temple remember long strings of numbers and write down personal information—like her age—in front of Matt, who might be younger, and who was supposed to care anymore but people did?

They sat together, waiting in a pair of inevitably orange molded chairs. Temple kept her sunglasses on to fend off the threatening headache.

An ambulance siren whined in the distance, then grew louder and louder, like a baby working itself up for a good long bawl. Just when Temple thought she would scream to keep it company, it choked off. What followed was worse. A man's cries—deep, guttural, repeated over and over. Only searing pain would make a man cry out like that. Temple's aches suddenly seemed minor.

A knot of people plowed through the waiting room, a small storm of activity in the stagnant pool of becalmed patients, and rushed back to the examining area.

One person in the group stopped, paused, then walked slowly over to chairs by the wall. Temple was watching the floor, too tired to hold her head up, when she saw the feet and legs stop in front of her.

She looked up. And up. And up.

"What are you doing here?" Lieutenant C. R. Molina asked with open surprise.

"Minor accident," Temple replied quickly.

Matt turned to stare at her, and drew Molina's notice. Temple watched Molina's policewoman's eyes rapidly tour Matt from head to toe, from clothes to posture to speculated vocation and possible vices.

"This is Matt Devine," Temple said, "the neighbor who brought me in."

"Nice to have good neighbors," Molina remarked cryptically, her expression as flat as ever.

She was looking at Matt Devine, boy dreamboat, Temple thought with irritation, and all Molina could do was look suspicious. She finished the introduction, because Molina obviously wasn't leaving without it.

"Lieutenant Molina of LVMPD."

Matt turned to Temple again, confusion in his eyes, and his lips parted to inform Temple that she could tell the police of her assault right here and right now very conveniently. . . . Sweet Shalimar!

"That man who was moaning," Temple said quickly to Molina, "must be in dreadful pain. Is he why you're here?"

"Yes, unfortunately. Nice meeting you, Mr. Devine." Molina's remarkable ice blue eyes rested on Temple with a hint of speculation. "Take care of yourself."

She wheeled and was gone. Temple let her shoulders slump. One protested. She had known that showing an interest in Molina's business would be the fastest way to get rid of her.

"That's Lieutenant Molina? And why didn't you tell her?" Matt demanded. "It was a perfect opportunity, if you know a police officer personally."

"Molina was on the ABA case. We don't get along."

"Still, it's her job—"

"Not the small stuff. Matt, I don't want to tell her, and I won't. Maybe I don't need to go to the police at all."

He was about to argue, but at that moment her name was finally called. Matt squeezed her hand as other eyes glanced up to follow her into the examining area. She didn't limp, but neither did her footsteps announce her assertive progress. Instead of a click, she padded as silently as Midnight Louie, only she owed her subtle approach to L.A. Gear metallic pink sneakers.

They made her feel like a kid, as the two men had made her feel helpless, as Matt's solicitude had made her feel like a teenager with a hopeless crush, as Molina's presence had made her feel found out. Hopeless and helpless.

"I hate this," Temple gritted between her teeth just before the nurse bearing a clipboard led her into an examining room.

"Come along, hon." The nurse was a chubby, cheerful soul with bright blond hair cut into a modified punk crew cut, plus the obligatory rattail trailing down her broad, white-covered back.

She took Temple's blood pressure and wrote it on the clipboard. She handed her a hospital smock. "Just undress from the waist up. Opens in the back." The nurse was almost out the door when Temple remembered an embarrassing fact.

"Uh, wait! You'll have to unhook me. My arm won't go back."

"Sure thing," the nurse said. "Should have remembered. You said your shoulder was really wracked up. Terrible what happens." And she glanced at Temple from under blue-shadowed lids, her eyes holding a puzzling trace of blame.

Tied by the nurse into the limp cotton smock and finally left to herself, sitting on the sanitary paper liner accorded each of the sequence of patients, her feet swinging free at the end of the examining table, Temple felt sore and tired and helpless.

She had a while to wait for that feeling to end; the

doctor didn't come in for twelve minutes. Now *he* carried her life data on a clipboard. He was an Indian man with skin the color of brown shoe polish, blue-black hair and fine features. Like many professionally trained natives of that land, he radiated a benign good cheer reminiscent of Gandhi. Dr. Rasti.

"Shoulder, arm, jaw and midsection." He enumerated her injury zones in a pleasant singsong. "You are an unfortunate young lady. Let us see."

Away went the charade of the hospital gown as he drew it back in stages to poke and prod and examine.

"Muggers, you say?"

Temple nodded. She had wanted to write "car accident," but then the police might want to know why it hadn't been reported. Besides, her injuries were not consistent with a close encounter with a dashboard; even she knew that. Dr. Rasti scribbled a long entry between the fine lines of her clipboard sheet.

His verbal diagnosis mirrored Matt's: no serious— seerius, he chirped like a friendly bird—damage; bruises and contusions. No X rays needed. Ice packs. Rest. A prescription for painkillers. Call your own physician if any symptoms persist unreasonably.

"As for here"—his hands thumped his white coat, his own chest—"perhaps bad bruises, discomfort. Will be fine." Then he frowned at the clipboard. "Muggers very bad. More than one?"

Temple nodded.

"Two? Big men, bad men?"

Temple nodded.

Dr. Rasti shook his head and regarded her narrowly. "Very bad. I will have nurse step in. Little more business needed."

Temple sighed when he left and started to pull her bra on. The nurse rustled through the door, hooked the back and helped her pull her loose top over her head.

The nurse held the clipboard, gave Temple a prescription, and finally flourished a brochure.

"Now, Miss Barr." She licked her lips. "Dr. Rasti is very worried. Your injuries . . . well, they are most unusual for a mugging. Usually scraped knees, a fractured elbow. Your injuries are the result of punches. I have a brochure from the Women's Shelter—"

"No. It wasn't a battering."

"Sometimes it's not easy to tell the difference. Sometimes it's hard to say. Please, just check out the Women's Shelter. You can call this number anytime, you don't have to leave your name. Talk to them."

"Thanks, but I don't need to. I'm not a victim of abuse."

"Nobody likes to think of themselves that way, but sometimes, when we love someone, it's hard to be objective. We know they don't mean it; we know they say they're sorry and they are—but they can't guarantee they won't be that way again. And again. It's a cycle. You have to take some action to stop it."

"I tell you, there's no need! All right, I'll take your brochure. But I think it's a free country and I can go now."

"Maybe I can help," came a voice from the hall.

A voice Temple knew well. She could have died.

Lieutenant Molina walked in, her professional face on. The moment she saw Temple, the self-possessed expression melted as Temple had never had the satisfaction of seeing before. All that taut confidence grew slack and confused for an instant.

The two women stared at each other in individual stupefaction. Molina recovered first, but she was on her feet and she wasn't half-dressed.

"I'll handle this," Molina told the nurse, in control again.

"Thanks, Lieutenant." The nurse vamoosed, brochure and all, but Molina held out her hand wordlessly for the clipboard. And got it. Now Molina was in full possession of all the facts of Temple's life. She loved it, Temple thought savagely.

151

"I can see," Temple said, fuming, "why poor people hate coming to emergency rooms, if they're going to be harassed as well as treated."

"Spotting battering cases is important." Molina scanned the bottom of the clipboard, her heavy eyebrows lifting once or twice. She looked up at Temple. "You took quite a beating."

"Yes, I did, and I don't need a verbal one now."

"The doctor and nurse did what they're supposed to. Any trained medical or police personnel would recognize that you were the recipient of a deliberate beating."

"Recipient. What a nice, bureaucratic way of putting it."

"Calm down. I know you're tough. I know you're stubborn. You don't have to pretend to be stronger than you are."

"Yes, I do, because I'm not six-blooming-feet tall and I don't get to carry a badge and a gun!"

Molina froze, then shrugged and backed up; then she did something amazing. She stepped out of her low-heeled shoes and dropped a couple of inches. "That better?"

Temple's righteous rage huffed and puffed and had nowhere to go. "Some. Listen. If I had been a victim of abuse, I'd be the first to cry 'Wolf!' Honest. These were strangers."

"Muggers hit and hurt on the run. They don't hang around for the fun of it."

"Maybe these were sadistic muggers."

"I don't buy that. Who is this Devine guy?"

"I told you. A neighbor. What a world if he takes me to the emergency room—and if he hadn't insisted, I wouldn't have come—and ends up getting accused of being an abuser! So much for the survival chances of good Samaritans."

"We have to ask these questions," Molina said patiently. "Doctors, nurses and police personnel haven't done it enough in the past, so women and children have paid for it. Did you know that one-third of the women who come into an emergency room are victims of abuse?"

Statistics hit home when argument would not. "No, I didn't know. That many?"

"And those are just the ones who come in. That doesn't count the tough customers like you who refuse to go."

"Ouch. Okay, I can see why you have to ask. But you have to listen, too. And intimate abuse is not my problem, believe me."

"So many deny," Molina said, then raised her hand as Temple bridled again. "Still, your story doesn't wash."

"Maybe because it's not the whole story."

Molina leaned against the wall. "Tell me."

So Temple did, hating it, but hating being thought an abusee worse. Molina listened, but her face never reflected her thoughts.

"You could identify the men?" she asked at last.

"I like to think so, but when you're in the middle of a thing like that, it's hard to look for identifying moles."

"We need you to look at some mug shots. Maybe tomorrow after you get some sleep."

"Okay."

"And they wanted to know Max Kinsella's whereabouts?"

Temple nodded.

"Did you tell them?"

"How could I? I don't know."

"So you say." Molina pushed herself away from the wall and resumed her shoes. She slid Temple a glance from under her dark wings of eyebrow. Lord, that woman could benefit from a little female artifice, Temple thought.

"Why now?" Molina asked when she stood, tall as ever, in front of Temple again. "Four months since Kinsella's disappearance."

Temple just shook her head.

"You need to take this seriously, so I'll have to tell you something I don't want to."

Temple perked up. It was about time the shoe slipped onto the other foot, even if it was a clodhopper.

Molina's lips worked reluctantly; then she came out with a hail of words as blunt as bullets. "After Kinsella disappeared, the night he disappeared, a body was found in the surveillance area over the Goliath's gaming area. Stabbed, once and well. The hotel's assistant security director. You know all the casinos have skymen on watch through one-way mirrors and video equipment over the gaming areas? Well, the man's body was found in an unauthorized peephole carved out of the air-conditioning vent. Only a clever and agile person could have managed that spy-hole, and getting someone else in it."

"You think Max—"

"A magician could have done it, but whether he ran because he knew his accomplice was dead and figured he'd be next, or just because the man was dead and he'd done it, I don't know. Nor do I know what was involved— abetting confederates at the tables below, or blackmailing cheaters, whatever."

"Whatever, Max's a murderer or the prey of one."

"And if someone's after him because he knows too much, they may not have bothered with you because they didn't know who you are, or where you were: until you came back to the Goliath this week. You did frequent the place when Kinsella was appearing there?"

"'Frequent.' Come on, Lieutenant, that makes me sound like a gun moll. Yes, I met Max there for a drink and dinner now and again. I went to a few shows."

"Didn't you know the act by heart by then?"

"The illusions may have been the same, but Max and the audience were different every night. That's what Max did; he never made anything seem the same twice."

Molina contemplated the interesting ramifications of that assessment without losing her cool, then nodded soberly. "They saw you again and decided to get some answers. That means they're familiar with the Goliath and that you're in danger working there. No chance you'd quit?"

"The show must go on."

Molina shook her head. "Then it'll go on with police all over the place. You're tiptoeing around something a lot uglier than you've ever imagined. You're lucky those two drivers had a set-to in the ramp, because even if you really don't know where Max Kinsella might be, those thugs wouldn't have stopped. They sound as if they enjoy their work."

Temple nodded. Lucky.

"All right." Molina stepped aside. "Come downtown tomorrow first thing for a mug-shot tour. I'll alert the staff. If those men want Kinsella, I want those men."

"Better them than him," Temple muttered as she hopped—ouch!—off the table.

"What?"

"I'll do what I can, Lieutenant," Temple said from the doorway. And then she skedaddled.

Matt's blond head hit her bleary eyes like a puddle of sunshine in the dreary waiting room. She headed straight for him and collapsed on the adjoining chair. It had been a long and traumatic evening.

"I'm free to go. No X rays, no casts, no permanent injuries. They tried to lay an abuse rap on me, can you imagine? And we need to stop for a prescription on the way home."

Matt glanced at the white slip in her hand and nodded, then picked up Temple's tote bag. He let it ease back to the floor again as Lieutenant Molina approached them.

She suddenly squatted on her heels in front of Temple, her piercing eyes and serious face impossible to avoid.

"I know you don't listen to officials much, but no matter how your injuries happened, you're a victim of a crime. You need to deal with that. Here's the number of a self-help group. Give them a call. You'll have a lot of rage; your self-esteem has taken a body blow, too. Don't be dumb. Talk to someone else who's been through it."

Temple sat in silence.

"She's right," Matt said.

Temple glanced at the number. Heck, maybe they needed a freebie PR person. "Okay."

Molina patted Temple's knee—Molina!—and rose. She flashed Matt a smile Temple had never seen, approving. "Thanks for the sensible support."

"I have to give it. I'm a hotline counselor."

Molina's expressive eyebrows lifted before she nodded. "Then you'll see that she does it."

"I'll see that she's encouraged to do it. Temple will do what's she thinks is best for her."

"What's best for her is what I suggested."

"Grrrr," Temple remarked softly as Molina walked away. "What an insufferable woman."

Matt grinned as he watched Molina's iron-straight navy blue back disappear. "Insufferably right. Tacky of her. Reminds me of a mother superior. Come on, I'll drive you home."

Home. A nice word. And nice to have someone to go there with.

Chapter 18

A Roommate to Die For

Temple felt about two hundred years old when she and Matt once again stood before her condo door. He unlocked it smoothly this time. She entered first, startled to find lights blazing. Electra Lark sat at her kitchen café table painting her fingernails black.

The moment she saw Temple, Electra bounded upright and whirled over in a blaze of highly colored Hawaiian flora. Her welcoming embrace—arms wide and fingers splayed to protect her wet polish and Temple's bruised frame—ended up as a gentle cheek-brush, during which Temple whiffed an unmistakable trace of Emeraude. Oh, no. . . .

Matt beamed like a Boy Scout. "I called Electra when you were seeing the doctor."

Electra nodded until her ear cuffs rang. "I used the passkey to get your gel packs," she told Matt. "They're already on ice. I bet you two kids are starved! I could order a pizza."

"I'm not really hungry." Temple toddled gingerly toward the living room. "Oh!" Her huge cocktail table stood by the French doors because her sleep-sofa had been opened and made up.

"We're not going to let you stay alone after what happened." Electra's tone brooked no disobedience.

"We?" Temple asked.

"Well, I made up the bed," Electra said modestly, implying that she didn't often stoop to such domestic makework. "Matt said he'd stay tonight."

"Oh." Temple turned to her new roommate. "What about your job?"

"I called the hotline from the hospital, too."

"I'm all right. I don't need baby-sitting."

Electra bustled between them. "Maybe we need to do it. Now, are these your pills? Hmm. Tylenol Three. You'll sleep tonight. I'll get you to bed, and then I'll get the ice packs. Then maybe we can tempt you with—I know, ice cream."

"Why ice cream?" Temple asked in amazement.

"That's what I always let myself eat when I'm sick."

"And it doesn't require chewing," Matt added. "I'll be right back. I need some things from upstairs."

"Fine," Temple managed to say over her—ouch—shoulder. "The guest bath is to the left off the office."

"Now, what can I help with?" Electra waved her morbid fingernails again as she followed Temple into the bedroom, her thong sandals vigorously slapping parquet.

Temple felt as if she were being trailed by an oversolicitous seal. "Forget the ice cream. What I really need is help getting out of these clothes." Temple plucked at her knit top and turned her back to the landlady.

"You poor little thing," Electra clucked warmly while she undid the zipper and bra. Temple gritted her teeth against pain both physical and psychic. Electra was only trying to help. "Where's your nightdress?"

"That's it."

"The Garfield T-shirt on the hook? Oh, cute."

Temple regarded the image of the self-satisfied tiger-striped cartoon feline regarding himself in a mirror under text that announced, "Gemini: Your double-edged nature means there's more for everybody, but you can never get enough of yourself." Cute didn't seem to describe it.

Lifting both arms to don the shirt was harder than it looked. "Electra, you're a Florence Nightingale to help me out. I'm sorry to be such a bother."

"I've been called a rare old bird before, but never a nightingale." But she blushed.

Temple plodded in slow motion into the tiled bathroom and glimpsed herself in the mirror. Not flattering, but at least she didn't look like Dracula's daughter with dried blood clinging to her lips. In fact, she looked remarkably normal, except for a subtle swelling in her face and an overall smudging of her makeup. No wonder so many battered women managed to conceal the ugly secret.

She ran the hot water tap, waiting for the warmth to rise up the elderly pipes, and finally dampened a washcloth. Wringing it out defeated her right arm, and she turned. Electra hovered behind her like a hotel maid.

"I can do that, dear!"

"Thanks." Temple waited for the cloth, then wiped her face one-handed. When she turned again, Electra was poised right there with the vintage blue aluminum tumbler and the pharmacy bag.

"Run a little cold water in this glass, and you can take your first pill."

The tiny bathroom, exquisitely tiled in a white and silver-gray pattern, was not up to a bumbling owner and a bustling landlady. They do-si-doed around each other and the pedestal sink, until Temple swallowed the pill and headed for the bed. Electra turned the ceiling fan on low and tucked her in.

Just in time. A knock on the ajar door announced the

return of Matt, bearing an armful of plastic packs loaded with blue goo. In moments he and Electra had mounted bath towels along Temple's right side. Her arm and shoulder soon were growing numb against a long, lumpy ski jump of frozen packs.

After installing her and turning off the lights, the pair decamped to the living room, from which Temple heard soft conversational tones—discussing her disaster, no doubt.

Alone at last. Everything throbbed when nothing distracted her from the pain. She was supposed to sleep, but she didn't feel like it.

A soft thump bounded atop the bed.

"Louie! Where did you come from?"

He stalked across the bed linens, wallowing over the swells of sheet and coverlet, and padded along her left side, stopping only when he would have to walk on her shoulder to continue.

Louie's big, furry feline face extended as he brought his jet black nose to hers, sniffing cautiously.

"You smell hospital." Or was it blood he noticed?

Louie turned his attention—and his head—to her body and arm, which he also honored with a thorough sniffing. Then he bent to paw the sheets and settled beside her, curling up like a kitten in the vee of her arm and body.

Midnight Louie had never permitted such a cozy position in their association. Temple gingerly patted the glossy back dome of his head, at which he laid his nose on his curled paws, seemed to sigh, and closed his eyes.

Great. Maybe *he*'d gotten into the potent Tylenol Threes.

Temple awoke in alarm.

She couldn't quite remember why her arm was propped on tepid plastic baggies, or why she felt like Midnight Louie's nigh-twenty pounds had been pussyfooting all over her in the night. The cat no longer lay next to her.

Moonlight leached through the fretwork of the French doors, throwing a pale plaid on the parquet tile.

Then it all came back to her. She sat up, panicked, heedless of the pain rapid movement brought. Her blood was battering at all her pulse points as if for exit. She couldn't breathe, couldn't catch her breath—maybe that's why her pulse was pounding, she'd been running in her dreams to catch her breath. . . .

A light sweat dappled her entire skin in an instant, chilling her in the relentless spin of the ceiling fan's Plexiglas blades. Hot flashes at her age? Well, she'd just turned thirty, she thought glumly. Combine that with recent shocks and it could happen. Wait. The pills! Strong, Electra had said. Maybe she was having a bad reaction.

Temple forced herself out of bed, hearing herself gasp for air in the tranquil silence.

Her bare feet stuck to the wooden floor as she skated for the door. It opened onto her living room. Moonlight from the bank of the French doors drenched that end of the room and bleached the walnut floor to white pine.

It also silvered the huge, alien form crouching low in front of the doors like an albino tiger. Temple skittered away into the living room proper—and found herself knocking into a larger, whiter unexpected shape.

"Temple?" a man's voice asked from the dark.

Max!

And then all the alien elements in the room—the two misplaced hunks, the man's voice—spun a little in her senses as she recognized them for familiar things out of place: her cocktail table turned stumbling block; her sofa turned bed; her neighbor turned watchdog-cum-counselor.

"Yes," she answered shakily. "I woke up suddenly. I couldn't remember at first."

"That was probably the Tylenol wearing off. Time to take another pill."

"Yes. No! Not just yet. I want to feel like myself for a

while." She sat on the misplaced bed's foot. "Did you see Louie leave?"

"Was he here?"

She nodded, then remembered that the room was dark and Matt wasn't used to its nighttime shapes. "Decidedly here, keeping me company in the bedroom. Maybe he went out."

"How? I never opened the French doors."

"The spare bathroom window is always cracked open."

"But that's three floors!"

"That's Louie's private exit and entry. Don't ask me how. Oh," Temple said despite herself, still feeling rocky.

"Are you all right?" Matt shifted in the bed.

Temple finally realized why she had such trouble making out his figure in the dim room. He was wearing his martial-arts outfit as pajamas; the pale material blended with the ivory-colored sheets. She had to credit him with coming up with a neat answer to the awkwardness of sleeping over. She wondered what he wore—or didn't wear—when he didn't have to be prepared for strange women barging into his sleeping area.

"Are you all right?" he repeated.

"I'm woozy from the pill, I guess." Matt waited. "And I think I just had a panic attack."

She could see the moonlight-gilded sheen of his hair nodding.

"That's why I'm here. Your body knows better than your mind what it's been through. You'll be extra jumpy for a while."

"Maybe I'll have reason to be."

"What do you mean?"

"I just realized something else. I'm afraid I was in mental as well as physical shock last night. I haven't been honest with you."

After a silence, Matt said, "How?"

"I didn't want to make it common knowledge, or maybe I didn't want to face facts. Those weren't two strangers that attacked me—I mean, they were strangers, to me. But they weren't to someone I know. Knew."

She heard the sheets rustle as Matt sat up and pushed them back. "What are you saying?"

"That it hadn't occurred to me, but they could come back, could come here. It isn't fair to let you do guard duty without letting you know that there's more to be worried about than me just freaking out."

"Why? Why are they after you?" He came around to sit beside her on the bed's edge.

"Not me. Max."

"Hummm."

"What do you mean, 'Hummm'?"

"Electra mentioned that you'd had a friend. A stage magician, she said."

"What else did Electra mention?"

"Only that he'd moved on."

"She didn't say how?"

"I didn't ask."

"Restrained of you. Well, Max overdid the magician bit one day, and vanished. Just like that. Four months ago. Left behind a few of his few favorite things. Me. A motorcycle I didn't know about, I've since learned. Some clothes and CDs."

"The men who assaulted you wanted him?"

"They wanted to know where he was."

"And you couldn't tell them."

"No. Wouldn't, either, if I could help it."

"Is that why you and the police lieutenant—"

"Why we don't get along? Sure, along with plain, rock-bottom mutual antipathy."

"I was going to say—why you know each other?"

"Oh. Well, we don't get along. God, I hated telling Molina about those creeps being after Max! She's after him herself, you know. Until tonight she wouldn't tell me why; even what she told me sounds like only half of it."

"Why, then?"

She glanced at Matt. The moonlight reached the end of the bed, so she could see his features, and he could read the truth of hers.

"The night Max vanished, he'd finished a run at the Sultan's Palace in the Goliath. That same night the body of the casino's security assistant was found in a secret hideaway in the ceiling—not the ordinary surveillance area above the gaming tables, but a hidden, unauthorized observation post."

"Coincidence," Matt said, shaking his head.

"Molina doesn't believe in coincidence. She thinks Max had the expertise to fashion that hidden post, to get in there, and to get someone else in there, maybe to kill that person."

"So why is she down on you?"

"Because when she came looking for answers about Max, I didn't have any."

"Or were you just not giving out any?"

"Maybe I wouldn't have talked if I knew, but I didn't know! And Molina didn't believe me any more than those men did, although I gotta say her interrogation technique, much as it leaves to be desired, is infinitely preferable to theirs."

"Poor kid," Matt said impulsively, his fingers pushing into the curls at the nape of her neck.

A kindly gesture, abstracted almost, but Temple felt a silken shiver down her spine that had nothing to do with panic attacks.

That's when she realized something else had awakened her and driven her out of the bedroom—loneliness under pressure, a need for comfort and care after a terrifying ordeal.

And here they were, all alone together. She wouldn't even have to worry about violating a bed Max and she had shared. No ghosts but the man dressed only in white martial-arts garb and moonlight.

She held herself still, neutral, and Matt's hand dropped away.

"Don't worry about me," he said. "I stayed because I knew that you wouldn't feel safe from those men for a long time, especially tonight. If they do come here, I'd be ready for them; I'm the human self-defense machine, remember? If they're really out to get you specifically, you should do more than contact that self-help group. You should study martial arts yourself."

"Oh, Matt! Who'd take me seriously? Martial Arts Mouse strikes again. These guys were big."

"Size has nothing to do with martial arts. They teach little kids."

"I'm not a jockette. The only muscles I've built up are in my feet."

"That's why it's ideal for you. It doesn't depend on brute strength. There's a studio only blocks from here. Jack Ree's a great teacher."

"Well, the gear is kind of cute"—she tugged on his full-cut sleeve—"but I'd get lost in it. And I bet I couldn't wear my high heels, right?"

"Not if you want to kick the menace out of anybody. We work barefoot."

"Never! Not in public."

"You really have a thing about it, don't you?"

"Appearing without high heels for me is like appearing nude would be for somebody else," she said firmly.

Matt leaned over to inspect her feet. "You're barefoot now."

"Except at home," she added with great dignity.

He pondered for a moment. "I can't stay here every night."

"Who says?" she couldn't resist saying. "Oops. Must be the Tylenol talking."

He was thinking hard and hadn't heard her, or had and wasn't going to comment. "I could teach you," he said. "Here. At home. Then you wouldn't have an excuse."

"Here?"

He looked around the room. "Not here. Down by the pool. I could borrow a couple mats from Jack. You don't work nine-to-five every day, and I've got afternoons off."

"Would I have to wear the cutesy pajamas?"

"I thought you liked mine."

"On you. And not even Cuban heels?"

"The only thing you're going have on your heels will be calluses."

"Sounds unappetizing."

"I'm serious, Temple. You might find out you're not as little as you think you are."

She shrugged. "You and Molina," she conceded sourly. "A couple of authoritarian do-gooders. Just for all your meddling, I'm going to find the G-string murderer, and tie him—or her—in knots with my new taikwanchi."

"T'ai chi or tae kwon do," Matt said, laughing. "Why should your finding another murderer get my goat?"

"It won't, but I hope it'll fry Lieutenant Molina down to her hard-boiled sole."

Talking to someone in the middle of the night was always therapeutic. When Temple returned to her bedroom—unaccompanied, darn!—visions of herself playing Karate Kid danced in her head until the fantasy became a dream and dream, morning.

She slipped into low-heeled slides and a wraparound sundress she didn't have to dislocate her arms to get into, and entered the sunny front room. Not to worry. No Matt. The sofa was a sofa again, with the bedding folded neatly on one arm. Matt must have learned such disciplined bed-making at boot camp or something.

She shuffled into the kitchen for something hot and bracing. With Matt gone, Temple enjoyed a certain, guilty relief. She could limp around the apartment without putting a brave face on her injuries, and without worrying about what her actual makeup-bare face looked like. She could even cuss under her breath.

And she did. It hurt to open the cupboard door and reach up for the mug, to turn on the faucet and twist open the instant-coffee jar. Running the microwave didn't hurt, thank goodness.

She turned from the cupboards, looking for some Equal to sweeten the straight black bitterness of coffee, and saw a foreign object poised on the opposite counter. Her shoe. Whole again. Heeled, so to speak. Heel and sole.

Temple smiled as she hobbled over to pick it up. Matt must have gotten up extra early and Super Glued the heel back on. She was standing there with a cup of coffee in one hand and mooning over a shoe in the other when her doorbell rang.

She glanced at the big pink neon clock. Eight o'clock. Who'd call that early? Unless Lieutenant Molina couldn't wait until nine for Temple to start her mug-shot search.

She reluctantly set down the shoe and wobbled for the door. She opened it on Electra's worried face.

"Did you have a good night, dear? I mean, did you sleep well?"

"Mostly," Temple answered vaguely. "Want some too-black coffee?"

"Never touch the stuff! Here, let me pour a little out, add a bit of water and . . . voilà!"

"Thanks," Temple said, accepting the diluted, drink-able coffee. "I'm not together yet, and I have to be at police headquarters downtown by nine."

"That's what I'm here for. Breakfast while you wait; assistant dresser; whatever. Do you want me to give you a ride there? The Vampire awaiteth."

"No, thanks. A bit too much agitation for me. I can get myself around once I get myself going. I wish—"

"Yes, dear—?"

"I wish I had another pair of ears and eyes at the Goliath for the strippers' competition. I won't be able to get in until ten or so, and I've got a feeling that the show has just begun to get on the road."

"Can you still do that job under the circumstances?"

"If they lost two PR people in a row, they'd really freak. Besides, it's too late for anyone else to come in cold."

"Maybe Mr. Buchanan is feeling better and can spell you."

"Electra, I'm going to be fine. I'll be better off with work to take my mind off things. And I wouldn't wish Crawford Buchanan on anybody."

Electra was banging through the cupboards in an effort to be helpful. She clattered the dishes, then handed Temple a cereal bowl. "Here's some milk."

"Thanks." Temple set down the coffee mug and took the tablespoon that Electra gave her, and crunched away at a generous spoonful. "Arghgk!" She ran to the sink and spat out her mouthful.

"What is it, dear? Is your stomach too delicate from the attack to—"

"Stomach nothing. It's my taste buds." Temple returned to the counter, picked up the so-called cereal container and squinted closely at the fine print. Since she had expected Matt, she had left her glasses on the bedside table.

"Electra, this is Louie's Free-to-be-Feline, not cereal! Aiyuch! No wonder he won't eat it."

"Oh, sorry! It looked like some trendy new cereal; something healthy."

"It's supposed to look like that," Temple commented sourly. "That's how they sell it to gullible humans. Cats are apparently harder to fool. Would you mind looking in the lower cupboard? I need some protein. I'm sure Louie wouldn't object to sharing some of the water-packed, dolphin-sparing fancy albacore people-tuna that's so bad for him with me."

Chapter 19

A Kinky
Cat-tail

Paging through mug shots was like looking at a yearbook of the terminally tough. Temple flipped past enough slightly skewed faces, tattoos, scraggly beards, sideburns and mustaches, scars and criminally close eyes to cast the gang members in several road-show companies of *West Side Story*.

"It's hard," she told the uniformed female officer who came back to check on her progress. "They were on me so fast, and they didn't look that unusual."

Officer Ontiveros, a woman of impressive muscularity, nodded, but offered a slim smile of encouragement. "The subconscious works all the time. Give yours a chance to testify."

So Temple turned page after page, wondering what Molina expected her to find: petty muggers or big-time muscle? Were her attackers even in this massive book?

At last she indicated three men who might have attacked her. "Obviously, I'm wrong about at least one," she said.

"That's okay, miss. It's a lead. The hard part will come if we dredge any of these guys up and have to go to lineup."

Molina must have been nearby watching, though that seemed unlikely. She strolled up just as Temple was about to be released from her civic duty, sat on the desk edge—no mercy the morning after—and looked down at Temple thoughtfully.

"Officer Ontiveros tells me you had some luck."

Temple nodded cautiously. She couldn't guarantee anything, she'd just done her best.

"I wish I'd had as much luck as you," Molina added.

"Oh?" Temple knew she was jumping hook, line, sinker and peach snakeskin high heels into something.

Molina rapped the manila file in her hand on the glass-topped desk. Temple didn't know why they bothered with the glass; the desktop was scarred by ballpoint squiggles, X-Acto knife cuts and coffee-cup rings.

"I never did unearth a photograph of Max Kinsella," Molina said. "Not a one. Quite a mystery man to the end."

Temple tried not to wince at that last phraseology. "The Goliath had tons of publicity shots," she said. "Head shots and eight-by-tens by the dozen."

"Not now, they don't."

"Oh, come on, Lieutenant. I saw those photos. I had 'em copied and distributed myself. Max didn't know PR from Puerto Rico. Maybe the publicity department didn't check the files."

"They did, and I did. Not a photo."

"What about the lobby placards?"

"Gone. Vanished."

"You're kidding! Those are collectors' items. This town was plastered with ephemera of Max. He was a big draw. You don't work the major hotels here unless you are."

"He draws a blank now." Molina managed not to sound triumphant. "And it's not just the absence of a paper trail. He left no trail at all: no driver's license, school records, employment. He's a Nowhere Man from—what did you call it? Ephemera." She almost tasted the word. "That means all the here-today, outdated-to-morrow publicity materials a show produces? The word does suit Mr. Mystifying Max. Looks like . . . some-body . . . made all those photos vanish. Presto chango."

Temple put a hand to her forehead. She was feeling punk, but had skipped her prescribed Tylenol because she had to get back to the Goliath and do her job. So not even photos remained of Max. Maybe she had dreamed him up.

Molina leaned forward, her resonant voice lowering confidentially. "You *are* contacting that self-help group?"

"Yes! All right? I'll go over next week."

"Fine," Molina said, backing off, drawing away. "You still sure that you don't have so much as a wallet shot?" she added.

Temple stared at her. "You'd use it against Max."

"Maybe, if we found him first, we'd save him from somebody else."

Temple sat back in the plain, hard chair. Her head hurt, along with a lot of other things. The hard truths she'd been hearing lately about Max, about herself, hurt, too. She wondered if she'd hate herself in the morning for saying this.

"I've got a poster," Temple admitted. "There should have been dozens still around. People like to collect post-ers."

"Great." Molina stood as if a bargain had been struck and it was time to go, probably straight back to Hades. "I'll stop by your place for it tonight. Say, seven?"

Temple nodded slowly. It hurt her head. She certainly

wasn't going out this evening. What better than to enter-
tain the Iron Maiden of the Las Vegas Metropolitan Police Department?

"Lieutenant! Telephone," bawled a man at an nearby
desk.

With a farewell nod, Molina moved briskly away.

Temple gathered up her tote bag, making sure everything was inside. She felt like a thousand-year-old lady
today, not daring to trust either her body or her mind to
go through even routine motions.

Unappetizing faces danced in the background of her
mind. Why would she want to finger those hoods? She
would only have to see them again in court.

A few desks away, Molina's low voice escalated into an
incredulous "What?"

Temple looked in that direction. Molina was bending
over the desk, scribbling furiously.

"Right," she was saying impatiently. "What time this
morning? Right away." She hung up the phone and
barked something to a man at a farther desk. He jumped
up, grabbing a khaki sport coat and some keys off a rack.

Molina was stuffing her kangaroo jacket pockets with
the paper she'd written on, her pen and notebook. She
glanced up at Temple watching her. "Did you drive here?"

"Yeah. I can do it—just."

"You up to stopping by the Goliath?"

"I was planning on it. I've got business there."

"So have I. Give me your car keys. I'll have a uniform
drive your vehicle over later. Let's get going now."

Temple complied and rose, teetering slightly on her
heels. Maybe they were a bad idea today, but then again,
they made a statement. "What's happening, Lieutenant?"
she asked.

Molina glanced over her shoulder at the other detective
right behind her. "Another stripper's been murdered.
Now let's go." The two officers didn't wait for Temple to
react, or wait for her, period.

She jammed her tote handles over her left shoulder and

hurried after them, feeling like Dorothy tripping down the Yellow Brick Road in her flashy new shoes, on marching orders from a distinctly enigmatic Witch of the North. She didn't relish encountering another Glinda at the Goliath.

Maybe Midnight Louie could play Toto.

Keeping up with the long-striding cops made Temple's head ache anew. She was hardly aware of passing through the bowels of the downtown cop shop, which would have fascinated her on a less stressed occasion.

After huffing up three flights of stairs, the party ended up at a rooftop lot. The male detective, apparently junior to Molina, got the car, a white Ford Crown Victoria. Suited Molina's autocratic style, Temple thought. Molina threw herself in the front passenger seat. Temple wrested the back door open and hopped—ow—in.

They were off.

"No siren?" Temple asked in the lengthening silence.

Molina twisted in the seat to regard her. "The victim is dead. Five minutes isn't going to change anything. You have a thing for sirens, or what?"

Temple flushed and sat back in the seat. She resisted an urge to perch, imagining what unsavory passengers might have sat here before her—pimps, pushers, child molesters. But this was an unmarked car. Maybe only unmarked citizens rode in it.

"Temple Barr," Molina explained to her partner. "Does freelance PR around town. Has a penchant for finding bodies." She nodded over her shoulder at the driver. "Detective Wayne Dindorf."

That was it for introductions, and so far no explanation why Molina had invited—ordered?—Temple along.

"The body was found this morning at nine," Molina droned from her notes for the sergeant's benefit. "None of the performers had arrived yet—must be late risers—so no one's identified it." She checked her watch, and the car spurted forward as the driver registered her gesture.

Now, that was clout, Temple thought enviously. A

mere flick of the wrist and some man puts the pedal to the metal. Temple wondered how male coworkers got along with Molina, or how hard it had been for her to get her position and keep cordial with men who might have—or might have felt they ought to have—gotten the lieutenant's job.

In the distance, the Goliath's garish towers glittered like fresh powder snow streaked with gold dust and blood. Their car rolled up under the entrance canopy and paused, the sergeant flashing his badge at the sandaled parking valet who rushed over. The valet backed off, kilt flapping, and the car stayed right where it was.

The moment they got out of the car, they were off. Temple trotted along in the wake of two fast, determined, long-legged people. Who needed Louie to play Toto? *She* was Toto. Crowds parted as if at the behest of Moses.

Molina led them straight to the ballroom where the strippers would perform. Nervous hotel security men guarded the closed doors. Temple recognized them for what they were at once. Hotel security men always wore street clothes and always looked like the Iranian secret police: grim, vigilant men with eyes like eagles' and an implicit ability to do all kinds of unthinkably nasty things if necessary. If they didn't look like that, welshing gamblers wouldn't sell their next of kin to pay up in a hurry.

Molina was not impressed. The men opened the double doors, and she brushed past, Dindorf and Temple in her wake.

The ballroom looked like the morning after New Year's Eve. Scattered chairs and equipment stood in place, but without a throng of people at work, the vast area was a deserted set lacking all vitality.

Not quite deserted. Temple followed the two detectives toward the pool of spotlights where a few forlorn figures stood.

No one was talking, which lent a furtive, almost funereal air to their presence. Temple couldn't decide whether the people looked sad, or guilty, or a bit of both.

Molina began announcing their party's names and ranks while still twenty feet away—Molina's and Dindorf's; not Temple's. This omission made her the uneasy object of quick, surreptitious glances. The others could be speculating whether she was a mystery expert on murder, or a chief suspect.

The identity of the welcoming committee became quickly clear: Arthur Hencell, WASPish head of hotel security; Lisa Osgood, a hyperactive young blond woman who handled hotel special events; and Hipolito Herrera, the pudgy middle-aged maintenance man who had found the body when opening up the ballroom for the day.

"Where are the people who expected to work in here today?" Molina asked.

"The Caravanserai Lounge," Lisa Osgood answered nervously. "We're, uh . . . storing them there until the police let them back in here. How long—?"

"Hours, maybe not until tomorrow. I'd find another place to practice" was Molina's encouraging answer.

"You're not sending any black-and-whites?" Hencell's question edged dangerously close to an order graced at the last moment with an interrogation mark.

"Don't worry. The coroner's ambulance and the M.E. will use the back entrance. Nothing awkward will be wheeled through the casino, only the usual money carts."

Temple folded her lips to keep from smiling at the security chief's livid face as he suffered Molina's sardonic reply.

Molina turned to the maintenance man with more warmth than she had shown the higher-ups. "What time did you—" Her question broke off suddenly, for no reason Temple could discern. And then, "*¿A qué hora descubrió el cuerpo?*" Molina asked in Spanish that flowed into one long phrase.

"*A las nueve.*" The man's face, his entire body, relaxed as he began an outpouring of Spanish, his hands and arms gesturing.

Molina nodded, and pulled out her notebook.

"Nine o'clock," he repeated laboriously in English at the end of his spiel.

His last hand wave directed Temple's attention to the metal skeleton of jungle-gym-like scaffolding that stood near the raised stage.

Something lay crumpled over the low bar nearest the floor. Temple's shiver started at her tailbone and worked its way up her spine to her scalp. Falling over Chester Royal at the ABA had been a macabre accident; she hadn't known the man was dead until it was too late to get hysterical about the fact.

This was the first dead body she had approached with the same cold certainty as the police. She didn't like the feeling, the sense that this investigation was about a collection of facts and circumstances rather than the tragic end of a personality, of a specific human being's hopes.

"*Ven conmigo, señor.*" Molina's head-jerk indicated only the maintenance man. Dindorf, his own notebook in hand, closed in on the other two hotel personnel.

Torn, Temple decided to follow Molina despite the language barrier. She needed to understand what murderous force was stalking the event she was responsible for. You couldn't do PR in an information vacuum.

Molina and Herrera had paused by the metal framework and stood looking down, like mourners at a grave, speaking quietly in Spanish. The language's musical cadence seemed to soften death's implicit ugliness. Temple eased closer, her heels muted by the garish carpeting. She couldn't see . . . the body, only flexed lace-stocking-clad legs lying together, like the Wicked Witch of the West's, as if their owner had fallen under the onslaught of sudden disaster, had never known what hit her, maybe. An emerald green spark winked at Temple in the dim light.

The shoes!

She brushed past the obscuring bulk of Señor Herrera to see.

"Oh . . . no."

Molina looked up. "You know her?"

Temple studied the fallen form, dancer-graceful even in death. She recognized the black cat mask she had suggested, even if she couldn't fully see the face.

"Know her? Not by any name other than Katharine. I saw her in the dressing room yesterday afternoon, before . . . my own mishap."

"This was no mishap," Molina reminded her.

"Couldn't she have fallen?" Temple asked hopefully. "Especially with the mask—" She stopped, realizing that her brilliant show-saving suggestion could have been fatal.

Molina pointed to the neck, which was obscured by a narrow black muffler, and squatted beside the body. "Did you see her in costume yesterday?" Temple nodded. "Was that part of it?"

"No. Her neck was bare, like most of the rest of her. The only new item is the mask. She must have made it and come back later to practice with it in private." Temple pulled out her glasses and put them on before leaning over the corpse. Poor Katharine, so hopeful again, so fatally doomed to lose. . . . "Wait! That thing around her neck— it's not a scarf; it's a tail!"

"Torn from the rear of her costume?" Molina asked.

"Probably. I saw her working out her Catwoman act on the grid early yesterday, but she didn't have it on in the dressing room. It was this clever tail, like the Cowardly Lion's in *The Wizard of Oz*. Some tiny remote control made it entwine and twitch."

"Then there'd be a wire." Molina studied the busy carpet pattern for a moment before her pencil darted out like a yellow snake and lifted a tiny curling wire from the floor.

She rose slowly, almost painfully. "Another stripper killed with a piece of her own costume. Interesting M.O." She turned to Herrera. "*Gracias, señor.*"

Her encouraging smile faded as she looked past him to Temple, the light laugh lines vanishing at the edges of her ice blue eyes. "And I'll want to know everything you know about the victim. Stick around until I finish setting up the investigation and get these hotel people off my back."

Molina turned and headed for the others, leaving Temple and Señor Herrera to contemplate the body, a study in the sleek black of her brief costume and the pale, luminescent white of her artistically revealed skin. The mask had worked splendidly, Temple saw, though she found the addition of black lipstick sinister rather than sensual. Only yesterday Katharine had experienced hopes and hurts. Sometime after their dressing-room talk she had made the mask and come back to try it in her act. She was going on with the show. Now it would go on without her. So would her kids. So would "he," the man who had needed to hit her. Temple would have something incriminating, at least, to tell Molina.

Hipolito Herrera knew none of that. He knew only what he saw: youth and death entwined in one sad, bizarre figure.

"*Muy linda*," he murmured, shaking his head. "*Muy triste.*"

Temple didn't have to speak Spanish to translate those universal sentiments. "Very pretty," she agreed. "Very, very sad."

Molina had bigger fish than Temple to grill. While Temple waited for her turn at interrogation, she asked Lisa to plug a phone into a ballroom jack, then settled near one wall with two chairs—one for a makeshift desktop—and the directory from her tote bag. Before she'd left the condo that morning, she had scribbled down the numbers of any callbacks on her answering machine. Until every last possible show is scheduled or scratched off the list, a PR person never rests. Neither pain, nor blow, nor dark of night, et cetera.

Her return calls went smoothly, although everybody commented that she sounded tired today. Temple didn't bother explaining that her jaw wasn't willing to open as much as usual, which made her usually free-flowing words ooze out like molasses.

By then the coroner's crew had gathered around the body, along with police photographers and forensic technicians. Temple would have loved to have watched this procedure, but she had work to do. She again snagged Lisa from the anxious trio of hotel observers and got directions to an office with a typewriter, then slipped away without anyone but the watchdogs on the outer doors noticing. As soon as her clerical work was done, she headed right for the Caravanserai Lounge, a sprawling array of cocktail tables lit by Aladdin's lamps under a chiffon ceiling tent strung with strips of fairy lights.

Midmorning attendance at the Caravanserai was usually light. Now every table was occupied by displaced dancers, most wearing workout clothes, a prominent few stripped down to performance shreds and earning passersby's stares. Smoke hovered above the motley crew like the steel blue haze from a volley of fired guns.

In the thickest of it, she found Lindy.

"Hi," Temple greeted her. "Here's the schedule for the local talk shows. Think you can make it?"

"If the cops let me." Lindy's foot yanked a vacant chair away from the table. "Sit down. You look frazzled already."

Temple used the copy of the schedule to fan away clouds of smoke. "No thanks. I have to get this copy to Ruth outside."

Lindy's laugh expired in the dry wheeze of a cigarette cough. "Sorry about the smokiness. Strippers are on the weed."

"Just nicotine?"

"Isn't that enough? Say, what's going on? Why won't they let us in the ballroom?"

"Plenty. You'll find out soon enough. Just be prepared to get some questions about it at the radio stations."

Lindy's tough face crinkled in sympathy. "Not another

fatality? Jeez. A strip show's supposed to liven people up, not lay them out."

"I'd better not say anything," Temple said, retreating before she started coughing. Her bruised ribs couldn't take the stress.

She switched to her sunglasses before going outside—great camouflage for brown eyes simultaneously turning blue, red and green.

Ruth's one-woman picket line had doubled. A reedy man with sparse hair on both head and upper lip and a couch-potato paunch now paced nearby. His sign read: MEN WANT WIVES AND TOTS, NOT SEX AND FLESHPOTS.

They weren't picketing together; they were arguing loudly, and drawing a crowd. Beyond them, the colossus scowled down with lofty pagan scorn.

"This is not a religious issue," Ruth was saying. She jammed her slipping sunglasses against her nose. "It's sociological and sexist."

"Brazen women don't have to be naked to offend the Lord," the man returned, glaring pointedly at her.

Ruth looked about ready to conk his bald spot with her sign when Temple pulled her aside and broke up the act.

"I've got the radio-station schedule," Temple said. "Lindy'll meet you here forty-five minutes before the shows." She dug in her tote bag. "Here are some blank cassettes. See if you can get the station to run a tape while you're on. You can cab it to the stations from here. Keep the receipts and I'll reimburse you. Okay?"

"Everything's okay except Lindy meeting me here," Ruth said. "I've had it with the holier-than-thou set. I'll meet her inside, maybe stick around and watch the goings-on. Learn something that way."

"You mean that sanctimonious guy is beginning to make strippers look sane and sensible?"

"Hardly." Ruth leaned her sign against the building. "I'm the only WOE member in Las Vegas," she said sheepishly. "It's hard being a protest movement of one. I like your idea of duking it out over the airwaves instead of in the streets. Say, you look a little wobbly."

Temple felt Ruth's supporting hand on her elbow and realized that she was feeling dizzy and exhausted. In unspoken agreement, the two women sat on the small retaining wall that bordered an azalea bed.

"I am a little beat," Temple admitted. "And—don't spread it around—but there's been another murder. In the ballroom. The police are there now."

"Another? Not a stripper again?"

Temple nodded. "I even met her—just last night. Living proof of your theory that strippers were often abused as children. Some kids like that never develop the self-esteem to stop being someone's victim. Katharine was a battered woman, but she seemed ready to split from the guy. I think this contest was her ticket out—out of the relationship, out of stripping for a living. She had this gag stripping service going—well, it's a start!" Temple added when Ruth looked dubious. "Now she's dead."

Ruth shook her head. "Who could be doing it?"

"I thought you might give me a clue."

"First off, there's the guy who beat her. Maybe he figured out she was leaving. Abusers usually freak when they lose their victims."

"But what about Dorothy Horvath, Monday's victim? Katharine's guy wouldn't need to kill her, too."

"Do you know anything about her?"

"Only that she had a gorgeous face and won the Rhinestone G-string two years ago. Katharine had a great body. I saw her work out; she was fantastically limber. She used this cat persona and she was grace incarnate."

"Sounds like somebody didn't like the competition."

Temple nodded, then glanced at the pacing man with the crudely lettered sign. "Or maybe somebody thought those women were damned anyway, and might as well be dead."

Ruth shuddered in the hot shade of the copper canopy.

"God, I'd hate to be a religious fanatic. I hold some pretty firm opinions, but I loathe thinking someone could kill a human being for a political or religious position."

"They've been doing it for millennia." Temple stood. "Good luck on the talk shows. I've got to get back. Lieutenant Molina wants to question me."

Ruth's eyebrows lifted over the top of her sunglass frames. "Are you under suspicion?"

"Only of being a nuisance," Temple answered, flogging her weary body back into the hotel's icy air-conditioning.

Chapter 20

The Sweet Smell
of Success

My dear mama, now departed, although perhaps not dead, always used to say that I took after my father. In truth, I believe that she herself wished to take after my father, but he was nowhere to be found.

Suffice it to say that somewhere there is a handsome, black-coated dude who knows how to live the good life of fish, females and serenade. I often picture the old guy basking upon some yacht, preferably a salmon or a tuna trawler, the sun glinting off his distinguished graying muzzle, seeing the world and wondering once in a while about how his spitting image is faring in landlocked Las Vegas.

He would have a dog to know that his long-ago offspring is slinking about the shadows of the Goliath Hotel trying to catch a whiff of a dead woman disguised as a pussycat.

There is method to my madness, if not much redeeming social value. For the fact is the late, lamented lady by now is a stiff and about to be given the bum's rush in a giant-size plastic baggie.

My olfactory mission is not based on mere morbidity, although my kind has been known to show a certain attachment to the aromas of dead fish, birds and mice.

No, it is not the scent of death that draws me, but a memory that teases at the edge of my awareness. It began when I examined the first victim of what has become a habit rather than an isolated tragedy. I smelled something then that was so elusive, yet familiar, that I must satisfy my curiosity. Does this second dead little doll bear the same scent? It is not that I have never inhaled the fragrance of a human before, dead or alive. I will never forget the musty odor of the deceased ABA dude, which I took for bookish mildew. Likewise, the scent of these done-for little dolls suits their circumstances: it is light, sweet and feminine, and I have encountered it before. Perfume it is not. This is more subtle. How maddening to possess a first-class sniffer and not be able to determine the exact bouquet that tickles my nostrils, if not my memory!

This is why, despite a half-dozen flunkies of officialdom bustling around the body, I lurk literally under their busy, oblivious feet, awaiting my opportunity. Some accuse my kind of sneakiness, but it is survival instincts that direct me to be discreet. The moment will arrive when a morgue attendant will turn aside, or a comment will distract their joint attention. Then I will dash in for the kill—or the diagnosis in this case.

Yet they are many, and no one leaves the body for a moment.

The fatal bag is produced, and I quiver in my boots. My sniffer is a world-class apparatus, but polyvinylchloride is one substance it cannot penetrate with any degree of accuracy.

At that moment, I hear the tread of large flat feet. A voice directs the assembled crew's attention to the body's former position, and the unearthly glow upon the noxious carpet that outlines the area.

For a few precious moments, little Miss Kitty is as unattended as a wallflower at the high school prom.

I seize the opportunity and run with it—run, in fact, toward her immobile body. My whiskers twitch with recognition. An insinuating scent wends its way to my flared nostrils. Miss Kitty has been branded with the same odor as her predecessor in death.

I pussyfoot out of sight, and hunker down under a banquet table swathed in white, floor-length linen. Beyond me, a crew of men bags the lady, and lifts her onto a cold metal gurney. She feels nothing, but my whiskers twitch in indignation.

I will not rest until I have traced this fatal scent to its origin. The killer.

Somewhere, on some forgotten swell of sea and salmon, the old dude would lift his venerable snout to the wind, and be proud of me.

Chapter 21

A Walk on the Wild Side

The palace guard was loath to let Temple enter the ball-room again until she used the password of Molina's name and rank. She doubted these private cops much feared the regular force, but they wanted them out of their territory as fast as possible.

Despite Molina's grumblings, the crime scene was clearing. Nothing remained of the body but a faint powdery luminescence on the carpeting—fairy dust from a Tinker Bell whom no one had cared about enough to clap for.

Molina joined her, looking harried. "Tell me about your encounter with the victim."

"Her name," Temple said pointedly, "was Katharine. With an 'a-r' in the middle. I picked that up from her pronunciation, so . . . precise. Like a child's who is lost and wants to make sure you understand perfectly so you can get her home again."

"Katharine? You're sure?"

Temple turned at Molina's sharp tone. "Of course. I hadn't been knocked half silly yet."

"I don't mean to contradict you—" Molina frowned, whether at her own train of thought or at what she was about to tell Temple wasn't clear. Molina consulted her notebook in the spotlight glare that was both too intense and too diffuse to read by.

"That's odd." She pursed her lips. "Everyone I talked to said her name was Kitty. Kitty Cardozo. She's well known around town; worked here for years. Has a kid attending UNLV."

"A kid in college?" Now Temple was puzzled. "She didn't look a day over twenty-four."

Molina's eyes stayed on her notebook. "Thirty-five. Started young."

"Stripping or having kids?"

Molina sighed. "They usually start both too soon. Now tell me about her."

"Did . . . anyone take off the mask?"

"For the final photographs, after the coroner arrived."

"Then you saw—?"

"The bruises and contusions were present when you saw her, then—when was that?"

"Four-fifty. I was on my way out."

"You stopped in the dressing room. Why?"

"Soaking up local color."

"You seem to prefer your local color blood red."

"That's below the belt, Lieutenant. Yeah, I was curious about the murder. I had a feeling—"

"Yes?"

"Something seems funny about it . . . them. Like they're messages."

"They're messages that some sick men out there get off on killing women, especially those in sexually titillating lines of work."

"You're sure it's a man?"

"Aren't you?"

"Both victims were serious contenders for winning the contest. Dorothy had won before and her face would launch a thousand flashbulbs. Katharine—Kitty—had a body that would freeze film into *Playboy*-ready shots, and the skill and grace to show it off."

"So you think a competitor killed them. I suppose a physically fit woman could have killed either one. But I'm not interested in your theories, Ms. Barr."

"Just the facts, ma'am."

"Exactly."

"Okay. I found Katharine—Kitty, in the dressing room. Actually, I heard her sob first. She was hiding among the costumes, pressed up against the wall like a hurt child. You know how an animal hides when it's scared, with its tail or ears sticking right out in plain sight, as if you can't possibly see them. That's the way she was hiding. I saw her shoes first."

"You would," Molina interrupted.

"What'll happen to those shoes, and her costume? They were so clever. Kitty made them herself."

"Police property room, until after the trial, if there is one. Go on."

"Anyway, I coaxed her out, and that's when I saw her face. Little did I know my own would look a lot like it in a few minutes. Kitty was afraid of a man. She kept asking if 'he' was out in the hall."

"There goes your jealous vixen theory."

"Maybe. Kitty could have had two enemies. She said that she would be all right, that she was ready to make the break from this guy; that's why he hurt her. He wanted to ruin her chances of winning the contest, because the money would help her get on her own. But she was going anyway; I know it."

"How?"

"By the way she spoke about her plans, her business. She called herself an 'entrepreneur'; sounded like a kid selling lemonade."

PUSSYFOOT

Molina's gaze dropped to her notes again. " 'Grin 'n' Bare It.' "

Temple nodded soberly. "A gag stripping business. 'Good clean fun,' according to Kitty. She was heartbroken to have her face ruined for the competition. Even makeup wouldn't cover everything, she said. I can see now she's right."

"Yeah. The dark glasses indoors are a nice punk touch," Molina said, not unsympathetically. "Anybody else been bothering you today?"

"Only the police and the ballroom security guards," Temple answered, deadpan.

"Go on."

"That's it. I suggested a cat mask to match the rest of the costume, and she lit up like a kid who's getting a Nintendo for Christmas. I left her happy and high on her act, only—"

"Yes?"

"Only she wanted me to know that she hadn't been crying because she'd been hit, but because it hurt her chances to be in the contest. I wondered then why it was so important not to cry when you're hit."

"And now—?"

"Now I know."

"So. You left her with so much hope that she went out and made the mask, then she returned after regular hours to work out with it—why?"

"Privacy. She probably needed to find out if it would handicap her vision, make her clumsy. She was poetry in motion. And she didn't want anyone to know what had happened. If she performed smoothly in the mask on a trial run, she could show up in it for the rest of the rehearsals and no one would ever suspect it hid something."

Molina flipped her notebook shut. "See the self-help group. Stay out of my investigation. If you think of anything more, tell me. Go home now." Molina paused. Her next sentence came out of the blue of suddenly angry eyes. "I'm going to get this bastard."

Molina marched back to the knot of police.

Temple, aching all over, was tempted to take Molina's advice. That was the problem, she was taking Molina's advice on too many things lately. Time for a little authority-flaunting.

She went back to the cocktail lounge, where idle dancers were starting to order lunches and drinks. The gathering had the halfheartedly festive air of a picnic forced indoors on a rainy day: they had to be here; they might as well make the best of it.

So should Temple.

She avoided Lindy's table. It was too easy to gravitate to someone she knew. A guide to a new milieu was useful, but not if the escort kept Temple from taking chances and learning something not in the guidebook.

Temple paused beside the table of the only silver-haired woman in the area who didn't owe it to bleach. "Mind if I sit here?"

"Go right ahead."

Temple sat down and sized up her table partner: a grandmotherly sort, her hair tightly permed, wearing one of those plaid cotton dusters that don't constrict the wearer and pass for street wear among the Golden Age set. Front buttons, decorative bias tape trim on the pockets and a Peter Pan collar kept it from qualifying as a muumuu, but just barely.

"Are you competing in the Over-Sexty division?" Temple asked politely, managing to not even stumble over the coy title.

The woman's scandalized look quickly turned into a chuckle. "Heavens, no! I'm much too old and fat for that in any category. What are you thinking of, girl? These contests have *some* standards."

"Sorry. I don't know much about it. I'm doing public relations work and am trying to get oriented."

"PR?" A gleam brightened the woman's pale hazel eyes.

"Well, then, you'll want to know about my Kelly. Here she comes now."

Temple turned to look in the direction that attracted her tablemate's beaming maternal gaze.

A long-stemmed brunette was mincing between the crowded tables, carrying two glasses and two bottles of beer from the bar, and a small bowl of popcorn clenched doggy-style in her teeth.

The prodigally endowed daughter made a professional waitress dip at the table to disencumber herself of the food and drink, then glanced curiously at Temple through the black fringe of false eyelashes top and bottom.

Mama Kelly did the honors. "This here's the competition PR lady, honey."

"Oh, hi. Get us tons of publicity, hear? I've got a super act."

Temple eyed Kelly's blue-gingham pinafore and matching, supernaturally bright blue eyes. Molina's eyes were arresting, but light enough a blue, however electric, to convince. This woman's contact-lens-store blue clashed with her disingenuous air of Southern comfort.

"You're mother and daughter?" Temple asked a bit uncertainly.

"I used to be darker and thinner," the mother said wryly, chuckling again.

"I used to be shorter," the daughter added with a wink.

Temple laughed. "And only Kelly goes onstage?"

"What do you think? I want to ruin her chances? Mildred Bartles is the name. How do you do?"

No one had said "How do you do" to Temple in a coon's age. She found it charming.

"Temple Barr. I admit I'm astounded. I figured most mothers of strippers wouldn't want to know what their darling daughters were doing."

"Then they are dumb mothers," Mildred answered genially. "Kids these days do what they want. You can either fight 'em, or join 'em."

"But not onstage?"

"No, ma'am. I'm a backstage mother. I help her rehearse, I sew all the costumes. Travel around with her for company. Life on the road can get lonely."

"Then strippers don't date the men from the clubs."

"Lordy, I should hope not!" The indignation came from the beauteous Kelly. Her cerulean eyes drilled into Temple's. "No matter how it looks, stripping is a business and it pays pretty fair. All that happens between the customers and the strippers is what you see onstage or out front. A little tease, a little talk, and—hopefully—a lot of tips."

"What if a man wants more?"

"Then I give him a freezing look and make clear he's out of line. Some girls," she added disdainfully, "are willing to be whores, but they don't last. The clubs don't want their dancers disappearing before pumpkin time, and the rest of us don't want to ruin our reputations."

By now, Temple didn't find the notion of strippers preserving their reputations laughable. "But you must know the public is highly titillated by your occupation."

"Titty-what, honey?" Kelly produced a dimple that proved she could tease offstage as well as on. "You got to ditch those big words. A lot of us didn't go no further than high school."

"People are curious," Temple said, "about why you dance almost-naked for an audience of the opposite sex."

"Oooh." Kelly shook her long fingers to indicate a topic too hot to handle. "Well, if we were whores, like they thought, we'd wouldn't waste our time and energy dancing first. We are performers," she said matter-of-factly. "Some of us are terrific and some of us are stinko. We bust our butts giving a good show, and then we're outa there. Listen, it beats waitressing, and I spent a lotta hours breaking my fingernails on trays loaded with forty pounds of restaurant ware. What's the difference? You give service for a lousy wage and make your money in tips. Except the tips are a damn sight better for strippers."

"Still, the club makes the real money in liquor sales."

"So does the restaurant."

Temple eyed the mother. "How did your daughter grow up to do this?"

Mildred Bartles accepted a full and nonfoamy glass of beer expertly poured by her daughter before musing on the past. "Since she was a tiny thing Kelly was a bolt-lightning of energy. Begged for dance lessons. It wasn't easy. Her father had run off. I was waitressing and no spring chicken—where do you think I got these varicose veins?" She thrust out a foot in a canvas wedgie. Temple glimpsed swollen ankles and veins like angry red crayon marks. "Kelly was too cute and too smart to end up like her mom. She started as ring girl at wrestling matches when she was fifteen, then got a job waitressing at a topless club."

"That's how most of us break in," Kelly said. "We see how the moves go. We also see how much better the tips are."

"But you're paid to cozy up to a lot of strange men."

"So is Meryl Streep."

"Some of those guys are pretty revolting."

Kelly shrugged her handsome shoulders, flapping the ruffled gingham cherub wings that covered them. "Most of them are just lonely. Harmless. They pay for attention, and they get it. It's a transaction. Damn few ever step over the line. They know what the girls are there for and how they make their money. It's worth it to them to stuff a rolled-up fifty in my G-string; better than gambling with it. And we're stars, girl, to them."

Temple believed Kelly, but she wasn't satisfied that the stripper's life was that simple.

"What about Dorothy Horvath?"

"Who?" Both Bartles spoke in tandem.

"The woman who died Monday."

"Oh, you mean Glinda." Kelly nodded sadly. "We almost all use stage names, and that was hers. Dorothy." She shook her head. "Doesn't sound like her. Maybe that was the point."

"She was getting away from her past then, remaking it?"

"Most of these girls," Mildred said, leaning forward to prop both elbows on the tabletop, "have had bad breaks, that's true. Some of it's pretty sad. Fathers that were beaters, or worse. I didn't let Kelly in for any of that. I could have remarried a time or two, but by then it was pretty plain that she was going to be a looker. I didn't want no stepfather messing her up just because I was as desperate for a man, or a man with a job, as a dog for a bone. No, sir."

"That's admirable," Temple said, meaning it. She didn't need Ruth and her statistics to know that stepfathers or a live-in boyfriends often abused the children of another man, and that their mothers didn't—couldn't, wouldn't—see it because of their own abused pasts, or their financial dependence or their fear of independence.

"So," Temple summed up, "you're your daughter's big sister. You support her, travel with her—"

"Hey," Kelly put in, interrupting a pull on her beer, "I support *her*. I told you the money was good."

"I meant emotionally, not economically," Temple clarified.

"We support each other," Mildred put in, pushing back one of her strapping daughter's errant little-girl curls. "Don't we, sweetie?"

"That's right," Kelly said. "We're a team."

Mama Rose and Gypsy these two were not; Temple sensed an easygoing affection between them that would be the envy of many mothers and daughters in primly proper families, often hopelessly estranged themselves. This duo liked and needed each other, despite, or because of, the daughter's supposedly seamy line of work.

She eavesdropped on her own thoughts, then analyzed them. "Supposedly"? Was she getting converted to life on the wild side? She suddenly recalled her own mother's horror when Temple had developed a yen for amateur theatricals in high school. The playhouses were invariably in "bad" neighborhoods and the other cast members, especially the males, were suspect from the first read-through until the cast party.

That might be an interesting angle for a newspaper feature: strippers' moms. Yeah. Temple eyed the cocktail area, looking for more story sources.

Ike Wetzel held court at a round, slate-topped table amid a harem of female strippers. The waitress was circling to deliver another round of drinks, her skimpy veils floating around her metal bikini.

Temple couldn't join that table, not even in her most professional capacity, without aligning herself with the harem, so she looked farther afield.

Four he-men in muscle T-shirts hunkered around a tiny cocktail table meant for the intimacy of two, long-neck beers rampant before them.

Temple supposed it was her duty to investigate the male side of the issue, but approached gingerly, wary of blazing pelvises. The guys seemed a lot more up front, excuse the expression, she told herself, about enjoying their notoriety.

She marched over the carpet and paused beside the gathered hunks. "Hi, guys. I wonder if you could answer some questions?"

"Anytime, pretty lady," said one.

Another rose and lumbered over to a nearby table, politely asking if a vacant chair was taken. Even if it was, would anybody in their right mind say so?

He efficiently swept it under Temple's derrière as she sat, and took his own chair again.

She tried to avoid nudging knees with anybody, but given the smallness of the table and the quantity of knees, not to mention their massiveness, that seemed impossible. Temple was used to feeling small among the rest of the population. With these guys, she felt like a fly in an elephant yard.

"You with 'Entertainment Tonight'?" a man with Schwarzenegger muscles and crew cut asked.

"No. I'm doing public relations for the competition.

But if 'ET' wants to do a competition segment, or if I can talk them into one, then maybe you guys'll get lucky and meet Lisa Hartman. But probably not," she warned them. "She doesn't do every segment in person."

"Shucks. What's your name?" asked another.

"Temple Barr."

"Temple's a neat name."

"Would sound great onstage," another put in.

"Any relation to Candy Barr?" teased the third.

"Only in our apparent addiction to . . . chocolate. Really, if you guys wouldn't mind talking about your work, I'd be able to put together a press release."

"Yeah, let us do release the press!"

"All right!" the others agreed, slapping the heels of their hands together while Temple blinked at such enthusiastic physical force. Maybe she had become subconsciously leery of big men since . . . no! She couldn't get paranoid. For all their muscular presence, not one of these guys was more than twenty-four, and they all exuded a wholesome, careless energy that was rather engaging. If only they'd been around when the bad guys had decided to do a drum riff of "Night and Day" on her torso . . .

So she asked questions, they answered, and she soon could put names—stage names—to individuals rather than clones.

Kirk wore his hair wild-man-long. It brushed his well-developed shoulders and gave him a wicked, rock-star look. He would ride a motorcycle (probably a Hesketh Vampire, without a helmet), although a woman of any experience at all would realize that underneath he was a moody, Marlon Brando kind of guy. You know . . . sensitive. Umm-hmmm.

Stetson's sun-streaked blond hair was long only in back. His tanned, muscled body radiated an outdoorsy, oil-rig-working, skin-cancer-defying, construction-crew kind of macho. The Last American He-Man. Performing was putting him through pre-med.

The crew cut was Butch, of course. Butch was all man, and all muscle, and one day he hoped to be Mr. Universe. And maybe be in movies, like Arnold. Saint Arnold.

And Cheyenne, lean, rangy Cheyenne: dark-eyed, dark-haired, racially and sexually ambiguous, a dangerous trait in the Age of AIDS, but attractive, perhaps for that reason. Cheyenne was truly the strong, silent type, and finally admitted after repeated questions that he was an actor, kind of. He had auditioned for a soap recently. Temple could picture him in seminaked, steamy close-ups, getting tons of fan mail from ladies who would never think beyond the obvious.

Finally, Temple got around to her eternal "Why?"

"The money's great!" said Butch.

"And it's fun," Kirk added.

"The chicks are really into it. You should see 'em," Stetson said. "Here at the competition doesn't count. It's an audience of your peers. You should come to a club and watch us."

"Yeah," said Temple, "the women perform solo, but you guys usually go onstage in a group. Why? Chicken?" It felt good to pass on Electra's challenge. The question also loosened whatever inhibitions they had left.

"Naw," Kirk said. "But it's true that guys are a new wrinkle in the club game. We're not supposed to package it and sling it around unless we're gay."

"Is that why you emphasize the muscles and the macho pose?" she asked.

Butch shook his virtually hairless head. "We're body-builders, first and foremost. That's what you gotta understand. We're used to performing at bodybuilding competitions in no more than a posing pouch. Stripping isn't much different."

"Except we get paid for it," Stetson put in.

"Man, those tips . . ." Cheyenne's smile was slow and sensual.

"You don't feel it's undignified—?"

"Hell, yes!" Kirk burst out. "But they don't ask at the bank how dignified your money is. Besides, it's a kick to watch women act like raving animals for a change."

"They know it's not real," Temple pointed out.

"Yeah." Kirk was definite. "It's not real, and that's okay. Too much of life is real."

"Like the murder of those female strippers," she suggested.

The young men's faces grew sober for the first time.

"Bummer," Kirk murmured.

Stetson shook his blond head. "It almost makes you feel guilty. We guys get all the hoopla and the good clean fun, and the girl strippers get the sickos."

"You think a psycho did it?" Temple asked.

"Who else?" Cheyenne asked angrily. "Look. We're doing this and no one will think we're trash because of it. But women—they're damned if they do, damned if they don't. Maybe none of us said it, but it's healthy to be up-front about your sexuality. But when they do it, women always get a bad rap."

She was surprised by their angry-young-men passion, by their guilt on behalf of their own sex. "I was going to ask if stripping is exploitive."

They nodded in concert.

"We exploit our audiences, you know?" Kirk said. "They exploit us. But we both know it."

"We make money," Stetson added. "We show off what we worked on, our bodies. We get to be somebody, not just some body. It's the same for the women, except . . . a lot of them use stripping to work out deep identity and self-esteem problems. And when the men pant and pay, it's not a harmless joke, like it is for us. It's history. Some men can prey on women in nasty ways."

Temple nodded. She liked these young men. Their work/art/identity was much more clear-cut than it was for the women. They were earthy, attractive; they knew the score. They would be safe to fantasize about. And to not take seriously.

"Thanks," she said. "You've helped." They couldn't understand that they'd helped with more personal issues than understanding the urge to strip or make money.

"My card." Cheyenne handed her a plain white two-and-a-half-by-three. Cheyenne, it read. And a phone number.

Everybody, she thought wearily as she walked away, is an entrepreneur.

Chapter 22

Golden Girls
and Boys . . .

She was "Barred" from the ballroom, so Temple headed,
like a lemming toward her irresistible doom, for the part
of a theater she knew, loved and understood the best.
Offstage. The dressing rooms. Why was she kidding herself? *The* dressing room was the only murder scene acces-
sible to her.

Something still nagged her, and it wasn't a nursery
rhyme.

Downstairs, the hard-surfaced halls broadcast the same
eerie sensation of desertion. Temple's heel clicks echoed,
duplicating the sound of her progress through the parking
ramp. She had thought herself alone then, too.

Suddenly, unintelligible voices joined the echoes.

She paused, and heard arguing tones, even some hot
words: "You're not doing it!" "I will!" "Won't." The
sounds came from the very dressing room she had wanted
to visit alone, darn.

Behind her, other footsteps were charging down the stairs, although less noisily. Temple ducked through the nearest door and pulled it almost closed behind her—not all the way; that would make a betraying click. She had never suspected she was so good at subterfuge.

Her heart pounded as if following in her earlier footsteps while she waited behind the door, glancing around to make sure that her shelter was truly safe.

Her worst fears were realized when she spotted a pair of peacock green sparks glimmering from the shadows. She was not alone! Luckily, she had seen this phenomenon before. Temple's retinas may not have reflected as spectacularly as these, but they did eventually adapt to the dimness.

She made out a sphinxlike piece of darkness that never lightened even when she could discern the glimmer of the mirror and the glitter of hanging costumes.

"Lou-ie!" she whispered. She tiptoed nearer.

One and the same. He lay like a sultan on the former Max's erstwhile wicker loveseat, his tail flexed in a graceful curve. Another double green glint flashed. Temple came nearer, bent down, and strangled a groan as she recognized Louie's sofa partner.

"Lou-ie! That's Yvette. Savannah Ashleigh's Yvette."

Louie blinked gravely.

"What? Once is for yes. Twice is for no?" Her next question would have made the parent of an errant teenager proud. "What are you doing here?"

He didn't answer, of course, and resumed grooming the pale cat's ruff. The overbred little hussy lounged on her side, slitty aquamarine eyes indolent, a throaty purr rumbling just above the subliminal level.

"Lou-ie! You're not fixed!"

He yawned and applied his tongue to his forepaw.

"I could get hit with a paternity suit. You don't know Savannah Ashleigh. Out!"

She picked him up. Weighed a ton. Still. At the door she listened, looked and found all quiet. She yanked it open to set the big black cat down on his four, fat furry feet.

The skin on his spine twitched indignantly; then he stalked away without a backward glance, tail erect and quirking just at the tip. Okay, Temple thought, we'll see if you're as good at getting out as you are at breaking and entering.

"All right, Juliet." Temple turned back to the dressing room and sighed in exasperation. She swept the dainty Yvette off the loveseat. It was like lofting an ostrich plume, so insubstantial was the shaded silver pedigreed Persian compared to Midnight Louie. "You little minx. How did you get out of your carrier? And where's your devoted Momsy when you need a chaperone?"

The carrier sat on the floor beside the sofa, unzipped. Temple prepared to whisk Yvette back inside and hope for the best. Maybe she was fixed. That made a lot of sense.

Yvette's limp little body thrummed like a cello string. Temple couldn't resist pressing her face against the frothy fur so like a silver fox's. Yvette's tongue felt like warm, wet Velcro as it licked the tip of her nose.

"All right, so you're irresistible. I won't take it out on Louie. But now back to your home-away-from-home. There."

Temple felt like a jailer as she zipped up the carrier. How on earth had Louie got in here? More to the point, how had Yvette got out of her carrier? That was one mystery she was not inclined to investigate. Both perpetrators had a speech impediment.

Temple soft-footed it to the door and peeked out. The hall was again so still that she could hear Yvette's contented, fading purr.

She left as quietly as she could, heading toward the scene of the first crime. Within that room, voices still rose and fell, although much more softly now. Two. Female. Well, it was a women's dressing room. Guess she could walk right in.

She announced her entry by pushing the ajar door open hard. Then she gave an indrawn shriek of alarm.

Two golden ghosts stood frozen face to face, shimmering in the glare of the makeup lights, as nude as classical statues except for gold lamé G-strings. At least they were ladies, sort of.

"Miss . . . Barr." One spoke, and broke the spell.

Temple followed Louie's example when caught red-handed where she shouldn't be, and blinked.

A gilt hand pounded its owner's golden breastbone. "June."

The other mirrored the gesture. "Gypsy."

Temple almost pounded her chest, too, and responded, "Me, Jane." Instead, she sank onto a nearby ice-cream chair. "Golly, you startled me," she said, realizing that by rights they should be accusing her of that.

"It's the gold metallic paint," the one on the left said. June. "We need to see what the light gels upstairs will do to it, especially with this opalescent glitter powder we're mixing with it. Sometimes it can go green. First we have to wait for it to dry."

"There's only one way to put it on," Gypsy added. "In the buff with a sponge."

"You paint each other?" Temple asked.

"Only the back parts the other can't reach," Gypsy said. "Twins make it handy. And we have to leave a discreet spot blank. Otherwise our entire skins would be covered and we'd—what's that word, June?"

"Asphyxiate."

"We'd croak."

"Ghastly, but the effect is phenomenal," Temple said. "You look like duplicate Greek statues . . . even your hair is gold and glittery. I can leave—"

"Don't!" June's voice sounded a little panicky. "Maybe you can settle an argument for us."

"You argue?"

"Not often," Gypsy said proudly. "But this time June's being a stick-in-the-mud."

203

"You're the one who wants to blow our whole act."

Temple sat up straighter, despite her fatigue, as befits an arbiter. PR people are problem solvers, first and foremost. "What's the matter?"

Gypsy sighed and sat down, first checking to insure that her derrière left no gilded imprint on the chair seat. Temple was relieved. With June still standing, she had a foolproof way to tell them apart.

"It's about coming out of the closet," Gypsy said.

"The closet," Temple repeated numbly. They were gay and in love with each other? Bizarro.

"No, it isn't that," June snapped. "Gypsy's got it all wrong. She invited *Dad* to the competition Saturday without telling me, even sent him a plane ticket. Can you imagine? Our parents don't know anything about . . . all this."

June's wide-armed gesture showed off more than the aura of the dressing room.

"I see," Temple said.

"No, you don't," the seated Gypsy argued. "Neither does June. It's a statement. Our father needs to confront our lives."

"What's to confront?" June asked. "We dance nearly naked, and are damn good at it. We make a nice bit of money."

"I want him to come to the competition."

"I don't!"

"He has to see what he did."

"Gypsy! You're not reviving that crazy story again."

"It's not crazy. I'm not crazy. It's true."

"Dad never touched me."

"He did me. Plenty."

Temple felt a cold chill in her stomach as she realized exactly what issue was tearing the single-minded twins' unanimity apart. Beneath their pert manners, their fit, agile forms and the glamorous gilt, lay an ancient rot.

"Why would he?" June demanded. "We always had everything the same. Same teachers, same clothes, same food, same sicknesses. Why would Dad mess with you and not me?" She almost sounded jealous.

"I don't know!" Emotion made Gypsy's voice tremble. "Maybe because doing it to only one of us would cause twice the pain. That's why I invited him. To see us both."

"Gypsy! Mom will know."

"Maybe Mom should know. Maybe Mom always knew what our father did."

June turned to Temple. "She's crazy! Isn't she?"

"She's your sister," Temple answered. "Do you think so?"

Her calm took the edge off of June's anger. "I don't know," she admitted. "Nobody's closer to me than my sister. How could I not know—how could she not tell me all these years?"

"Shame," Temple said.

"June." Gypsy reached a tentative, golden arm out for her sister, like Yvette batting at a fringe. "I didn't want to hurt you."

"But you'll hurt Dad."

"I'll make him see."

"See what?"

Good question, Temple thought. Was the child Gypsy secretly eager to perform for her molesting father? Did she crave his attention and arousal despite herself? Is that why she stripped, to tease the other men in her audience who could see and not touch? Or did she want revenge, to taunt their father with the fact that she was now a woman with a sexuality he could no longer control? Did she want to show that she had dragged the unknowing June into her own need for exhibitionism that his sickness had caused?

"What will he see?" Temple asked, echoing June.

"What we are. What we became. What he did to us. And that he can't do it anymore."

"Us," June repeated. "You said it was just you."

Gypsy sighed. "It was never just me, Junie. It was all of us. It's what our father did to all of us."

"Maybe we won't make the Saturday finals," June suggested almost hopefully.

"We always do," Gypsy answered.

Our Father, Temple concluded, was definitely not in Heaven. Nor would he be, if he came to the competition Saturday night.

Chapter 23

Nursery Crimes

It was a good thing Temple was not a Supreme Court Justice.

She had advised the Gold Dust Twins to see a counselor together, and then consider family counseling. Not a judgment of Solomon that cleaved to the heart of the matter, but a waffling, trendy modern way to deal with a form of human grief as old as Sophocles and Oedipus. She had then left.

"I thought you were headed home an hour ago."

At the words, Temple came to a dead, guilty halt while skirting the Goliath's Caravanserai on the way out. Molina's voice was right behind her; the law's long arm apparently had at last extended its reach beyond the ballroom.

She turned. "Ah, I needed a drink first."

"You'd have been better off if you'd actually had one," Molina noted sourly. "Don't you know when to quit?"

"I was just leaving now. Honest."

"Good. Rest assured that I will call you," Molina added with sweet sarcasm, "in case there are any major breaks in the case that you should know about. Now get outa here."

Temple hated to turn tail, but her energy was at its end. A chorus of aches and pains from her eyebrows to her knees had reached fever pitch.

Still, she felt like an AWOL from the French Foreign Legion as she dragged herself and her heavy tote bag through the clustered tables. Besides, the ambience had hooked her; the color and confusion of readying a show made her homesick for the theater. She hated it when frailties kept her from the thick of things. Imagine how many clues were floating around this mob, just waiting for an agile intelligence to pick them up. . . .

The sound of intense voices broke into her reverie. Two women stood at the cocktail tables that had been drafted as the competition's field desk while the ballroom was unavailable. One of the women was Lindy, scanning a sheet of paper and smoking up a storm. A second woman, whose black iridescent hair matched her iridescent black-leather motorcycle jacket, was giving her the hard sell.

"—just blew into town," the woman, who looked quite ordinary to Temple among this crowd, was saying. She hadn't removed her sunglasses. Temple wondered if she had any unsightly bruises to hide.

"It's awfully late to enter," Lindy objected.

"Any rules against it?"

"Not exactly—"

"Not exactly means no. When can I get into the rehearsal room?"

"That depends on the police."

"Say, hotel security is getting awful tight."

"It's not that," Lindy said, saying no more.

Temple trudged past the pair, amazed by contestants who would stop at nothing and even pay for the privilege of baring their bottoms. The bizarre conversation followed her like faint and argumentative rap music.

"Your stage pretty strong?" the new contestant was asking.

"You don't weigh *that* much, honey."

"Thanks, but it's not me. It's my bike."

"You use a *bike* in your act? I suppose that's encouraging to over-sixty types."

"Not *that* kind of bike," was the contemptuous answer. "Mine's a real bike. Weighs a thousand pounds."

"A . . . motorcycle?"

Not only Lindy was incredulous. Temple, almost out of earshot, stopped cold. She turned slowly to study the over-the-hill Hell's Angel.

"Listen," Lindy was telling her, "we've had grand pianos and baby elephants on our stages. I think we can handle one overweight motorcycle."

"Okay. There's my money. Count me in." The motorcycle moll moved on.

Temple backtracked, catching Lindy about to slip the entrant's sheet into a red manila folder. "Who was that masked woman?"

"The one in the sunglasses? I don't know. Never heard of or saw her before. That's not odd. She's in the Over-Sexty division."

"What did she put down on her form?"

Lindy pouted in concentration. "This has gotta be only her stage name. That's all we require."

"Which is—?"

" 'Moll Philanders.' I don't get it."

"I do! Any address?" Temple twisted to read it upside down. Then she cased the cocktail area, looking for a figure that reminded her of Elton John in drag.

The phantom contestant had settled at the Four Hunks' table. Temple's jaw dropped. The woman finally whipped off her seventies wraparound sunglasses to reveal green, snakeskin-patterned eyelids outlined in black glitter. The

Fab Four obviously found the effect awesome. They were hooting and laughing and nodding their trendily styled heads.

While they were thus diverted, Electra Lark looked coolly in Temple's direction and winked.

Temple turned again and hobbled out—yes, limping now, and so tired she thought that she saw a black cat dash from the shadow of one table-underside to another. Why just "a" black cat. Why not . . .?

"Et 'tu, Louie?" she muttered darkly. She had been naïve to think he would meekly go home just because he had been discovered. Had she, when Molina had told her to? At least the lissome Yvette was zipped up tight for the night.

She sat in the Storm after she finally pulled into the Circle Ritz lot and turned off the motor, sensing the temperature change as the icy interior air slowly warmed to the hot sun.

Her face felt like an aching mask, her body like it wore an iron cast. She hated to give the Mother Machree of the LVMPD any credit, but she did indeed need a rest.

Temple extracted herself from the car, free to groan now that no one could hear, and stumbled inside. No one joined her on the elevator or passed her in the hall, but that was typical. Most residents had nine-to-five jobs that kept them away for predictable hours.

At the turn of a key she was home again. The condo was empty, cool, serene. She stood motionless beside the door, trying to sense any intruder. Then she slipped off her shoes and peeked into the office and the bedroom in turn, but the condo was secure. Hers alone. Sometimes that unplanned solitariness wasn't too bad.

After rummaging in the refrigerator, she came up with a bacon-bit, tomato, lettuce and tuna sandwich. Had to polish off the open tuna can left over from—hah!—breakfast. A generous mound of Free-to-be-Feline sat in the bowl, untouched.

She bent to haul the half-liter bottle of Blush Light from the bottom cabinet and pried off its metallic collar with her long, strong fingernails. Lacking the energy to stretch up for the wineglasses on the highest shelf, she paused. Inside the lower cupboard she found an odd root-beer mug, filled it with ice and poured in the pale coral wine.

"So it's crass to have wine over ice," she told her ever-present Invisible Critic. "I am home alone, and I'm going to relax and enjoy it."

She headed for the bedroom, dragging her tote bag over the crook of one arm, her hands full of tuna sandwich and a frosty mug of wine.

One high heel was left high and dry in the living room; the other was walked out on in the bedroom doorway. The moment the tote hit the unmade bed, Temple pulled out the day's notes. Cheyenne's card fell to the coverlet. Did he do massages? Prob-ab-lee. She dropped the card on the nightstand and laid her glasses atop it.

The tiled bathroom awaited like a Big White Set from an Astaire/Rogers movie—sleek, moderne and ready to reverberate. The elderly white porcelain tub was long, deep enough to drown in and had a divinely wide, old-fashioned rim.

She turned the faucets to the position where hot and cold blended into a pulsing stream of pure nirvana, set her sandwich and mug on the tub edge, and began peeling off her clothes—slowly, not like a stripper, but like someone whose muscles screamed at every motion.

For once Temple was grateful that the fifties bathroom did not, repeat, did *not* sport a full-length mirror. Temple leaned over the pedestal sink to check her face in the mirror-fronted medicine cabinet mounted above it. Thanks to the would-be Westmore brothers' impromptu facial behind the Goliath, she could skip eye shadow for several days. Technicolor bruises tinted the skin around her eyes, and now were turning a rotten-banana yellow along the edges. Yellow was a sign of healing, but also too ugly to disguise as a heavy hand with the magenta and purple eyeshadow.

She stood on tiptoe to peek at the bruises on her torso. Still at the blue-plum stage in size and color, ugly and deep. Temple winced to realize that, despite their best efforts, those men hadn't really gotten around to seriously hurting her.

From the now-muffled rush of the faucet, she sensed that the bathwater was rising. She dipped in a toe, then climbed over the high edge and sat gingerly, her skin twitching at the sudden lap of hot water before settling into it like a nervous cat into a petting hand. Aaaah. She lay back, munched some sandwich, sat up to chugalug a little wine.

She thought of Electra going undercover at a strippers' convention, and laughed. Moll Philanders, indeed! Crazy old girl. And was Louie really still on the premises, or had she hallucinated him? Not to worry, not with two prime crime solvers like Louie and Electra on the scene in her stead. Sure.

Temple sighed as a sense of slow draining dripped down her arms like an IV of molasses-thick wine. Tension and worry were siphoning down her fingertips into the warm water. The tub was deep and long enough to float in when it was filled to the top. It would be, because she had bought this plastic thingamajig that sealed off the overflow drain, just so she could float like she had when she was a kid. The advantage of being petite.

So Temple drifted in the soapless, clear water like a fetus in amniotic fluid, detached, isolated, the seeds of future thoughts spinning disconnectedly around her.

This is Wednesday. The contest is Saturday, when Daddy Gold Dust is in for a big surprise. Three more days to get through before it's all over. And it is all over for Dorothy and Kitty. Kitty. Another "y"-ending name. Had Kitty been the birthday girl on the cake? Was her real name Katharine? Sure. Katharine, that was what she had been called in grade school, the name that the scared kid peeking out from the costume niche had used. Kitty had come later, Kitty for short. Kitty was tougher, Kitty had reason to be. Poor kids. One dead on Monday, one on Tuesday.

Temple sat up with a splash. Monday's death, and Tuesday's. And Monday's child is fair of face, but Tuesday's child is . . . far to go? No. Works for a living? No. Monday's child is fair of face, and Tuesday's child is . . . all space. Ace. Mace. Place. Is bace/dace/face/gace/hace/jace/case/lace! Is lavender and lace? Mace/nace/pace/race/tace—trace/brace/grace. Grace.

Tuesday's child is full of grace! Not anymore.

She leaned forward to jerk the faucets shut, then stood, grabbing the porcelain tub grips, dripping onto her sandwich as she stepped down to the bath mat and pulled the towel off the chrome bar behind her.

The hotel-size Turkish towel swaddled her like a graceless sari. At six-four, Max couldn't stand squinky towels. She waddled, wet and enervated, into the bedroom to dial the Goliath. Still knew the main switchboard number by heart.

She asked for Lieutenant Molina, and finally got her. Then she told her the theory.

Silence. "You think the killer is following this nursery rhyme?" Molina asked. "Just because you linked the two victims to the first couple lines?"

"Maybe! But that's not the important thing. If the murderer is following the rhyme, there'll be more deaths—or attempted ones."

"You know the next lines?"

"No, but I could call the library. I wanted to tell you first."

"Commendable, but the, ah, ordeal you went through could throw off your emotional equilibrium. You're liable to see shadows behind every bush for a while."

"And serial killers in every nursery rhyme?"

"I didn't say that, but your theory is thin, to say the least. Anyone could twist the rhymes to apply to most of the women here. They're all 'fair of face and full of grace,' or could pass for it on a cloudy day. Sorry. Get some rest, and leave the detection to the pros."

Temple sat and dripped on her bedspread after Molina had hung up. She called the library anyway and jotted down the eight lines the librarian looked up. Wednesday's child was full of woe; according to the tales she had heard about the strippers' pasts and private lives, that was probably another universal truth. Woe. That was the name of the organization that Ruth Morris belonged to. Was Ruth in danger? When had she been born? But no: she wasn't a stripper. Far from it. What came next? Thursday's child, she saw, scanning ahead, "has far to go."

So do we all, she agreed with Molina. So do we all. Too bad Electra was at the Goliath, or Temple would try her theory out on her. Or on Matt.

But she didn't have his number, she was too tired to go up to his apartment and she was probably all wet anyway.

She read ahead to Friday's child. Loving and giving. Saturday's child "has to work for its living."

And Saturday all these children turned sex icons would be doing just that, gyrating for dollars. And for other, less tangible rewards that had their roots in the past.

She must have fallen asleep on the bed, wrapped in the damp towel. The room dripped with blinds-drawn, deep afternoon lethargy when she awoke to the sound of jangling. Not jangling, ding-donging. Her glorious doorbell.

She stumbled to the light switch, then blinked at her watch until she could read it. Six-something. She rushed for the door, tripping over her discarded shoes.

Luckily, she had not been too exhausted to use her chain lock. Turning the deadbolt seemed more than her aching arm could handle, but she finally edged the door open enough to peer out.

"Oh, Matt! I was thinking of you. I mean, I was thinking of you just before I fell asleep—" No, that wasn't cool, might as well cut to the gory chase. "There's been another murder at the Goliath!"

He took her non sequiturs with Matt-style equanimity. "I'd like to hear about it, but can I come in first?"

"Yes, but I'm not dressed. I'll be right back out."

She undid the chain and left it swaying while she retreated to the bedroom. Not that the huge towel wasn't perfectly modest; it just made her look like a resuscitated mummy, and walk like one too.

In the bedroom, Temple threw on her handy wraparound dress and low-heeled mules, then checked herself in the bathroom mirror. Nothing makeup could do for her now. The tuna sandwich had gotten soggy absorbing the hot water, and the ice had melted in the glass mug, creating an unappetizing liquid the color of pink lemonade.

She opened the tub drain to let the water gurgle out, grabbed the paper by the phone on which she had scribbled down the rhymes, and hustled into the living room.

Matt was standing by the French doors, arms folded and legs braced. From the back he was well built enough to pass for a Newd Dude, but less intimidatingly muscular. Self-absorbed bodybuilders were likely total losses as romantic interests, anyway.

He turned. "I didn't mean to wake you. I just stopped in to see how you're doing."

"Okay. I spent two-thirds of the day at the Goliath and was more tired than I knew."

"I stopped at the penthouse to ask Electra to keep an eye on you, but there's no answer."

"Oh, Electra . . . she might be doing errands, riding around. You know."

"No, I don't. She usually sticks close to the Circle Ritz in case a wedding shows up."

"I'm sure she'll be back later." Temple felt it was Electra's business to tell anyone what she was up to.

Matt rotated his lightly tanned wrist to check his

Timex. Temple saw a thin white line where it had shifted. None of the strippers had tans with unwanted white lines, she would bet. She had heard the women chattering of tan booths and untimely burns. Too bad they didn't know that a touch of reality is so much more inciting to the imagination than premeditated perfection.

"I just thought of something," she said.

"Yes?" Ever-helpful Matt, ever ready to listen.

"I've been spending so much time among the strippers, and something about the men just struck me." She paused. It was probably a dumb question. "Maybe you'd know, being into physical fitness."

"Wait a minute. I like to swim and I've studied martial arts since high school. That's not 'being into physical fitness.'"

"Well, being a man, then." He couldn't object to that. "These guys are really Arnold Jrs., overbuilt, if you ask me. But none of them have hair on their chest—and not much body hair anywhere else that shows. Is it because they take steroids, or what? Or do men who have no body hair become strippers? Fascinating, isn't it?"

Matt smiled. "I have to answer a lot of difficult questions at the hot line, but I've never gotten one like that. It could be steroids, Temple. And I'd guess that if they went to all the trouble to build that muscle, they wouldn't want anything obscuring it. I've heard some guys who wrestle shave their chests, and even their legs."

"Their legs! You mean these big, macho guys go through the same rigmarole as women?"

"So I've heard."

"Maybe they get it waxed," Temple mused. "That would last longer than shaving such big areas. Can you picture these guys lined up in a salon covered in hot wax?"

"No, but evidently you can." Matt was laughing. "You don't miss anything, do you?"

"I'm just curious about people, and being around so many professionally pretty people is mind-blowing. I wonder if men really find women who work at being that calculatedly 'female' attractive? Frankly, the guys' overinflated muscles and bulging veins and jeans turn me off instead of on. It's all too-too. Is that terrible of me? Am I not with it?"

"Just sounds to me like you know what you like."

"Real people," she said promptly and firmly.

He was quiet for a moment, his eyes sobering. "Then the magician's disappearance must have been quite a shock."

"Oh, yeah. But then, who is real? As I get to know these women strippers a little, I see their toughness and their tragedies, and I like them. They may be selling a perfect fantasy, but they're far from perfect, and they know it. I don't understand if the skin game is kicky and liberating, or a symptom of repression and oppression and obsession and all those other big words. Maybe I don't understand it because I never qualified for it."

"What do you mean? You're attractive."

"I'm okay. I like me. Some men like me. But I'm nothing to stop traffic, and I don't try to be. Some of these women were born with breasts the size of watermelons, and otherwise slim. What are they going to do for a living in this society? I can see how they got there. It's realistic, but at some time they must have suffered for being a different kid. And their semifreakdom makes them mucho moola. Others . . . were made, not born, formed by abuse, yet stripping seems to free some of them, and to further degrade others. I'm confused. I don't have a strong moral or philosophical position on the state of the art. Or even know if it is an art."

"At least you try. You question. Have you ever considered that black guys who are tall and can shoot baskets face the same problems? Should they use their natural advantages, make money young, and forget about whether they're being exploited until they're older?"

"No. I never compared *Playboy* centerfolds, say, with

big-money student athletes. But you're right. They've both got something they can sell: being young and in shape. I should judge: I never had those temptations."

"Why not?"

"Look at me! I looked twelve until I was past twenty, and now that I finally hit thirty, I look twenty. Well? Don't I?"

He looked her over, so much more thoroughly than he ever had before that Temple regretted her impulsive challenge. Why draw anyone's attention to your perceived deficits? Bad PR.

"What's wrong with that?" Matt asked at last. "They sell expensive creams to get the same effect. Someday you'll be seventy and look fifty."

"But I'm never taken seriously! Everybody's always saying I'm too young or too small. They think that my brain matches my stature. They think I'm cute!" she snarled. "They especially think I'm cute when I'm mad."

He put up his hands. "Not me. Listen, Temple, I understand your frustration."

"Why? I'm sure everybody takes you very seriously. Face it, you're one of the born-beautiful people, and you don't even work at it."

Tactful, calm Matt Devine suddenly tensed. He turned away, hands in his pockets. "You say you don't find the perfect bodies in a strip show real. What about the other way around? What if 'perfect people' never find anyone else real?"

"Oh. I'm sorry. I shouldn't have personalized it. You know what I've been working against."

"You hate being typecast by your size. I hate my so-called looks. I don't think of myself that way, but everybody else does. I have to wonder if they're fooling themselves, and if they're fooling me."

"I suppose," Temple ventured, "that women have chased you since Day One."

He nodded, not happy at the memory. Was that how the women with big boobs felt? Valued for their outsides and not their insides? You could get cynical and use it. Or you could be honest and come to hate it.

"Well," she said, clearing her throat, "I might be tempted to try myself, except that I'm recovering from my own emotional Waterloo."

He turned back, with a smile that would melt an igloo. "Why try? You have all those physical handicaps, remember?"

"I *am* 'cute.' Some people find that appealing."

"And you're fated to hate the ones who do."

She nodded. "Are you fated to hate the ones who are attracted to you?"

"I hope not," he said, just lightly enough that she knew the heavy stuff was over. For now. "Saddest of all are the people who hate themselves." Matt glanced at his watch face, frowning. "Is something wrong?" Temple asked.

He went to sit on the sofa arm, then rubbed his neck. Maybe Cheyenne would come out and give him a back massage.

"I'm punchy from switching shifts," he admitted. "And I didn't remember until this afternoon that I have a regular caller who missed me last night when I was here instead."

"Oh. I'm sorry that I—"

"It's not your fault. She was on the brink in her personal situation—cutting it close, that's all. Abusive boyfriend or husband; never said which. I'll be at the phone again in half an hour, and she never calls until evening." He paused, concern still puckering his face. "I just checked with my substitute, but she didn't call at all yesterday."

"Maybe when she heard you weren't in she rang off without leaving her name."

"We don't use names, not even the counselors, only code names, like CBers. Sometimes they're pretty revealing anyway."

Temple nodded. "Like stripper names. Pseudonyms say a lot. Can't you reach her somewhere, somehow?"

He shook his head. "Anonymity is the heart and soul of a hot line. I can't find her, she can't find me." He sighed. "She's probably all right. Just like you."

"Yeah."

"So tell me about the second murder?"

Temple sat on the matching arm. "Terrible. I know now how you must feel about your clients, because I met this girl last night just before I left the Goliath and had my head-on with the Goon Squad. She was in a bad way, but I thought I'd cheered her up. This morning, she was found dead. Strangled with her cat's tail."

"Her what?"

"She was costumed as Catwoman. Someone ripped off the tail and strangled her."

"That's a lot kinkier than the ABA murder."

"Maybe book people are better at writing and reading about murder than doing it."

"Crawford Buchanan handed you a hot potato, after all."

"Don't remind me! But I did get a crazy idea, at least Lieutenant Molina thinks it's crazy."

"How crazy?"

"That the murderer is following that old rhyme about 'Monday's child is fair of face.' Monday's victim had a face to die for. The girl yesterday was a magnificent gymnast—'full of grace.' "

"You think that there'll be more murders?"

"Molina doesn't. She says that everybody over there is fair of face and full of grace, even the men."

"Lieutenant Molina doesn't look like the type to be grading men."

"I added that part, all right? But no men have been killed. Yet."

"Just what you don't need, Temple, all that sensational publicity when you're recovering from your own troubles." Matt shook his head. "You could have knocked me over with a feather when Lieutenant Molina came up to us in the emergency room. From what you said, I pictured some beefy veteran who liked throwing his overweight around against defenseless solid citizens like you."

"Don't let the A-line skirts fool you. She may dress like a nun, but I bet Molina can be meaner than a K-9 attack dog."

"Not to you?"

"She doesn't cut anyone much slack."

"That's not her job. You and I can afford to be bleeding hearts; we're removed from the misery and danger out there. I've got my phone line and—when you're not stumbling over bodies—your work concentrates on good news, not bad."

"Not lately," Temple said glumly.

Matt stood and yawned. "I'd feel better about leaving for work if Electra were here."

"There are other tenants."

"But none who know what you've been through. Here." He reached in his shirt pocket and pulled out a card.

Must be her lucky day, Temple thought. This card had no name on it, just a number, a 731 exchange, and a word: "ConTact: Crisis Intervention for the Nineties."

"What kind of callers do you get?"

"Everything imaginable. Rape victims. Physical- and sexual-abuse victims. Alcoholics. The suicidal. Compulsive drug addicts and gamblers. The mentally distressed."

"How awful to hear so much grief."

"It can get intense, but the counselors are insulated by the phone, and by the anonymity. We hold the fort until we can put them in touch with the community agency that can help them in the long term."

"You said every kind of caller imaginable. That include obscene callers?"

"Not yet, but we get some pranksters, kids killing time. They don't fool us. It's hard to mimic real misery."

"Amen," Temple said, accompanying him to the door. "Maybe I should lighten your load and give you a naughty call now and then."

She had meant it as a joke, and like a lot of jokes it struck closer to home than was meant.

Matt's ears reddened suddenly. Temple could see that even from behind. Wow, she thought. For some reason, that comment had pushed his buttons.

By the time they reached the door, the moment had passed. He held it open for her to pass through.

"Oh, by the way," she said, smiling. He looked perfectly collected. Too bad. "Thanks for fixing the shoe. I felt like Cinderella when I found it in the morning."

"Shoes are easy to fix. Souls are harder."

"Matt, I hope she calls. I hope she's all right."

"And I hope that your theory about the murder pattern predicting more deaths is wrong, but you have an uncanny sixth sense about these things."

"Molina says I'm crazy and now you say I'm psychic. I'm not sure which is worse" was Temple's mock-glum comment as she closed the door.

At least he was laughing when he left. And so was Temple, until she remembered that Lieutenant Molina, her own personal Rumplestiltskin, was stopping by at seven o'clock to collect what Temple had promised.

Chapter 24

Poster Boy

Molina was right on time. She arrived about twenty minutes after Louie had lofted down from the bathroom window and stalked with bored, stiff-legged laissez-faire for the one piece of furniture upon which his black hair would leave the most obvious trail, the off-white living-room sofa.

Lord knew where Louie had been since the Goliath, but Molina must have come straight from the hotel or head-quarters downtown; she was still wearing her dreaded casual cotton suit. If Temple saw another A-line skirt on her, she'd scream.

"An unusual building," Molina remarked when Temple opened the door to her ring. Molina's routine glance around ricocheted off the interior angles of the pie-shaped rooms, off the subtly vaulted white plaster ceiling so soft and cool it seemed like the top of a sensuous silk tent.

Molina teetered on the entry-hall parquet, uncertain which way to move. Temple could tell that the unpredictable slice-of-pie layout upset her four-square investigative mind. The chessboard-tiled kitchen floor, a symphony in black and white eerily accented by a pink neon clock and radio, didn't help.

Feeling smug, Temple clicked down the hall to the living room, all business. She really hated Molina's being here, inspecting the space she and Max had shared, making comparisons and inferences and judgments. At least the place disoriented the policewoman more than anything Temple had yet seen her confront.

Turning by the cocktail table, Temple caught Molina jumping as Midnight Louie vaulted off the pale sofa onto the floor, looking miffed, as if offended by the very proximity of the law.

Of course it was only some arcane feline reaction, but he certainly did not seem to be unrolling a welcome mat for Molina. Temple was relieved that the scamp had finally bothered to come home from the Goliath.

"That's the cat from the ABA," Molina noted.

"Brilliant deduction. But Louie was never from the ABA; he was just visiting, like the rest of us."

Molina watched the cat swagger slowly to the French doors and sit to lick a front paw. "He sure is a big bruiser."

"Watchcat," Temple said smugly. "Did you learn anything important at the murder scene? Anything I should know about when the press comes hounding around?"

"Not much," Molina said briskly. "I brought the birth dates of the two victims, in case you want to play some more with days of the week."

"Thanks."

Temple accepted the gaudy piece of Goliath notepaper—an embossed gold pyramid straddled by guess what? It looked like a cross between legal tender and a Charles Atlas ad—and tried not to smile. Molina's handwriting was like a doctor's, loose and hasty, but she could at least read the numbers.

Time for a payback.

"The poster's in the bedroom," Temple said. "I'll get it."

She hadn't expected Molina to follow, but the detective did. The nerve of some people! Give them a badge and they think they can barge in anywhere.

Temple turned. "If you want to wait in the living room, I'll be right back."

"I don't."

"Well, you ought to. I didn't offer you a guided tour."

Molina's smile, being rare, seemed suspiciously disarming. "This place is fascinating. Psychologically, I mean. You said once that Kinsella found it?"

"Yes, but I approved it."

Molina looked around with Midnight Louie's expressionless curiosity. "Not a right angle in the place. Interesting."

"You don't need to trail me into the bedroom."

Molina leaned nearer, lowered her bitter chocolate voice even further. "Clues," she whispered darkly, mockingly.

Temple hadn't thought the woman capable of such drama. "What do you expect to find? Colonel Mustard with a meat-ax in the boudoir?"

Molina shrugged. She wasn't retreating, and at her size that alone made a massive statement.

Temple turned and marched on, wishing looks could kill because then she'd turn and do the dirty deed with a grimace in the front room.

She hadn't felt up to bending over and making the bed that morning, of course. Nor could she hang up her clothes with her bum shoulder.

"Welcome to the physically challenged ward."

Molina's quick eyes skittered over Temple's belongings, missing nothing but dismissing everything. "Where's the poster?"

"In the dark at the back of the closet." Temple opened the folding doors—an exotic South American wood Electra had told her bore the poetic name of purpleheart. That was the award she deserved for putting up with Molina . . . a Purple Heart.

Rows of high-rise clear plastic boxes confronted Molina. "You could hold your own shoe sale," the detective commented.

"Why would I? I want to keep every one. Now"—Temple dove into the closet's far end, thrusting hangers aside and pushing between swaying curtains of blouses and skirts—"here it is." She handed Molina a long, thin roll of paper.

The lieutenant uncurled the end, then paused to brace herself. Temple realized that she had never seen Max in the fleshtones. She watched Molina unroll the poster carefully, but quickly, as if eager to get the unveiling over with. Molina's face showed virtually nothing. Virtually. Only long-practiced control kept her reaction so unreadable.

"Hair—is that really black, or dark brown?" she asked.

"Raven black."

"And his eyes were really this green?"

"Like a cat's. Could see in the dark, too."

Molina grimaced slightly. "Height. Weight."

"Six-four, and I never asked."

"Any . . . identifying marks?"

"I said he could see in the dark; I never said I could."

Molina cocked her head as she studied the poster. Her vivid blue eyes moved around the two-by-three-foot surface held taut between her extended arms.

She brought it to the bed, picked up a midheeled blue satin mule from the floor to anchor the top and pinned the bottom edge with the mate. Then she stepped back to consider the image.

"Did it ever occur to you, Lieutenant," Temple asked in strained tones, "that it might be as hard for me to look at that poster under these circumstances as to hunt through the mug-shot book for the faces of the men who attacked me?"

Molina whirled to face Temple, then her eyes dropped. "No. I'm sorry." She turned back to the poster. "Quite . . . intense, isn't he?"

"The present tense. You give me hope, Lieutenant, of revenge if not reunion."

"You were right," Molina answered absently. "He wouldn't be easy to kill. Was he a good magician?"

"Unbelievable. He wouldn't work with an assistant. Didn't like airhead dollies, didn't need anybody to distract the audience from him."

"Didn't want it," Molina added.

"No."

"Hmm."

"You can have it copied?"

Molina's dark, blunt-cut hair bobbed. "I'll see they don't damage it."

"Why?"

Her head didn't turn. "You kept it, didn't you?"

"Stored it."

"Hmm." Molina lifted the anchoring slippers, let the poster slowly roll out of sight from the bottom, like a drawn shade. One of her fingers touched the bit of Magic Tape that had been pressed down on the back.

"Is that all you need?" Temple asked pointedly.

Molina turned. "Sorry. Did you keep anything else of his?"

"That wasn't in the deal." Temple sighed, then relented. She'd gone this far, and she was too tired to resist. "Only some CDs, and some clothes I hadn't gotten rid of yet."

"Clothes?" Molina's head lifted like a hound's.

"Back here." Temple swept her own belongings to the left to bare the closet's far, shadowed end where the odd shirt, sweater and jacket hung.

Molina stepped up and began paging through the clothes. She plucked out a sweater, a thick-woven wool turtleneck, and took it to the French doors for inspection.

"Irish-made," she declared, sounding as cut and dried as a customs official.

Temple nodded, not surprised.

"Odd for Las Vegas."

"Winters can get chilly here. Besides, Max performed all over the country—Minneapolis, Boston—the world even."

"But he left this behind. Expensive. Odd. Might indicate . . . and blue. Beige and blue." Molina grew so lost in thought that she seemed to be mooning over the sweater.

"Lots of men wear those colors," Temple said, aggravated that Molina would dismiss her clever "Monday's child" murder theory, yet waste this much time on an abandoned sweater. "Ever notice that the manly among us are limited to a deadly dull and restricted palette?"

"No." Molina cast Temple an amused glance as she stood there in her deadly dull navy suit. Navy or khaki or gray. Organization woman.

Molina abruptly returned to the closet and replaced the sweater. She retrieved the rolled-up poster from the bed. "I'll get it back to you as soon as possible."

Temple nodded, impatient for her to leave.

For once, Molina took the hint and stalked out of the bedroom into the light-drenched living room. She looked around as if memorizing it, then turned to Temple. "This neighbor of yours, Devine. Was he living here when Kinsella disappeared?"

"No. Why do you ask?"

"You two seemed to get along. I wondered if that was something new."

"Awfully interested in the men in my life, for a policeperson, aren't you?"

"Maybe I'm just envious," Molina said.

"Why?"

"Short women get all the tall men."

"Matt isn't that tall."

"Tall enough."

Temple's mind flashed back to a mental picture of Matt rising to meet Molina at the emergency room. In her low work heels, Molina stood a trifle taller than his five-ten-or-so. Barefoot, they'd be dead even.

"Oh, come on!" Temple found herself saying disdainfully. "You beanpoles have nothing to complain about. You get to play basketball and be models."

"Short girls get to be cheerleaders and prom queens."

"I never was!"

"I never modeled."

"That's only because you never plucked your eyebrows!"

Molina reared back in surprise. "The natural look is in."

"Not that natural. And not back then. Even with Hairy Ape eyebrows, tall girls get taken seriously and get voted to be class president and they *marry* basketball players! There isn't one thing about short girls that tall girls envy, admit it!"

Molina considered, then shrugged. "Short girls get to wear high heels."

Temple, speechless, stared back. Then she clapped her hand over her mouth before she began laughing.

Molina didn't laugh . . . not quite. She waved the long white roll of the poster. "Thanks for the loan. Watch your step."

Molina let herself out before Temple could pull herself together and do it. How did they get into eyebrows and high heels? And Matt as well as Max?

She looked around. And where the heck had Midnight Louie gone now? She could use some feline aid and comfort.

Chapter 25

The Kitty City Connection

The phone on the nightstand had an electronic panic attack, jolting Temple wide awake. New-fashioned phones rang like a hysterical Moog synthesizer being choked off in the middle of an aria, she thought, grabbing the red plastic high-heeled shoe masquerading as a telephone. According to the amount of light filtering through the miniblinds on the French doors, morning had arrived.

Temple cradled the heel against her ear, hopeful that Molina had reconsidered and wanted to know more about her theory.

"Hi, kiddo!"

"Electra? I called you last thing last night, but you weren't home. I was worried."

"Piffle. You think anyone would give me trouble in that outfit? When did you do your last thing last night and call?"

"Nine-thirty. I was a little tired."

"Heavens to Boadicea, dearie! I wasn't done gossiping until midnight. Want to come up for some whole-wheat pancakes and tofu?"

"Yeah!" Temple's enthusiasm expressed a hunger for the forthcoming information, not the menu. "I'll be there as soon as I'm dressed."

"Don't bother to dress for breakfast." Electra chuckled. "After a few hours in the Goliath dressing rooms and at Kitty City, clothes seem downright unnatural."

Getting *into* them had struck Temple as unnatural lately, she told herself after she hung up and jumped out of bed. She was slightly cheered to find her right shoulder loose enough to wiggle into a pullover top.

Louie awaited in the kitchen. He lay on the black-and-white tiles making like a grinless Cheshire cat: parts of him faded into the black and stood out against the white. At his length and width, he sprawled over several tiles.

"How about some almost-fresh tuna on your Free-to-be-Feline?" Temple scraped the last of the can's contents atop yesterday's allotment of dry food.

The cat leaned his nose nearer to sniff, but did not deign to rise.

"Louie, you need a better diet at your age! The vet is going to think you're an incorrigible case."

Taking her own nutrition lecture to heart, Temple swallowed her regular regimen of bullet-sized vitamin pills with a glass of tomato juice before snatching today's fire-engine-scarlet patent-leather tote bag from the sofa and racing up to Electra's penthouse apartment, her heart going pitty-pat. She was not only about to get inside information on the competition from a source she could trust; she would finally see the inside of Electra's place. Even Max had never broached this sanctum scantorum.

The elevator was particularly cranky that morning, clanking up the two floors. It disgorged her with a final, miffed metallic squeal. Temple walked the few steps to Electra's set of double doors and rang the mother-of-pearl doorbell. Craftsmen still used touches like that in the fifties.

The heavy wooden double doors muted a mellow echo of her own doorbell, but in a moment one swept open.

The muumuu was predominantly yellow and violet, splashed with tasteful streaks of lime green and turquoise. It flowed, a Technicolor wave of polished cotton, from Electra's neck to her bare toes.

"Come in!" the landlady ordered. "Don't you look snappy today! Let's see."

"Thanks." Temple had coordinated her red-and-white knit sailor top with a short navy pleated skirt and white, navy and red Jourdan pumps. She spun decorously, until the pleats fanned out.

"Lovely. So normal, after what I've seen lately. I decided breakfast on the patio would be nice. It's still shady." Electra took Temple's wrist to lead her through the mirrored vertical blinds that lined the entry hall, creating a fun-house effect.

In a room beyond, Temple stared at the blond fifties television cabinet she had glimpsed once before. Atop it still stood a huge, green glass globe on a tarnished brass base, whose design represented either colliding Studebakers or copulating elephants, Temple couldn't decide which.

Even as Temple followed Electra into the next room, she was aware of drawn-blind dimness, of massive shadowy pieces of period furniture—*several* sofas, for instance—and the evasive scent of eucalyptus.

A genteel thump in a farther room made her stop, resisting Electra's firm pull. "What was that?"

"Nothing," Electra said.

"But I thought—" A movement brushed along the baseboard edging the parquet floors. Then the bottom fringe on a buxom forties sofa undulated like a hula skirt. "Electra, do you have pets?"

"You cannot own an animal," Electra replied haughtily.

"Pests, then?"

"What kind of a landlady do you think I am?"

"Then ghosts?" Temple suggested in exasperation.

"I'm afraid not. Not that I haven't tried. Séances have been held up here since the building was erected."

"That's fascinating. I'd like to—" Temple was jerked through an open French door into the rude shock of daylight.

This high, on the fifth floor, the low-lying clutter of Las Vegas vanished as if it had never been. Only the tall towers of hotels probed the sky as the desert's faded rose, gold, azure and green bled toward the horizon like running watercolors. The mountains, hazy blue in their serene distance from the hot, yellow-white hurly-burly of the city, kept company with frothy clouds tinted with the exact flattering shade of a baby pink spotlight.

The view was the least of it. The entire rooftop was upholstered in green—covered with potted topiary trees, beds of plump-leaved succulents and cacti with textures as weird and varied as anything on earth.

"Hurry," Electra said, "you don't want your pancakes to get cold."

Temple eyed the only table. A large circle of glass rested atop an abomination: a ring of chubby, gilded plaster Oriental figures with raised hands that were either modeled on Wu Fat in "Hawaii Five-O" reruns, or the big-bellied Oriental god of luck reproduced in an infinitude of cheap versions.

Atop these gaudy, somewhat ungainly gentlemen—floating on the glass like lily pads on water—were rainbow-colored carnival glass plates, cheap giveaways from days gone by, now dear.

Temple regarded stacks of plump brown pancakes centered on the wavy-rimmed plates. A dollop of white stuff resembling sour cream or Zymonal reposed beside them.

At least there was coffee. She took a sip from a steaming Porky Pig mug.

"Chicory," Electra announced as she sat, watching

Temple fight not to spit out her mouthful. "Now try your wheatcakes. If you must have something unhealthy, here's a tub of no-cholesterol vegetable oil."

Temple eyed this concession warily. As far as she was concerned, butter was butter. Pretenders weren't much tastier than axle grease, but the heavy-textured pancakes needed something. She used her knife tip to scoop out a blob of the pale stuff.

The tofu beside her pancakes shook like Santa Claus's belly as she smeared her cakes and dug in. Not half bad, if you chewed fast. Electra was dribbling something that resembled rat droppings atop her cakes.

"Raw bran," she explained.

"Okay," Temple said. "What about the raw facts? What did you find out at the Goliath?"

"Lots." Electra tilted her head as she chewed a bite, toying with her shoulder-dusting earrings, a cornucopia of apples, cherries, bananas and pineapples so appropriate to the breakfast hour. "What do you want to know first?"

"About Dorothy Horvath. I actually met the second victim, and saw for myself that she had an abusive lover. But Dorothy was the first, and she's still a mystery to me."

"Dorothy—oh, you mean Glinda. Yeah, they all knew Glinda." Electra pushed the half-dozen colorful wooden bangles ringing each arm up like sleeves as she braced her elbows on the cool glass tabletop and leaned forward to tell Temple all.

"A lot of these dancers live on a very simple level. They don't worry about who's gonna be president, or pollution in Mexico City, nothing global or political. Survival is their prime directive, as they say on 'Star Trek.' The only higher education they got was in the College of Carnal Knowledge, and that too early. They figure the world handed them a raw deal, and they're going to make the best of it. A lot of them pick bad boyfriends and make bad loans. A lot live from day to day, and blow any windfalls on froufrou for the stage, or lots of cheap civilian clothes, or drugs. Or on bad boyfriends again. A lot are what you'd call single mothers—not like Murphy Brown. They had kids when they were still kids themselves. If they're working for anything besides the bright lights and a G-string full of tips, it's to keep those kids from getting the same raw deal they got. But they still pick bad men— bikers, the big bad wolf kind; smooth-talking club owners who run their joints like a company store and bleed the girls by fining them flat; abusers."

"I get the picture," Temple put in.

"I don't want to sound like I'm putting them down. They're doing their best with a bad deal. Poor Glinda— that face of hers was worth a million bucks, but the brain behind it wasn't worth enough to make a local call at a pay phone. They say she acted like a ten-year-old. Never quite understood what happened to her—or why, or why it kept happening again and again. She could move on that stage like liquid lightning, but she was a patsy for any smooth operator with a rough reputation who came along. She was going to lose her kids to her first husband, an upright type whose contempt drove her into exotic dancing and who was using her work as a reason to get custody of the kids. Some of the dancers are fighters; some aren't. Glinda wasn't."

"Maybe that was why she based her act on *The Wizard of Oz*. She wanted to be whisked away to a better world."

"Or she wanted to go home to a place like Kansas that she never had. Sad story. Sad girl. Guess hubby has the kids for sure now."

"What about him? Where does he live? Could he have—?"

Electra fanned her hands to stop Temple's jackhammer questions. "I thought of that, too. Still stationed abroad after the Desert Storm call-up. And he was a shoe-in to get custody anyway, from what the other dancers told me. Glinda kept missing her court dates, so afraid the system wouldn't help her that she made sure it didn't."

"It's hard to understand self-esteem so low that it can be that self-destructive," Temple said. Her fork skated a bit of pancake into the pile of tofu. "I can see it, from my one encounter with the kind of a world that sticks out a fist and strikes you down every time you move. Eventually, you'd stop moving."

Electra patted Temple's hand to the accompaniment of jangling bangles. "Glinda hoped, in that looney, kiddish way of hers, that winning another Rhinestone G-string would establish that she was an artist, an entertainer, that it would help her get her kids.

"That's what I was trying to say, these dancers aren't fools, but they fool themselves," Electra went on. "They can use the business, or the business can use them. Some girls barely eighteen perform for ten grand a week at uptown clubs. They don't have to take tips or talk to customers or touch them. They're exotic dance queens like in the classy old burlesque days. Other girls the same age are bussed around from town to town and dump to dump, paid ten bucks a night and all the tips they can writhe out of men, no more than bar girls selling drinks with their bodies. The sleazy club owners fine them their tip money for so-called 'infractions,' and then fire them if they want to develop their careers by taking time off to be in a contest like this. Some club managers are little more than pimps, forcing green kids into dancing until they're afraid they can't do anything better. Then there are the seasoned ones, the hardheads. Nobody does them out of their pay, they come and they go of their free will, and essentially take the money and run. Most of them run back to stripping, though, because no other job they could get pays those kind of tips, or offers that kind of spotlight."

"Whew. You heard it all. What about Katharine—Kitty Cardozo? She wasn't like poor Glinda North. She had nothing to lose, except a woman-beating man worth getting rid of. She had her own business—"

"She *got* the business, Temple, just like Glinda. Wait'll you hear the stuff I dug up. That's why I was at Kitty City. Who do you think it's named after?"

"Lots of strip joints play on cat names. The Pussycat Lounge down Paradise, *Le Chat Noir*—"

"Only one is named Kitty City, and that's because Kitty—your Kitty!—started it. Or her then-husband did. Twelve years ago. Named it in her honor. She was the star. Then they split. Kitty claimed she owned half, but had no papers to prove it. It seems she trusted them to the office safe, and guess who got custody of *that* when she walked out?"

"Her husband?"

"The one and only. What a sweetie. Say, I might have a new career. Kitty City doesn't use novelty acts, but they're willing to let me try out." Electra tossed her head. Not much of her moussed midnight-black hair moved, but her earrings shimmied like everyone's sister Kate. "The Vampire and I just might blow their carburetors."

"You're kidding!"

"Swear to Sally Rand! I'm telling you, I could have a sixth career here."

"Speaking of which, what about your wedding chapel clients while you're tripping the light fantastic?"

"Listen, there are two dozen wedding chapels in Vegas. Let 'em eat rice cakes somewhere else for a couple of days. The Lover's Knot will still be here tomorrow. This is fun!"

"I'm glad you're enjoying yourself. You certainly got a lot of information. I bet Molina would give her best penny loafers for half of what you know."

"Don't count on it. That woman is all over that place like a bad dream. I've been interviewed by one of her associates already." Electra paused. "Not bad. About fifty-three. Decent build. Cute little bald spot."

"Electra! You're beginning to sound like one of the dancers. Keep your mind on business."

"Okay. Here's something I kept hearing, and finally this little voice starts ringing in my ears, sort of breathy, like Marilyn Monroe. Maybe I'm channeling her, who knows?

Anyway, it keeps saying: What name keeps coming up, dummy, in all the gossip? And guess what does?"

Temple was at a loss, especially after the Marilyn Monroe allusion out of left field. "Joe DiMaggio?"

"No, silly! Even—get this!—even Savannah Ashleigh has a connection. The word is she's judging this competition because, if she doesn't, some photos from her past might show up in the North American *Examiner*."

"That supermarket rag!"

"Yes, well-read but not good for the career in fil-mah."

"You talked to Savannah Ashleigh, too?" Temple was impressed. Electra knew how to get in there and boogie.

"Oh, yeah. She admired my earrings. I promised to make her some. Glinda did a stint at Kitty City, too. And that's where Savannah got her start more years ago than she'd care to let on. Supposedly, some sleazy photos of her would have hit the street if she hadn't agreed to judge this year's competition. Actually, everyone thinks that some scandalous photos in the right places could jump-start her stalling career, except hers are so old that she no longer displays the top form she used to, and the contrast would be shocking."

"So Savannah, Glinda and Kitty all worked, even began their careers, at Kitty City?"

"Them, and more. It's a big club, in a big-club town."

"You're not saying that the same man who cheated Kitty of her interest in the business and is blackmailing Savannah, who gave Glinda her start and who wants you to audition is—"

Electra nodded. "The one, the only, and the oily. Ike Wetzel."

Chapter 26

. . . All Must Come to Dust

The aqua Storm sprinted through the colossus's braced legs like a cartoon car—bright and fast. As it pulled under the hotel's metallic entrance canopy, a parking valet came scampering in his Ramses kilt to open the driver's door. Temple was happy to exchange a dollar bill for the precaution of avoiding the parking ramp.

She faced her reflection in the Goliath's mirrored revolving doors. She felt less stiff and sore today, and even looked a little more . . . perky. Too perky. Her impromptu outfit made her resemble a patriotic tap dancer, she thought, whisking into the midst of her reflected spinning selves, then around and out into the Goliath lobby.

Today she was going to take this town by the tail and whip the convention PR into apple-pie order. The ballroom would be open again, the troops gathered, and she had lots of juicy new information to confirm and expand upon. Best of all, Electra would still be undercover.

The landlady had told Temple she had resolved to continue her charade "as long as it takes" to clear the competition of the pall of bad press. Temple was relieved to have a reliable inside source, but had wondered aloud just how far Electra was prepared to take her stripper persona.

"To the limit the law allows," Electra had declared doughtily. She even refused Temple's offer of a ride to the Goliath.

"I've got to take the Vampire in for a tech rehearsal. We got the music keyed in yesterday."

"What music?"

"The music for my routine," Electra said indignantly. " 'Born To Be Wild.' You don't think you can just show up and claim to be a stripper without an act?"

"I didn't think about it at all."

"Hmph. Good thing *I'm* the undercover operator."

"I think the word is 'operative.' "

"Whatever. Don't worry about me. I'll be in later. Strippers sleep late. You don't want me to blow my cover, do you? You'll hear me coming."

What have I wrought? Temple asked herself, pausing before the ballroom doors as she remembered Electra's parting words.

Today no security men were plastered against the doors, legs braced and faces stern, like miniature colossi. Better. Normalcy was returning. Temple sailed inside unchallenged, full of the spirit of Scarlett O'Hara. Today was not only another day, it was an unfolding origami paper sculpture, rife with surprise and elegance.

"Hi there, T.B. Coming in a little late, aren't we?"

Temple hit the breaks on her Jourdans at the sound of that ever-so-deep baritone, and turned in its direction.

Yes, Crawford Buchanan occupied a ballroom chair against the wall. He was riffling through some papers as pale as his silk-blend oyster trousers and yuck-yellow shirt. A straw fedora hid most of his silver hair and a brass-headed cane leaned against the wall beside him. He looked like a decadent English invalid.

"What are you doing out of the hospital?" she demanded, not meaning to sound as annoyed as she did.

He tremulously patted the left side of his chest. "The boy is better. They released me, with odious instructions on diet and exercise. I decided to begin my new physical-fitness regimen by ambling over here and seeing how you were doing."

"Just dandy until now."

Buchanan fished a folded newspaper tear sheet from among his papers. "Actually, 'dandy' doesn't appear to do justice to such happenings as a double murder." He flashed the *Las Vegas Scoop*'s front page with ten double-column bylined inches on "Jack the Stripper-ripper Strikes Again at Goliath."

"I'm doing this PR job because you keeled over, and you're knifing me in the back with sleazy stories on the tragedies?"

"Now that I'm no longer handing PR, the stress is gone," Buchanan said. "No conflict of interest, I think you'd say. I did the first story from the hospital," he added modestly. "You mind checking it to see if all the facts are right?"

She snatched it from his hand and read the first lurid subhead. "'A Comely Come-on from an Ecdysiast'! Crawford, even you admitted that the poor Horvath woman wouldn't have given you the time of day in a Swatch factory."

"I wanted to convey a feeling for the victim when she was alive and beautiful. Haven't you heard of the New Journalism?"

"'She eeled past me in a scent of roses and regret'—oh, God! You don't even get to the first murder until the fourth paragraph. And the last subhead, 'Catwoman Caught by Batman'? Crawford, this is salacious, self-aggrandizing and totally fictional."

"Thank you," he said complacently, reaching to take his treasure back. "Don't wrinkle it."

Temple refolded the tear sheet and slapped it atop the

papers piled on his lap. "Stay home. Stay out of print. Stay out of my way, or I'll see that WHOOPE sues you and your fish wrappings to kingdom come."

"I got you a job," came the injured whine. "Most people would be grateful."

"Want to do something to make me really grateful? Retire."

Temple stomped away over the black spaghetti of cables still strewing the carpeting. Electra's pancakes were beginning to back up in her stomach, and she really didn't want to taste them again. It would be a perverted kind of poetic justice if *she* ended up with a heart attack and Crawford Buchanan replaced her.

"Whoa—! You're a real fireball today."

Temple stopped by the smoke signal hovering above one of the scattered ballroom chairs—Lindy's. Ike Wetzel sat in the chair next to her, puffing on a cigar.

"I've just had a chat with my predecessor," Temple said. "He's written a smarmy story about the murders for his scandal sheet."

"I know." Lindy waved some of her own smoke away and patted a vacant chairseat. "Sit down. We're not worried about that. No one takes 'Buchanan's Broadside' seriously."

Wetzel brooded for a moment, then broke into the conversation. "Frankly, much as I hate to say it, the murders are getting us some big-league press coverage."

"I was going to write a blanket press release," Temple said, "then set up a system to funnel interviews and make sure that marauding press people don't disturb the contestants."

Wetzel laughed. "Forget it. Listen, strippers get so much bad press that all this attention for some plain old murders is gravy. These girls love to stop whatever they're doing for an interview. Pictures are even better. Don't sweat it."

He rose, his cigar ash perilously close to falling off, and headed for the stage.

Temple watched him, an overbuilt short-legged man, a walking inverted pyramid of touchy pride and prejudice. His every word and mannerism made plain that he didn't expect to have his will crossed. He could hit a woman he considered lippy.

"How long were Kitty and Ike married?" she asked Lindy, looking down quickly to judge the woman's reaction.

Lindy drew on her cigarette until she frowned from the effort. "You've been busy. Maybe seven, eight years. They broke up about three years ago."

"They couldn't still have been seeing each other?"

"Never say never."

"Did he . . . hit her?"

Lindy shrugged and screwed her cigarette butt into a slick of watered-down scotch at the bottom of a hotel glass. "Who knows? Could have. Ike's a funny guy. Changes. Like he was always against his girls competing in the contest. Fired them if they took the weekend off to do it—that's not unusual, a lot of clubs don't want us to waste time on things like dreams. Just fling that ass and sling that booze at the customers. So Ike was real hard-nosed about WHOOPE, the whole deal. Then, this year, he lightened up. Got himself put on the board. Said we were gonna do it right. Strange guy."

"Strange business," Temple added. "Don't any women own clubs?"

Lindy's dark eyes widened. "Say, you read my mind. I'd like to get something like that going. But clubs cost money. A night's lights can run twenty-five hundred dollars; rent three grand a week and up. Then there's liquor trouble, fight trouble. Clubs need bouncers. It's a man's game."

"Do you know who Kitty was seeing recently?"

"Some guy."

Lindy's disinterested tone promised no new revelations. Temple had heard the dancers confiding every fact of their private lives—"I'm in love with this neat guy";

"My kid got ninety-three on his math test yesterday"; "Hey, hon, I'm so worn out from last night I don't even want to wiggle my butt"; "I'd like to beat the shit out of my old man"—but dressing-room girl talk revolved around guys and kids and bum pasts, all generic, like the customers. Facing such a transient, casual milieu, even Molina would have a hard time solving a murder times two.

Temple had watched the action near the stage while brooding on the frustrations of getting juicy gossip from a rolling stone.

"At least you all have access to the stage setup again," she said. "The prelims are tomorrow, and showtime is only fifty-some hours away."

"Yeah. Except now that we have the ballroom back, the cops have banned us from the dressing rooms."

"What?"

"Just this morning. We got here around ten to find yellow tape stretched across the hall. Everybody's been changing in the wings."

"Crime scene tape? But why now—?"

"Yeah. Took 'em awhile to get around to putting it up. Cops must be like the lazy stripper—a little behind in their work."

Temple glanced quickly to the ballroom wall. Buchanan's chair was empty, the cane gone. She scanned the room, trying to see past all sorts of arresting getups. There—the would-be Mark Twain garb. Luckily, pale colors stood out in a crowd, especially one where the dominant color was black. Buchanan was wandering around the floor ogling the female strippers. No doubt his press credentials aided and abetted. She assessed the acts available, and hoped they would suffice to keep the miserable weasel occupied while she headed downstairs to find out why the police would waste their time putting up crime tape two days too late.

Lindy was right. The back stairs were no longer the discreet, deserted route they had been. A yellow tape blocked the bottom, and beyond it stood a uniformed officer.

Temple descended anyway, wishing that her high heels were not so percussive.

"You can't enter, ma'am," the officer told her when she paused on the bottom step.

She liked the additional elevation. "Can I at least ask what's going on?"

"You can ask," he said.

"Isn't it odd to cordon off a crime scene after the lab people have been and gone?"

"They haven't," he answered.

Temple opened her mouth to ask another unwelcome question when the rising wail of a distraught woman interrupted her. Obviously the woman was deeply anguished.

Temple stared at the officer, puzzled. "Is Lieutenant Molina——?"

Molina herself suddenly stepped into the picture, like a magician, all at once. Temple jumped, even though she knew Molina had merely been out of sight down the hall, and had stepped forward when she heard Temple's voice.

"You know a Savannah Ashleigh?" Molina asked.

Temple nodded, recognizing the exasperated note in her voice despite the official monotone.

"She's hysterical. Do you think you could get a sensible word out of her?"

Temple shrugged slowly.

"Let her through," Molina told the officer.

He pulled the tape free of one wall.

"Well, come on," Molina said.

Temple hesitated a moment longer. With her high heels and six inches of riser, she was exactly Lieutenant C. R. Molina's height. She hated to abandon such a rare advantage. Muffled wails were too great a temptation to resist, however, especially when they were movie-star muffled wails.

"What happened?" she asked Molina as she stepped down.

"Your theory got blown to Vancouver."

"By another murder?"

"Two," Molina said succinctly, starting down the hall.

Two. How did a killer mimic a one-a-day nursery rhyme with a double murder? He didn't.

Temple hated the fact that she always had to trot to keep up with Molina. Down here on the concrete floor, her two little tootsies sounded like a convention of hackneys.

Molina led Temple to a dressing room across the hall from the ones she had visited. Temple noticed that the door to the big one was open, but the private one was shut.

This door was ajar. In the mirror Temple glimpsed something old—the Ashleigh mane of platinum blond; something new—the glitter of an evening gown draping the actress; something borrowed—a white square of handkerchief linen that could only belong to someone sensible; and something pink.

The woman was not so much sobbing as gasping for breath. "Gone," she wailed. "Just gone." And then she gave a long, whining moan.

"Did she know the victims?" Temple asked in surprise.

"You tell me. They were found in her dressing room."

"Who were they?"

"We're still checking. Sister act."

"Not . . . twins?"

Molina nodded. "Know them?"

"Met them. June and Gypsy . . . gone? How?"

"We don't know yet."

Temple was going to ask another question, but Molina forestalled her. "Look, they were found dead, naked except for a thin coat of gold paint. Identification's been a little slow. Tracing the path of that gold paint down here has been a lot slower."

"That's why the area's barred."

"Right."

"And Savannah Ashleigh found the body? Bodies."

"Dialed nine-one-one. A perfect witness. Too shaken to

leave the area. The first squad on the scene found her in the dressing room, like this."

"Gone," Savannah wailed again, in utter bereavement.

"I had no idea that they were that close," Temple whispered.

"Whatever. See if you can settle her down. We can't interrogate a siren."

Temple edged into the room, seeing her cheerful outfit in the mirror. She felt like a clown, but there was no way to approach Savannah gently, not with these heels on this floor.

She slipped the shoes off and left them by the door. She could see in the mirror that, behind her, Molina lifted one eyebrow in mute surprise, like Mr. Spock. Come to think of it, they had a lot in common.

Temple approached Savannah. "Miss Ashleigh? Miss Ashleigh?"

At the sound of her own name, the panting picked up tempo. Savannah's eyes were wide open and dazed, as was her mouth. Her long-nailed hands clutched the pink purse on her lap, twisting its straps, tightening on its sides as if it were dough she was kneading.

"Gone," she repeated.

If Savannah Ashleigh had been able to put the variety of tone and inflection into her film lines that she put into that one word here, she would have had a remarkable career.

"Yes," Temple said, "sometimes people are gone. But we are here."

Savannah Ashleigh stared at her blankly.

"I'm Temple Barr, the new PR person. We talked Tuesday, remember? A lot of the national media is coming in for the show, did I tell you?"

Savannah's head began shaking in petulant denial. "Media? What do I care? Gone! Gone, gone, gone!"

"I know it's upsetting. I found someone dead once myself."

"Dead? Dead . . . dead?" Her wide eyes went wild as her voice hit the high notes of hysteria. "She's dead?"

"Both are dead."

"Both. Both?"

Temple could see why Molina had let her talk to Savannah. She tried to picture the lieutenant subjected to one-word answers, repeated noisily and ad nauseam.

"That's what the police say," Temple said.

Savannah's head bowed over her lap, over the pink bag in her lap. Her glamorous bleached platinum hair looked like an old woman's disordered mop. And then Temple understood. She reached for the bag, but Savannah wailed and clutched it closer.

"Dead. And gone."

Temple was at least able to pull off the woman's hands and brush away enough hair to glimpse the "Yvette" sewn atop the bag—not a purse, but a cat carrier. From the crushing way the actress clutched it, the contents were obviously absent.

"What happened?" Temple asked. "You came in, went down to the dressing room, left Yvette and went upstairs again. When?"

The word "Yvette" worked wonders. Savannah looked up, her face as radiant with shared knowledge as young Helen Keller's at the breakthrough moment in *The Miracle Worker*. No one had been speaking Savannah's language before. She had been shocked to discover the bodies, but what had devastated her was simultaneously discovering the absence of her cat, Yvette.

"Yvette," she repeated in heartbreaking tones. "Who? Why?"

"Am I right? The dressing room was fine when you came in, changed and left Yvette."

Savannah nodded through tears that would not fall, her face twisted into a mask of tragedy.

"What time was that?"

"Nine," she wailed.

"And when you came back?"

Savannah shook her head. Time was not a priority with her. "Later."

"And the bodies were there, dead."

Savannah nodded ponderously.

"You called nine-one-one?"

Another lethargic nod.

"And then you remembered Yvette and went back? That was very brave. But Yvette was gone."

"Ye-es. Gone. You say dead—"

"Not Yvette. Not . . . yet. How could she have gotten away?"

Savannah's Hollywood-white teeth bit her bottom lip until it matched their pallor. "I left her in her carrier and shut the door. I thought she was safe." The sentence ended on another long wail. "Safe . . . safe," Savannah repeated like a mantra, rocking. "What will . . . the killer do with Yvette? Do *to* Yvette? A killer's got her!"

"Maybe Yvette ran out when the women or their murderer entered. Yes! She could be hiding among all the costumes down here. You know how cats are: won't come out even though you beg and plead. Give it time. I'm sure she's all right. Who would hurt a cat?"

"Think so?" Savannah was sniffling slightly now, a good sign that the hysterics were ebbing. She pressed the police-issue handkerchief to her delicate nose, then recoiled at the stiff linen and tossed it onto the dressing table.

"It's the likeliest scenario," Temple said. "Cats are too clever to get caught by anybody, even a murderer."

"Yvette was so sweet, so trusting—"

"She's still a cat, and you don't often catch a cat napping when it comes to crime."

Savannah nodded with childlike trust. Temple peeled her rigid hands away from the crumpled carrier.

"Yvette will need this when she comes home. Why don't you leave it open down here? Give her a chance to come back when it's quiet again and curl up. It's only a matter of time."

"Promise?" Savannah beseeched, her big hazel eyes floating in a pond of tears. "Promise she'll come back?"

Oh, great, Temple thought even as she nodded reassuringly. Now she had to produce a missing cat as well as face up to the fact that the puzzling and terrible death of two more women had proved her murder theory nothing more than child's play.

Chapter 27

Louie in a Jam

I am no Einstein (and would never allow *my* hair to go so obviously untended) but even a Roads Scholar of the self-made variety can see that the dressing rooms and ballroom of the Goliath Hotel are no fit environment for the likes of the Divine Yvette.

In fact, nothing would get me within one hundred yards of this scene of dirty dancing and naked death, were not this sweet little doll of my acquaintance in the vicinity. From the first, the Divine Yvette has been forced into a position that offers the worst of two worlds. She has been left untended, yet confined to a canvas cage; abandoned and trapped at one and the same time.

Naturally, I have kept a close eye on the Divine One's disposition and comings and goings. It is no great feat to arrive at the dressing area early in the morning in anticipation of Yvette's arrival on the arm of her mistress, Miss Savannah Ashleigh.

Usually the latter can be counted upon to arrive no earlier than ten in the morning, and then only under duress. However, I wish to take no chances and post myself in the cavernous costume storage area by nine, the better to avoid attention.

I admit that I am playing more here than the love-stricken swain. In the back of my mind is a notion that I may have an opportunity to get a better look at Black Legs. Given the demise of the lissome lady in the ballroom while wearing an ensemble, such as it was, that paid tribute to my breed, I am more eager than ever to cross paths with this murderous abuser of little dolls, be they human or feline.

As I await the arrival of my feline friend, I recline on and under the ruffled train of a Flamenco skirt, inhaling an unhealthy attar of powder, sweat and mothballs. Such contemplative times are my favorite. I picture myself tracking and cornering Black Legs in the fatal dressing room. I see an admiring circle of humans agape at my exploits. Miss Temple Barr sheds tears of remorse and promises never again to take me to the House of Dr. Death. There will be another photograph in the local rag, of course: tiresome, and hard on the peepers, but I am so photogenic. Perhaps also a small reward—a goldfish, say. Or several. And the lovely Yvette standing by, unnoticed by the applauding police and officials, her big blue-green eyes beaming with pride and adoration.

I hear the night maintenance man shuffle out. Other occasional footsteps come and go. My ears prick and flatten at each advance and retreat of shoes. High heels clatter past twice, but not in the rhythm favored by Miss Savannah Ashleigh (arrogant, yet languid) or my own Miss Temple Barr (brisk and snappy). Softer footsteps come. An odor of chemicals pushes past the ajar door to my sensitive nostrils. My whiskers twitch, then my back. I shut my eyes at this noxious smell. Miraculously, it blends with the other unpleasant scents and becomes a background note, sharp but less shrill among the many others.

At last! Miss Savannah Ashleigh's sullen steps. She stumbles outside my lair and mutters a rude expression. I wince to think of the Divine Yvette's pink-and-silver ears flattening at the sound of such language.

Her mistress clatters and curses on, toward the dressing room they share. All is quiet for a time. I rise, stretch until my belly touches the floor (contrary to the impression of some, this does not happen without my making a special effort) and amble to the door.

Other voices murmur from the farther dressing room, the very location in which Miss Glinda North went West and I first encountered Black Legs. I detect the sound of makeup jars being unscrewed and an ongoing family argument. The sweetest sound of all is that of Miss Savannah Ashleigh's heels scraping along the concrete as she retreats up the stairs.

Alone at last. I am halfway to the dressing-room door before you can say "Puss-in-Boots." Luckily, theatrical sorts do not close dressing-room doors behind them, always expecting a hurried return. Also, they are not much on privacy unless they are up to something of a naughty nature.

So I throw myself casually against the door just below the doorknob, and my weight pushes it open enough for me to enter without cramping my midsection.

First I sniff. The Divine Yvette is a victim of air pollution as well; an odious drugstore perfume poisons the air. I carefully avoid a gleaming slick of spilled powder and walk to the love-seat. There, beside its white wicker legs, rests the soft-sided cell containing my long-lost love.

She has long since sensed my arrival, and is waiting with round, limpid eyes at the mesh window to her cell. I must silence her welcoming cries with a quick lash of my tail. Who knows when her mistress will return?

The Divine Yvette accepts my admonition gracefully. She is, she tells me with a tender purr, happy to see me again so soon. Miss Savannah Ashleigh has been most trying of late, as nervous, in fact, as a cat in a Doberman kennel.

"Speaking of which," I tell her, "it is high time for me to attempt what I came to accomplish."

What, she inquires sweetly, is that?

I explain that I am here to bust her out of this sissy cell.

At first the black-tipped hair lifts along her spine, sending shivers down mine. The Divine Yvette protests that she must not leave the carrier, that she is not "safe" outside of it.

"Bullfinch feathers!" I answer. I tell her that she has been sold a bill of goods. Besides, with me here, she could not be safer.

She lowers her head to lick nervously at her ruff, a soft silver collar that shimmers with an unearthly glimmer. Then she bats her silver eyelashes and agrees with me.

I lift up to examine the carrier's fastening—a long pink-painted metal zipper that takes two right turns before it stops. This is Miss Savannah Ashleigh's fatal mistake. Had she purchased a trap with a pawproof closure—say, one of those blasted doorknobs—my goose liver would have been cooked. (Not that I mind a little warm food from time to time.) But a zipper is kitten's play. Since I encountered the Divine Yvette's pink-canvas house, I have been practicing, in fact, on a few of Miss Temple Barr's dresses in the privacy of her closet.

I lean over the pink metal tab on the operative end, hook an incisor in the convenient hole, and pull with all my nineteen-point-eight pounds so thoughtfully revealed to me at the House of Dr. Death. The sweet metallic squeal of zipper teeth parting is my reward. Despite some trouble at the corners, between my tooth and its teeth, we make tracks together to the end of the line.

Yvette, who has been straining to watch me achieve this feat, pokes her adorable little face up through the pink canvas flap. I cannot restrain myself from a long nose-to-nose encounter, followed by billing and cooing of a feline nature. It does not behoove a gentleman to go into specifics, but let us say that I am no slouch with what you could call hot licks.

The Divine Yvette confesses that she has never been so transported.

"You see, this is better than a cat carrier any day," I point out. When I look into this flimsy cage while preparing to assist Miss Yvette out, I notice a pile like a pink angora mouse in one corner.

Oh, says Miss Yvette with a soft little trill, those are my beauty supplies.

I paw through them, never having seen the like, and overturn a steel-tooth comb and a powder puff (the erstwhile pastel mouse) with a satin ribbon on one side on which is written the ineffable name, Yvette, in silver script.

PUSSYFOOT

I flip this frippery over again. "Do you mean to say that Miss Savannah Ashleigh powders you? For fleas?"

Oh, no, Miss Yvette answers, shocked. Miss Savannah Ashleigh powders her, she tells me, so that her hairs will be clean and fluffy and smell good.

I can attest to the efficacy of this beauty regimen as I push the front of the carrier flat, the better for Miss Yvette to step out. An almond-scented wave of fur brushes past.

I am about to take matters in their foreordained direction, when my alert senses detect voices growing louder in the hall. I have not been forewarned by the sound of nearing shoes, a puzzlement that immediately becomes an annoyance.

"Quick!" I hiss at the Divine Yvette, slapping the empty carrier farther into the shadows and pushing my companion rather rudely underneath the sofa.

Not a moment too soon. A trio of feet enter, two bare but painted with the gaudy color of the twenty-four-carat trim on a Cadillac Seville, the other wearing black sneakers. No wonder I heard no approach. Beside me, Yvette's airy whiskers tremble at the dust we have bestirred beneath the sofa, but I clap a paw over her nose before she sneezes.

"Here it is," announces one of the barefoot girls with cheek of gold (from my position I can see more of the scenery than the Divine Yvette).

"Let me finish you off," a new voice suggests.

I hear a plastic cap being unscrewed and am nearly leveled by a strong odor with an undertone of glycerine. Beside me, the Divine Yvette trembles in fear.

I begin to appreciate her reaction, for I do not like what is transpiring in the room beyond us one bit. The two girls talk, as girls will who are undressed and used to it, of many things.

"We have never argued like this before," one says apologetically.

"That's because we never faced the past," the other answers.

"Your past," the first says, "is not my past."

A silence increases the tension. Then the second girl says, "Be sure to leave an apple-sized spot."

And the first says, "Oh, that's cold. Oh, well, almost done."
And the second says, "I feel kind of . . . faint."
And the first says, "Gypsy?"

Next I hear the boneless thump of a body to hard concrete. The Divine Yvette's body is plastered to mine. I can feel her heart beating like a berserk metronome. Peering out with my chin on the floor, I see a golden horizon of legs and arms and torso. Another golden girl bends down beside the first, utters a little Yvette-like cry, and crumples beside the first.

Beyond them stands Black Legs. I curse myself for not peeking sooner and tense to spring out for a good look. What can Black Legs do to me?

The Divine Yvette curls her long nails into my shoulders, clinging for dear life. If I shoot out from under the sofa now, I will scrape her off like yesterday's mud.

While I watch helplessly, Black Legs leaves on quiet cat feet, unidentified.

Chapter 28

Louie Takes a Powder

Matt Devine was shadowboxing, Asian-style, by the pool when Temple returned to the Circle Ritz at four that afternoon.

She paused under the shade of the solitary palm to watch until he finished an arcane sequence, straightened and smiled at her.

"Did your regular caller reach you last night?" she asked.

He shook his head and walked over. His white exercise clothes were clean and unwrinkled; nothing about him spoke of heat or effort. The man was supernaturally cool, Temple thought, not for the first time. But his face was troubled.

"She didn't call. If she hasn't—I doubt she will again."

"What do you think happened?" Temple asked with concern. She hated people dropping out of her life before their stories were resolved. Matt made his living by dealing with such frustration.

Matt sat on the lounge chair, despite its dusting of wind-blown oleander petals. "What happened? Good or bad; nothing in between. She could have solved her problem and left the abusive guy. She could have gone back to him, broken. I'll never know."

"You're sure about that?"

"I've got a feeling. That's what you go by when you counsel people over the phone, in the dark. Instinct. I feel that . . . she's gone, one way or the other."

"She was in an abusive relationship, but had hopes of getting out?"

"Yeah." He regarded her with new curiosity. "Not a new story."

"And she had called every day until, was it Tuesday night?"

"When I wasn't there, right," he answered a bit self-accusingly.

"Hey, she still didn't call, even if you had been there. Ever think of it that way, Mr. Guilt Trip?"

He smiled ruefully. "You're looking better, and you must be feeling better, if you're delivering pep talks. When are you going to get serious about working out, 'earning some self-defense?"

Temple sighed heavily, then sat on the end of the lounge chair now that Matt's weight stabilized it. The shade was pleasant, the sound of the muted traffic predictable, almost peaceful.

"When I feel up to physical education. Right now, I could use a pep talk myself," she admitted. "They found two more bodies this morning."

"What?" Matt sat up so quickly that the lounge foot almost collapsed.

"Hey! Yes, now it's four dead in all. Not even Rambo could stop the national press from overrunning the event—although the organizers seem strangely indifferent to the notoriety. Molina and the Las Vegas Metropolitan police force are convinced they're after a serial killer hung up on sexy women. They've got enough uniformed officers running around the Goliath to make them part of every act. Oh. And Crawford Buchanan showed up today. He's doing just dandy, well enough to be out working on a sleazy tell-all about this mess for the Las Vegas *Scoop*."

"What about your theory?"

"That," she said darkly. "Molina gave me the birth dates for 'fair of face' and 'full of grace,' but now that 'full of woe' has been knocked piewacky—two dead at once and a day skipped—I don't feel like pursuing my fantasies. At least I was able to help Molina."

"That would be the day. How?"

"I'd talked to the victims—twin-sister strippers, who went by the names of June and Gypsy."

"They were twins?"

She nodded. "Did an act in metallic body paint as the Gold Dust Twins. That's what killed them, the paint. I'd talked to them about how lethal that stuff can be if you don't leave a bare patch of skin somewhere to breathe. From what Molina said—and this was before the autopsy—there weren't any obvious bare spots. And they knew better."

"So the killer had to get close enough to paint them without their getting suspicious before it was too late?"

Temple nodded, then bit her lip. "Unless . . . they'd been quarreling. Gypsy had invited their father to the competition without June's knowledge. She claimed he had sexually abused her as a child, but June denied it."

"Not uncommon. Denial is the backbone of the dysfunctional family."

"But it would be weird, to abuse one twin daughter and not the other. Maybe the father thought it didn't count that way. Anyway, June was against Gypsy's 'statement.' So one or the other of them could have painted her twin solid gold, waited for her to collapse, and painted herself."

Temple watched Matt absorb her somewhat confusing scenario.

"Murder-suicide. It's possible." Matt rubbed his chin, an unnecessary gesture. With his blond coloring, he'd never suffer from five-o'clock shadow. "Did you get the twins' birth dates?"

"Why bother? Molina gave me the first two, but now my theory is impossible. Besides, Molina isn't talking to me unless it's an interrogation."

"When has it been any different between you and Lieutenant Molina? In the meantime, why don't you check on the birth dates you've already got?"

"Is that therapy, counselor?"

"Common sense. Use what you have."

"Right." Temple stood, then checked her wristwatch. "I guess the public library is still open, darn it."

"Why the library?"

"Who else has one of those perpetual calendars that shows what day of the week it was for the last one hundred years? Speaking of which, that's about how old I feel. Have you seen Louie lately, by the way?"

Matt shook his head. "Not hide nor hair."

Everybody was AWOL, Temple thought as she went upstairs. Electra was practically living at the Goliath. Temple had heard a distant vroom-vroom at about three P.M. that indicated the Hesketh Vampire was going through its paces onstage. Louie was almost always gone, as he had been ever since . . .

Temple turned the key and opened her mahogany door. Dead ahead on the slice of kitchen floor visible stood the banana split dish overflowing with brown-green pellets.

She marched over, picked it up and dumped the contents down the garbage disposal. They made a quite satisfactory racket getting ground up, she observed.

She next did what Matt had suggested. The library's reference-desk personnel sounded harried, but easily found the needed calendar. Temple read the woman on the other end of the phone the dates: March 4, 1963, and April 22, 1958.

One was a Monday, and one was a Tuesday. In the right order.

Temple screamed and jumped up before the phone was fully hung up. No doubt the library staff was used to bar bettors and other unstable inquirers.

She sat down again, sobered. Since when did women-hating, brutal serial killers of strippers docilely follow nursery rhymes?

She went to the bedroom to change, still mulling it over. Clothes lay everywhere—on the closet floor, near the bed.

Temple stiffened on the threshold. She had been so obsessed with the Goliath murders that she had almost forgotten her own peril. Had those two men come back and trashed her bedroom? Why hadn't she learned how to lay grown men flat with one well-placed kick? Maybe those thugs weren't just after Max. Maybe they had something to do with the Goliath murders . . . She was already too deep into the condo to retreat from intruders who might be lurking at her back, and the phone was across the room. But why hadn't they attacked her when she was calling the library from the living room? An abiding respect for public institutions?

Ridiculous.

And her clothes. Most of them had slipped off the hangers. She went over to inspect the damage, and picked up a red knit dress. The zipper was undone. What kind of room-tossing hoodlum stops to neatly undo the zippers? She looked around some more.

Oh, no! Her Hanae Mori green silk, crumpled again, on the floor! She whipped it aloft, unable to help admiring the fall of emerald silk folds. Another gaping zipper. Were these guys metal freaks, or what? Something had wafted to the floor when she lifted the dress.

She looked. A powder puff. The fluffy dressing-table kind. Pink. Ugh. She bent and picked it up. A diagonal white satin ribbon on the back bore the brand name in flowing script. Yvette. The puff part glimmered with opalescent flakes. A subtle whiff of Emeraude assaulted her nostrils.

So Temple now knew what had inspired the name of the actress's cat. But how had Savannah Ashleigh's powder puff arrived at the Circle Ritz? On the wings of a dove?

Chapter 29

Born to Be Child

"What are you doing here?" Lieutenant C. R. Molina asked a trifle bitterly Friday morning. "There hasn't been another murder."

Molina's world-class blue eyes—Temple could give credit where credit was due—lay stranded in maroon circles. Her hair was more lusterless than usual, and she was unconsciously twisting the loose class ring on her right hand. At eleven o'clock, both women were already pretty frazzled.

"I don't know," Temple answered, aware of a mirroring bitterness in her own voice. "WHOOPE apparently doesn't need PR advice since the murders have made it world-famous. I guess I'm about as effective as you are, Lieutenant."

"PR is window dressing. Murder is people's lives."

"I know. And I still think—"

"I don't care what you think."

"I know. But you do care what I know."

"What do you know?"

The ballroom was bustling in preparation for afternoon and evening preliminaries. Seminaked men and women fussed with costumes, props, lights, music. Technicians lent state-of-the-art finesse to the process. Media people buzzed around, thrilled by the crude energy, the obvious glitz, the titillating lure of sex and death.

No one police lieutenant, no one PR woman could do a damn thing to stop it.

"I knew," said Temple, "that Kitty Cardozo was abused, and was fighting it. I suspect that she was calling a local hot line with the same message she gave me: she was breaking free, she was going to live her own life."

"Matt Devine?" Molina asked tersely. "She was calling him?

"Like clockwork. Until Tuesday night."

"What happened Tuesday night?"

"I was attacked. Matt skipped work to stay at the Circle Ritz with me. Kitty was killed."

"Devine stayed with you?"

"Yes. Strictly defensive, Lieutenant."

Molina moved her nervous hand from her ring to her forehead, where she brushed back her thick hair. "I checked him out."

"Matt?"

"No college record, no degrees. No driver's license in this state. The hot line director stonewalls on his background. You seem to have found another mystery man."

"With all this going on, you had time to play peekaboo in Matt's life? My life? Again?"

"Maybe you have a pattern: mysterious men and murder. By the way, we haven't found anything out on your attackers."

"Attackers-schmackers, so what! You probably think I hallucinated that, too. Listen. You didn't like my nursery-rhyme pattern. Well, it works! I did my own checking out, with the public library. Both of the first victims were born on the right days."

"And murdered on the wrong ones? Is there a right day for it, Barr?"

"How about today?"

Molina visibly stiffened. Temple was impressed with herself. Height didn't matter here, or position. Only results. She had a feeling she was beginning to think like a hard-nosed homicide lieutenant.

"So." Molina deliberately modulated her voice to noncommittal silk. "Tell me what the library said."

Temple did.

Molina nodded. "It does fit. Perfectly. Do you realize what a . . . twisted mind it would take to follow your plan?"

"No more twisted than a random stalker."

"It doesn't figure. Whoever's killing them is taking a tremendous risk. Some of these killers have massive egos; they enjoy the game of taunting the police. The murderer has got to be someone close to the competition. Now you say it's someone who had access to their birth dates."

Temple shrugged. "Look at a driver's license in an unguarded purse. Call the library and find the right date."

"And bypass victim B, C and D because they were born on the wrong day of the year?"

"Why not, if you've got a cornucopia of victims?"

Molina was silent again, thinking. "There must be . . . three hundred entrants in this competition."

"Three hundred and four," Temple said with PR person precision.

"Almost as many as days in the year."

Temple nodded.

"Your whole approach is crazy."

"Maybe we've got a crazy killer."

"Hmm. What do you want?"

"The birth date of the latest victims. I don't even know their last name."

"Standish."

"As in 'Miles'?"

"So the records say."

"And the date?"

"June first, nineteen sixty-seven."

"That young?"

"That young. You're pretty young yourself."

"Sixty-three. Hey! I guess I am."

"Where are you off to? What are you going to do?"

"Call the library," Temple answered, sprinting away.

The phone that Temple had requested the day before still sat on a chair by the wall. She had to call information to get the Clark County Library number. The librarian consulted a perpetual calendar and was quite certain. June 1, 1967, had been a Thursday.

"Thursday's child has far to go," Temple repeated speculatively. But what about Wednesday's? Why had Wednesday's child ("is full of woe") been left out?

While she was sitting there puzzling it out, the corner of her eye caught a flurry of black leather coming in at seven o'clock low. Temple braced herself for Switch Bitch, but when the figure arrived, she got Motorcycle Moll.

"Electra! You haven't been home."

"Tell me about it. Listen, did you know that Glinda North—Dorothy Horvath—was lesbian?"

"No. Um, what has this to do with anything?"

"Well, she wasn't great bait for a sex-crazed heterosexual serial killer."

"Was that really why she was afraid of losing her kids?"

"You bet." Electra's black-lipsticked mouth took a grim downturn.

"But . . . she was a stripper."

"You've met Switch Bitch?"

"Oh, yeah."

"Don't let the wrong half of that name fool you. She's a work-in-progress. In the name as in the person, and the commercial, it's what's up front that counts."

Temple's preconceptions did a U-turn. "Switch . . .? You mean—?"

"This is strictly confidential," Electra added. "Lifestyle choices aren't anybody's business, and I don't usually tattletale. But this is a multiple murder case."

"Why would a transsexual and a lesbian work as strippers?"

"They're both making a point without having to get down and dirty about it, like a prostitute," Electra said. "The transsexual gets to show off the body work, and the lesbian gets to make money off men without having to get screwed by them. Makes a lot of sense. What doesn't is that I have a funny feeling about the murderer, now that I've inbibed the ambience. Maybe it's Marilyn. She was used long before she got any clout, you know, and she knew it. Poor kid. Poor tossed-around kid."

"Electra, I hardly know ye."

"Trust me. Marilyn says . . . my instincts say that this killer is totally looney."

"You don't need a doctoral degree—"

"Flush the killer out."

"How?"

"Play the game. What if—what if one of the victims came back? Didn't lie down and play dead?"

"That works on TV if the killer thinks he or she missed. But everybody in the competition saw the body bags go out of here."

"You're forgetting that the killer may be following a different logic. Even if I were only half looney, I wouldn't like seeing my victim walking around. I might snap. Do something stupid."

"Or dangerous. And how could you fool the killer? Oh."

"An idea, dear?"

"Kitty Cardozo added a cat mask to her costume just before she was killed. It would be easy to resurrect her with someone the right height and weight." Temple thought a moment longer. "Like me. I'd have to color my hair, though."

"Can I interrupt this beauty discussion?" Molina's

voice came from over Temple's shoulder. When the tall lieutenant wanted to eavesdrop, she could do it literally. She eyed Electra's black leather "Wild Bunch" getup. "Haven't I seen you before?"

"It wasn't in a lineup, honest," Temple said. "This is my landlady, Electra Lark."

Molina nodded slowly. "You were the J.P. who officiated, if you can call it that, at the parody of a memorial service for Chester Royal at the Lover's Knot Wedding Chapel."

"Sure was," Electra admitted breezily.

Temple was amazed that Molina recognized her chameleon landlady, then recalled that Electra had colored her hair black on that occasion, too.

The lieutenant turned to her. "Well?"

"Well what?"

"What did the library say about the Standish women's birthdate?"

"Oh. You don't want to know."

"I'm standing here, aren't I?"

"A Thursday," Temple said.

Molina digested that for a few seconds. "That makes Wednesday's murder a day late and a dollar short."

"Unless Wednesday's child was killed elsewhere—and the Standish twins were killed after midnight, so both of them were Thursday's victims."

"Looks like they were killed around midnight, but I'll need the medical examiner's report to confirm that. And there weren't any similar deaths in town last night. Besides, why would the killer change M.O.s now? Every victim was a contestant."

"Too many police around? Too much attention?"

Molina shook her head. "The birth days must be a crazy coincidence. The killer is saying more by using elements of the victims' costumes as weapons. Perhaps he's expressing a hatred for their manner of work, for women as sex objects in general."

"Say, Lieutenant," Electra put in, "speaking of sex objects. We were just discussing an idea—"

"Electra, no!" Temple warned.

"Don't you think that the killer would go ape if you had one of the victims parading around here in costume like she was alive? That kitty costume Temple was telling me about would work perfectly. In fact, Temple's the right size—"

Molina's face stiffened with rage. "Amateur theatrics belong in TV mystery shows. Nobody'd fall for that old chestnut, anyway. And if you think I'd let a civilian go traipsing around in a murder victim's costume on some long shot that it might unnerve the killer, you're crazier than the murderer."

"I'd never do it," Temple interjected hastily. "Thighs."

Molina turned on her like a junkyard dog. "Thighs?" she barked.

"I don't wear anything that makes my thighs look like flesh-colored Jell-O, and stripper costumes don't leave anything to the imagination. Although I would wear the cat shoes," she added meditatively. "They were really cool."

By now Molina was trying to control laughter rather than anger. "It's too bad vaudeville is dead," she finally said. "You two would make quite an act." She turned to Electra. "You knew Max Kinsella, then?"

"Oh, sure. He was such a doll."

"Odd. Ms. Barr is a lot less enthusiastic about him."

"Now," Electra retorted. "All Max owed me when he left was a month's mortgage, and Temple took that over, poor kid."

"Yeah. I saw that the mortgage is in both their names." She turned back to Temple. "That could make things inconvenient if you want to move in the seven years before he's legally declared dead."

"Seven years—I never thought of that." Temple caught her breath. It was one thing to adjust to Max's being gone for good; another to write him off as dead and figure out the legalities.

"Think about it," Molina advised before walking away.

Electra chuckled as Molina left, shaking her head. "It's a cackle to rattle her cage. I still think you'd make a great Kitty Two."

"I don't want the job, Electra. I've gotten into enough trouble lately. Darn. That Monday's-child scheme is so close to perfect. It's like having a quatrain where one line won't rhyme no matter what you do."

"Maybe that's too clever, dear. I can see it's distracting you. What about all the dirt you were digging up on Kitty City?"

Temple sat back down on the chair, staring at the phone. "What do you think of Ike Wetzel, Electra?"

"He better stay out of the bathtub if I'm anywhere nearby with a small electrical appliance plugged in."

"Mad about the guy, huh?"

"God's gift to the masochists among us. Maybe each of the dead strippers crossed him. I can see him taking pleasure in enforcing his will on the unwilling. Poor Lindy puts up with a lot."

"Ike and Lindy?"

Electra nodded. "Didn't you know? Oh, he's made the rounds. Savannah Ashleigh, Kitty Cardozo. He always picked winners, though, at least in the early days; women who were going to climb out of the holes they were in."

"That *is* odd, Electra. From what you said he ran a closed shop. His girls did what he said, or they didn't dance at Kitty City. He was even down on the competition when hometown dancers didn't have to put in travel days to get here. Then, this year, he changes his tyrannical tune and is all love and kisses with WHOOPE. Why?"

"You laid it out: a perfect cover for murder. He's not openly mad at anybody for being here. All his old loves and former victims are gathering in one place, like sitting ducks. He's a competition cosponsor. He has total access to the facilities and nobody thinks a thing about it."

"So," said Temple. "I don't have a jot of PR to do. As the great C.B. noted early on, even a baby could get publicity for an event with as much sex appeal at this one. Now, with murder on the menu, it's a media feeding frenzy, and my clients are enjoying the buffet. They're being interviewed left and right, and everyone knows about the competition Saturday night. Saturday. That day's child 'has to work for a living.' So do I." She slapped her knees and stood. "Since I've got nothing else to do, I might as well solve the murders. And Molina was downright derisive about your idea, Electra. Let's make her eat it."

"Right on!" Electra's hands slapped Temple's palms. "Partner. Where do we start? Want me to whip up—pardon me, Switch Bitch!—a kittycat lookalike costume for you?"

"No masquerades that Molina can sneer at, no quivering thighs, just hard cold facts that'll freeze her assets. Bring me someone who knows the real poop on the Standish twins."

"The last victims? But they don't fit."

"That's why they're the key. I'm going to find out why if it's the last thing I do."

Electra nodded, the anodized aluminum moon and stars in her left ear colliding with the sterling silver comet. The heavens were in collusion.

Chapter 30

A Stitch in Time . . .

"Another opening, another show."

Temple was as capable as anyone of responding to the backstage hullabaloo that attended the dress rehearsal of everything from the rawest amateur theatrical to the biggest Broadway hit. Competition preliminaries were much the same.

Yet it was hard for her not to brood. By now Molina had made a stunning about-face and taken Electra's flaky idea of reviving Kitty Cardozo. Temple hadn't minded for a moment that a petite and pretty Asian undercover officer used to playing hookers would don the dead stripper's identity. Professionals each had their roles, and risk-taking was Officer Lee Choi's prerogative. Besides, she had the requisite raven hair.

Temple's depression didn't kick in until three P.M. Friday, when she glimpsed Officer Choi strutting about the wings, a perfect body double for the dead woman. Those high-heeled cat shoes were awesome.

More than that, she hated being reminded of the living Kitty Cardozo she had met briefly, whose hopes and hurts she had glimpsed, as Matt Devine had heard of them over the phone. It seemed cruel to animate the carapace of the woman, her performing persona, one that she had planned to set aside for good soon.

Almost as bad was watching Electra as Moll Philanders participate in the backstage bustle, hovering over the Vampire in its below-stage position near one of the stage elevators, mingling with undercover officers and strippers as if born to be wild indeed.

Temple, meanwhile, had been consigned to cold storage.

"I understand that you consider it part of your job to be on the scene for the preliminaries," Lieutenant Molina had told her. Temple was beginning to hate hearing that Lieutenant Molina understood. "But I don't want you mistaken for Kitty Cardozo. Despite the hair, you're the same build. Don't confuse matters. Stick to the dressing room downstairs where it's safe."

"I used to think parking ramps were safe," Temple objected.

"They weren't," Molina snapped.

The lietenant herself was done up as a stage technician in blue jeans and oversized T-shirt, her dark hair drawn back into a sweat band. The new look didn't fool Temple for a moment; Molina would broadcast authority in a Bozo the Clown costume. How myopic was a murderer supposed to be?

"Downstairs!" Molina ordered as if Temple were somebody's misbehaving canine, when the performers and tech people were in place and all the real fun was about to start upstairs.

Chaos reigned in the dressing rooms. Savannah Ashleigh was having hysterics over some missing rhinestone earrings. Since Yvette's disappearance she had become even more the quintessential spoiled movie star. In the common dressing rooms, strippers thronged back and forth, modesty a foreign concept, as they fussed with last-minute touches.

A dozen panicked voices cried for safety pins as costumes revealed their eleventh-hour genius for falling apart. Hair that had performed docilely for weeks would not curl, pin up or stay put. Hair spray clouded the air.

Zelda, the competition's buxom wardrobe lady, ran to and fro, a jingling wire ring of safety pins fixed like a badge of courage upon her motherly breast. She ran to first one victim then another, saving the day with safety pins and calm, fixing fingers. Part dorm mother, part madam, she tarted up her girls for the preliminaries like a society mama primping daughters for a debut.

Wilma, the costume lady, was there, too, wearing a bright pink smock-top over her black slacks as if she were pregnant, and whisking out new T-back G-strings for suddenly insecure strippers who felt their acts needed a little more flash.

Temple winced to see a run developing on Wilma's supply of black lipstick. The macabre color had been ultra-effective with Kitty's cat mask. Now everyone had seen it on Electra, who found it the perfect partner for heavy metal and leather. Switch Bitch was commandeering the last tube as six others pressed around, pleading to try it.

Temple rolled her eyes as she caught Wilma's harried glance. Madness, all madness.

The first onslaught of performers suddenly deserted the dressing room like a flock of frightened birds. Who's on first? Forget it, Bud and Lou, not you guys. The other strippers soon followed, unable to resist rating their peers from the wings, even if watching made them nervous about their own acts.

Zelda moved to Savannah's dressing room. The actress wasn't needed today, but wanted to perfect the timing on the six costume changes, each representing a queen of burlesque, that she would accomplish during the final competition. If there was any method to her acting, it was in being the consummate choreographer of her own image.

Temple sat in an abandoned chair in the community dressing room, her feet in their spirited electric-blue spikes braced on the concrete floor. A Milky Way of spilled iridescent powder glimmered on the long makeup counter before her. In the sandwich of reflecting mirrors, she glimpsed her own blue back, a clutter of makeup littering both countertops, and Wilma sitting in her customary seat nearest the door, her ring of teeny-weeny spandex G-strings lying unmauled for the moment.

The dressing room speakers broadcast backstage chatter from the wings and the muffled blare of the sound system spinning its discs. Someone was shouting for quiet.

Temple rose and went over to Wilma. "We're kind of useless now."

The older woman nodded, serene.

Temple let her fingers riffle through the gaudy-patterned G-strings, elastic-puckered flights of fantasy. "Do you ever sell this stuff to civilians who want to perk up their lingerie wardrobes?"

"Heavens, no. The department stores have enough bustiers and bikini bottoms to satisfy ordinary people nowadays. Those models aren't strong enough for the stage, though. That's why my girls buy from me."

"How did you get into doing this?"

Wilma's broad face frowned. A more down-home, ordinary woman you could not find. Her work-thickened fingers roved among the sleazy, shiny fabrics meant to showcase sleek thighs and taut tummies.

"I sewed for my daughters when they were in gymnastics," Wilma said in a dreamy, reminiscent monotone. "Bright, sturdy costumes. I got used to working with stretchy material, which is tricky. These girls need the same."

"Your girls must be grown now."

Wilma nodded. "Grown. Gone. I still sew."

"And you still have girls who need you."

Wilma nodded again.

Above them, the remote drone of backstage chaos continued. Upstairs, Officer Choi was strutting her stuff as Kitty Cardozo for an audience that included a possible killer. Suddenly, Temple didn't resent being removed from the scene of the police trap. She wasn't a cop or a private dick. She was an onlooker, like Wilma, a temporary face on the fringe of this exotic life-style, though Wilma had made a habit of attaching herself to this milieu. These girls would never outgrow her. Their faces and names might change, but their needs never would.

"Why do they do it?" Temple asked, pulling a chair over. Its four feet screeched across the concrete, as if protesting the dislocation. She sat and squelched the sound.

"Do you have children?" Wilma asked out of the blue.

Temple shouldn't have been taken aback by such a question, but she was. She hadn't heard it in a while. Max would have been great with children. On the other hand, in other ways, Max would have been terrible with children, because he was one himself yet, in a still, small, irresponsible corner of his soul.

"No," she said. Such questions never required a complicated answer.

"Then you've never seen the amazing innocence of a young child close up. Never seen how . . . trusting kids are. How smiling, utterly loving, and attractive. My girls—all curls and tiny white teeth and laughing eyes. Gigglers. In love with the world. Maybe I was young and pretty like that, but I've long forgotten it. You see it in a child and you wonder what we've all forgotten. You envy them."

Temple watched the woman's work-worn face soften with memories. Years and wrinkles fell away. The straight strands of her unstyled gray hair seemed to curve and grow brown again. Was part of having children, Temple wondered, ending up lonely and nostalgic for them?

"I don't know about that," Temple admitted. Her most recent maternal instinct had been fretting over Midnight Louie's feeding regimen and intermittent absences. "But I've seen photographs, school photos, in the paper of some poor kid who's been abused to death, and I'm always amazed that a child living that kind of nightmare can still give the camera a dazzling, hopeful, trusting smile."

"The world spits on that trust." Wilma's white-knuckled fist shook her G-string ring. Her hands were large, the knuckles coarse and swollen, Temple noticed. Sewing must hurt the arthritic joints. A rumpled clutter of G-strings fell back to the countertop. "All that lovely innocence, mangled by its makers. Poor girls. Poor girls. Don't understand. Didn't see themselves. And them, the corrupters, they blame the seductive power of innocence. Innocents, that's what all these girls are"—Wilma looked bitterly around the dressing room, judging every tawdry detail in the makeup lights' glare—"though they don't believe it, though they'd laugh and say they know better now. Corrupted innocents."

"Big words," Temple said. Old-fashioned, hellfire preacher words. "Are your daughters . . . in the business?"

Wilma nodded, her neutral-colored eyes distant. "Somewhere."

"You've lost touch?"

"Lost them, yes."

"I'm sorry. Was it a bad marriage?"

"Worse than I knew. I thought he only hit me, that that's all he did. I thought I could take it, that I had to take it. I was so scared, so sure I had to be doing something wrong to make him mad. I stayed as long as I could. Too long."

"What happened to your daughters?"

Her bleak eyes deadened further. "I found out he'd

been messing with them, all the time. They were terrified of him, too."

"How old were they?"

"When I finally found out? Six."

Temple's indrawn breath whistled between her teeth at the awfulness of it. "Then you took the kids and left?"

Wilma's head shook almost imperceptibly. "Then I had a breakdown. Nobody talked about such things then. Incest only happened in the Bible. I was committed to an institution."

"And the kids?"

"Stayed with him. He was the father, and the mother was—incompetent, they said." Wilma's lips distorted into a crooked smile that reminded Temple of a controlled, silent scream. "I was pretty confused and upset. No one believed me. And the kids were too scared to tell. He'd seen to that."

She looked at Temple, her eyes clearing. Her tone became more vibrant, almost as if she were snapping out of a trance. "Oh, say, hon, did you get banged up too?" A strong, twisted hand reached toward Temple's cheek.

Temple found herself dodging the gesture, even as she was shocked by how rude that was. "I'm fine. Just a . . . dumb accident."

Wilma's sympathetic expression grew weary. "Yeah. Sure. But look, I got some terrific cover-up in my bag. You'd be surprised how many of these dancers come in banged up from here to Sunday—legs, arms, faces. Try it."

Temple took the small tube of makeup, which claimed that the contents would cover burns and birthmarks. She'd never used this heavy-duty stuff before, so she gingerly dabbed some at the edges of her eyes. In the mirror, the lurid coloration that had seeped through her usual cover-up vanished.

"You're such a pretty girl," Wilma said in the same, sad monotone. "You don't need to take that. You don't need to work here."

"I'm not a battered woman," Temple said swiftly. "I was mugged. And I can't let a setback like this keep me from working. Here, can I buy this tube—?" She reached for the tote bag on the floor.

Wilma's hand, hard and warm, caught her wrist and held it, before she could extract her clutch purse.

"You don't have to pay. I never charge anybody for that stuff."

"Thanks."

"A girl like you, brought up right, you shouldn't be here."

"I won't be, much longer." Temple tugged her hand free, straightened in the chair, took in the eerie emptiness of the dressing room with the sound of onstage life coming in faint and fuzzy over the loudspeaker.

"How old are you?" Wilma asked suddenly.

"Thirty," Temple answered. An icy spasm clutched her stomach.

"Thirty. A good age. Old enough to know better. Young enough to not feel yourself falling apart yet. When's your birthday?"

"I'm a Gemini," Temple said, stalling for time. Her mind was dancing like water on a hot griddle, sizzling with warning. Birthday talk seemed so sinister. . . . No one had been a bit interested in birthdays lately, except her and the murderer. No—! Birthdays expressed Wilma's motherly instincts. Temple wouldn't even think this way if she hadn't been so overstressed and overworked, seeing death in unlikely places, in innocent faces.

Wilma was nodding, taking out needle and thread to repair one of the G-strings, as she considered Gemini. "May-to-June. A nice time of year to be born. Not a bad time to get married, either, or to have children, or to die. You're a June baby, though, right? Right in the heart of Gemini?"

"June," Temple answered reluctantly.

"What date?"

"Why?"

Wilma's sparse eyebrows lifted in surprise. "I do a little cake for my girls' birthdays. It's no problem; they dance it off. You youngsters could eat an elephant and still look like toothpicks, with all the prancing you do. And all to that awful, loud, repeating music."

"You bring cakes for each one's birthday?"

Wilma nodded. "Homemade. My last was a Lady Baltimore. Nobody makes Lady Baltimore cakes anymore. But nothing's too good for my girls."

"I noticed some half-eaten cake in this dressing room earlier in the week."

Wilma gave another complacent, grandmother-sewing kind of nod. "That was my Lady Baltimore, what was left of it. They gobble it up like little pigs."

"Then you . . . know their birthdays?"

"Course I do. Couldn't make the cakes otherwise. When is yours, dear? I'll make you a Red Devil's Food; haven't made one of those for ages. When's your birthday?"

"June," Temple temporized, "and not for almost a year. Wilma, what do you think about the killings?"

"Terrible," the woman said. "Terrible things. What was done to my girls was terrible."

Temple had a feeling that Wilma was not talking about the murders, but about the wrongs that preceded them. "Then you knew Glinda and Kitty, and the twins?"

"I know all my girls," she said.

"Did you know that Glinda and Kitty had abusive men in their lives, and that one of the twins was molested by her father?"

"Only one?" Wilma's face slackened with shock. "Only one twin? No, it must be that only one admitted it; the other denied it. Denial is very common in such cases."

Wilma sounded like a parrot mouthing the party line dispensed in some shrink's office, but then, she ought to know that routine, Temple thought.

"That's true," Temple agreed. "How sad that those

women won't be here to perform tomorrow. And they all celebrated birthdays so recently."

I remember doing cakes for them, but were their birthdays that recent?"

Temple ticked off the dates on her fingers. "Dorothy/ Glinda was March; Kitty was April; and the twins were June—Gemini like me. Isn't that odd?"

Wilma shrugged and tied off a knot. She picked up a polished chrome sewing shears to cut the thread. "Everybody has to be born sometime."

"But isn't it odd that the victims' birthdays are almost in sequence through the calendar: March, April, June. Except that May is missing."

Wilma paused to think. "No, it's not."

"It's not? You mean that there's another victim nobody knows about?"

Wilma pursed her lips. "You had to know the girls. You had to be around to listen. Gypsy and June. Everybody knew they were stage names. Everybody figured they referred to Gypsy Rose Lee and her sister June Havoc."

"They didn't?"

"Yes, they did, except that June was June's real given name to begin with. You see?"

Passing laughter reverberated in the hall for a moment as a last gaggle of strippers rushed upstairs. Wilma rose and drew the dressing-room door shut on the sound.

Temple's mouth opened and her hands clenched. "I don't see anything," she admitted.

"Maybe I shouldn't tell you this." Wilma resumed her chair but set her sewing things aside. "They hated it themselves, and tried to forget it. Sometimes twins are funny about things. June and her sister were born a few minutes apart."

Temple nodded. "On June 1, 1967."

"No." Wilma was definite. "I heard it from their own lips. June was born on June 1, 1967. At twelve-thirteen A.M."

"And—omigod. Gypsy was born the night of May 31st, and christened . . . May!"

Wilma smiled fondly. "They hated all the school jokes about 'May' and 'June.' I think they even hated being separated by as much as midnight. Those girls were so close. It would have been cruel to kill one and leave the other."

An ugly thought trespassed in Temple's mind. "Just as it was the height of cruelty to abuse one, and not the other! Gypsy was right. Her father had victimized only her to intensify his manipulation of the girls. And she's the one who changed her name, May, because she had come to loathe the man who called her by her birth-name only to violate her."

Wilma's face wore a prudish expression. "I wouldn't know about that, except that Gypsy was set on inviting their father to the competition. I wonder if he knows they're . . . gone? I wonder if he'll find out when he comes?"

"More to the point, would he even care?"

"No. If he cared about anything other than his sick needs, he wouldn't have done what he did, hurt his girls beyond fixing. You can break human beings, but you can't mend them. You can't baste them together again. Nobody takes care of the broken ones. I gave the twins their cake June 1st. May yearned to *be* June. Maybe she wanted to share her sister's innocent memories. Now they won't have to remember anything ugly."

"So May 31, 1967, had to have been a Wednesday," Temple mused, drawing her forefinger through the glittery line of opalescent powder that Wilma sold and that Dorothy, Kitty, June and Gypsy had used. All gone now, dust from a dead butterfly's wing. Beautiful, fragile fairy dust, like Tinker Bell's. Temple had seen that sheen somewhere else . . . on a powder puff. Savannah Ashleigh had used the same stuff on Yvette. And had bought it from the same source. And Midnight Louie—

"Gracious!"

Wilma's exclamation made Temple jump. The woman was squeezing her fingertip until it reddened. She had pierced her finger with a needle.

"Have you got a kerchief?" Wilma asked.

"I'll look." Temple, confused, her heart pounding, trying to think when all that came into her mind was the unthinkable, lifted the tote to the countertop and slapped its contents to the Formica piece by piece until she delved deep enough to find out.

Her clutch purse with its cargo of cash, credit cards and driver's license was the first item out, then her bulging day arranger and address book, then her cosmetic bag, then . . .

Wilma had picked up the clutch purse and unsnapped the flap. Temple was about to protest this incursion on her most valuables. Then she remembered the little plastic window inside that displayed her driver's license.

Wilma was smiling and nodding at that very item.

The license, Temple recalled, listed her address, her number, and her DOB, as police shorthand put it. Date of Birth.

Stricken, she stopped rummaging through her belongings to stare at Wilma. Opalescent dust, even on a powder puff meant for a pampered pussums. Oh, Louie, that wasn't a fuzzy "mouse" you dragged home for the heck of it, but a vital clue! The murderer had left a trail in powder. Temple's renegade forefinger drew an exclamation point in the glittery dust that had decorated four dead bodies and one cat.

She knew who the murderer was. Unfortunately, the murderer knew exactly who she was now, and that she knew.

Wilma set Temple's clutch purse aside to snap open the huge silver ring to release a spandex G-string. She was a beefy woman with strong hands and a mission. Temple realized that she had just made her hit list.

Chapter 31

. . . Saves Nine

"I really need to check what's going on upstairs." Temple got up to step past Wilma.

The woman rose like a double-knit wall and blocked her path. Temple glanced down at Wilma's black slacks. Her thighs strained the fabric. Big rough hands closed on Temple's fragile wrist bones.

"You forgot your purse," Wilma said.

"It's fine down here. You watch it."

Temple tried to move but found herself frozen by an unmoved, an unmoving, an unmovable counterforce. She looked into Wilma's expressionless face, meaning to argue, and saw inarguable purpose.

"No one will hit you again." The woman's promise was as vehement as a threat. "No man will abuse you. You won't have to sell yourself on the stage because of what they did to you."

"I'm not a stripper! I'm a public relations specialist. I haven't been abused, only mugged. Wilma, please—"

"No one will come down here now. Too much of a show going on upstairs. Even the guards and the hotel security men stop to rubberneck. Nothing distracts men's attention like little girls made to perform for it. No one saw me. Not once. No one hardly ever notices me anyway. Too old, too ugly, too useful. My girls won't have to suffer anymore. All my girls. I'm sorry I didn't give you a birthday cake, but I can't let you go on. You might say something, and I can't stop until I find my own girls. I'm fast, and strong. It won't hurt. Try not to think about it, and it'll all be over."

Temple quivered as she felt the bones in her wrist constrict within a relentless grip. The only thing that could still move was her mouth.

"Wilma, that's just what abusers tell their victims: it won't hurt; it'll be fast; try not to think about it. You don't want to be like them, Wilma!"

"It won't be like them. You'll sleep. You'll be at peace. You won't ever hurt again."

"But life hurts! You can't stop pain by taking lives. Kitty Cardozo wanted to live; she had plans. Glinda was hoping to get her kids back. The twins were working out their problem their way, and you denied them that. You denied them their triumphs as well as their tragedies."

Wilma's strong hands forced Temple back into the chair by pulling her wrists down.

"Listen," Temple said. "You'll ruin your pattern. It's Friday. Friday's child is—" She blanked on the next words; she blankety-blank blanked, just when she needed them most!

"Friday's child is loving and giving," Wilma recited in a dulcet sing-song for her. "And you're a Friday."

"How can you know? Be sure?"

"I always had a head for figures. Not much school learning, and maybe not much sense, but numbers stick. I know the perpetual calendar like a nun knows her rosary beads. It's all up here."

Wilma released Temple's left wrist to tap her forehead and then reached for the G-string she had freed.

No way, Temple thought. Her free hand flashed out, found the big shiny shears on the countertop and picked them up. She shuddered to imagine what would happen if Wilma got them away from her, so she slashed and thrust at the woman's loose top like a mad Japanese chef, trying not to think of what she was attempting to do to flesh and bone.

Contact. Resistance. The shears bouncing off something hard only to dig into something soft. Temple moaned. Her restrained wrist felt as if it were caught in a meat grinder. Wilma's grip was forcing her out of the chair and to her knees on the floor, as the woman's other hand drew back to slap the scissors from her grasp.

Temple steeled herself and drove the blades toward the oncoming palm.

Then, plummeting from above, came a black tarantula, all dangling legs and falling furry bulk, plunging directly atop Wilma's head.

Wilma screamed. Temple screamed. The tarantula screamed.

With a crack like a firing rifle, the closed dressing room door sprang open under the bulk of a man's body. Two men's bodies entered, followed by a familiar woman's body.

Temple was sitting on the floor, holding her wrist.

The men had jumped Wilma, bearing her down beside Temple and pinioning her wrists. The shears lay—open and innocent of anyone's blood—a short distance away.

Wilma's face was bathed in bloody rivulets, though; scarlet threads ran into her eyes and gasping mouth, soaked into her pink top.

Lieutenant Molina was standing in the doorway, a semiautomatic in her hand, looking very worried and a bit guilty.

The tarantula uncurled from its sinister ball-shape and strutted over to Temple, albeit a bit stiffly. One of its five furry legs hoisted aloft to brush Temple's face as Midnight Louie rubbed back and forth along her shoulder, back and forth.

"Is she all right?" Molina asked her men. She was eyeing Temple, so they did, too.

"Looks okay," one said, before grunting and bearing down on Wilma, who was fighting his partner's handcuffs.

Midnight Louie began purring loudly enough to attract everyone's attention.

"Give that cat a badge," one of the men suggested out of the corner of his mouth.

Temple stared at the cat, then threw her arms around him. "Oh, Louie, I can't believe I almost had you declawed!"

"Poor baby," Electra crooned. "I brought you a Black Russian."

She set the drink, which looked like motor oil on ice, on the counter and glared at Lieutenant Molina, as if daring her to object.

Temple sat in the same fatal chair that had originally been Wilma's, her wrist wrapped in the G-string meant to throttle her. Thin strips of leopard-pattern spandex made an excellent support bandage, and Molina, born camp counselor that she was, had done the honors.

Louie, basking in the warm glare of the makeup lights, sprawled atop the counter, looking regal. The only trace of his recent heroic measures was the dried blood faintly visible on his claws, which were flexing in and out in perfect time to a soft baritone purr of satisfaction.

"I can't believe"—the Lieutenant looked at Temple again—"that with all your fiddling with birth dates and birthday rhymes you never checked out your own."

"I was too busy to fool around with that stuff."

"I can't believe," Electra put in, glaring at Lieutenant Molina, "that you would set up Temple as a sitting duck down here."

"I can't believe"—Temple finally got her two cents in—

"that Officer Choi was just a cat in wolf's clothing, an honest-to-badness double decoy."

"I can't believe," Molina said in her turn, "that your cat is really going to drink that Black Russian."

"Oops!" Electra pulled the glass away, but not before Louie's whiskers had received a chocolate-colored coating.

"He deserves it," Temple said stoutly, but she sipped the drink Electra put into her right hand. "You really had this place bugged?"

Molina shook her head. "Wasn't necessary to bug it; the two-way system was already in. We just patched it into Savannah Ashleigh's dressing room. And waited."

"And waited until I was at death's door," Temple said. "A good thing that Midnight Louie had decided to camp out here."

"Cut the theatrics. We would have been in time," Molina said. "We did need conclusive evidence."

"Conclusive to *me!*" Temple objected. "I don't get it. How did you know what to expect?"

"For one thing, you can be sure that I never would have seriously gone for the corny Catwoman decoy trick you two came up with. As it is, it'll take years to live that one down in the department." Molina sat on the countertop and crossed her arms. "You're a born magnet for murderers, Barr. I figured that if I let you go about your unauthorized business, someone would get annoyed enough to try to off you."

"Temple came too close," Electra put in. She looked fierce in her fringed leather chaps and motorcycle jacket. "That's her secret for attracting murderers: outsmarting them."

"She almost outsmarted herself this time," Molina retorted. "Okay. Same deal as last time. I'll need a statement tomorrow morning. Think you can drive with that wrist? Or should I send a squad car to collect you?"

"I'll be fine," Temple said. "Do you want me to bring Louie?"

Molina stood. "That, thank God, won't be necessary. Stay out of trouble until tomorrow. Please. We need your statement."

Temple sighed raggedly when she left. "Gee, Electra, this drink is hitting me like a freight train. Am I still here?"

"You sure are, honey!" Electra hugged Temple's shoulders, then backed off when she winced. "The wrist?"

"The everything. I've had it. Can you get me home?"

"Only on the Vampire."

Temple stood up. Her legs still worked. "What the hell, Electra. Let's go."

"What about Louie?"

Temple turned and looked at the cat, who winked one semihooded green eye. "Let him find his own way home. Apparently he's better at a lot more things than we know."

Chapter 32

Louie Bows Out

I am, of course, not invited to the finale of the stripping competition. At nine, I am considered underage for attending such adult shenanigans.

In truth, I do not have the heart for it. The Divine Yvette has returned to her gilded cage. All right, it is pink canvas, but nonetheless a cage.

As for my prescient presence on the attempted-murder scene, I admit that it is all a sham. I haunt the premises only because of my obsession with the Divine Yvette, who finds freedom a heavy burden to bear.

Of course, my eleventh-hour dive atop the murderer's head makes me a hero in those blue-green eyes. Some may think that the imminent peril faced by my dear consort in accommodations at the Circle Ritz, Miss Temple Barr, has spurred my bold attack. Such persons are unaware that the hidden presence of the Divine Yvette is more to the point.

PUSSYFOOT

When the lady in question peeks out of her sanctuary behind the costume rack some time later, I am still reclining on the countertop, having made the most of the abandoned Black Russian in the dereliction of all human personnel. Even Miss Temple Barr has granted me the right to come in as late as I like.

Yvette lofts atop an empty chair and regards me with dewy eyes.

Even now every sentiment she expresses rings in my ears as if it were an endless yesterday. "What a hero," she informs me with a heartfelt sigh.

I offer her the dregs of the Black Russian, but she wrinkles her perfect pink little nose. "No, Louie. I do not need any more stimulants—"

"Alcohol is a depressant," I growl with my usual prescience. I can see who is going to get depressed here already.

"I must return to my mistress." The Divine Yvette pushes a heavy silver whisker back from her gleaming black lips. Her eyes grow round and sorrowful. "I must admit that these have been the most . . . piquant days of my life, but I am not happy on your level, Louie, trodding the common pavement until my soft pink pads grow coarse, pushed hither and yon by whomever would brush against me. I am used to a life of international travel, to seeing sights uncluttered by grime and graft. I am used to the haven of my carrier, and the attentions of my mistress."

I have not the heart to argue. I could protect her from all she finds too crude, but she will not believe me.

"It is for the best, Louie," she tells me, her sad eyes growing greener by the minute. "My mistress is in a career slump. With my returned presence, she may manage a comeback. I am all she has. Return me."

It is not as if Miss Savannah Ashleigh is about to discover a cure for cancer, much less feline leukemia. I shake my head sadly. Some might misinterpret the gesture as an attempt to dislodge a flea. The only flea in my ear is the plea of the Divine Yvette.

"Louie, Louie," she purrs poignantly. I recall a popular party song of that title, but am in no mood for partying. "Even though I must go, you must remember this: we will always have the Goliath."

I growl an answer. At such times, I am not articulate. Then I remember our stolen hours on the premises, the three A.M. glide on The Love Moat, the scent and sight of her opalescent powder in the almost-dark of the cave, when we exchanged more than whispers. She was always afraid of water, of motion under her own power, of independence.

"Please," she rumbles throatily, and what is an honorable dude to do?

I leap down to the floor in one bound, and assist her off the chair.

A light still beams in Miss Savannah Ashleigh's dressing room. The Divine Yvette minces, one fine, furred foot set in front of the other, toward the ajar door. Even I can hear the muted sobs within.

Yvette noses open the door, turns to give me one last, lingering look that would melt a snow leopard, then shoulders her way through.

I hear a gasp. A cry. "Oh, Yvette! You're back. Momsy is so glad her baby-waby is backy-wacky!"

I stifle a gag. It would be impolite to deposit a hairball outside the Divine Yvette's door.

At the sound of a zipper being opened, I turn and walk away.

Miss Temple Barr is waiting up at the Circle Ritz. No doubt the caffeine in the Black Russian has given her the heebie-jeebies. I loft through the bathroom window, and she pounces on me with a full food dish.

"Louie!" she cries. "See! No more Free-to-be-Feline. This is Salmon Surprise, from Kat-sup. And no declawing, so help me."

She mentions nothing of the other abhorred procedure, and far be it from me to remind her. At the moment she is hanging over me like a pendulum and massaging my neck, while cooing my name. The Divine Yvette she isn't, but I have been in worse spots in my nine lives.

Chapter 33

Electra City

Matt Devine stepped around to the passenger door of the
Storm and opened it.

Temple couldn't just say no when Matt had offered to
drive tonight. How could she explain knowing that he had
no license? He must have had one once upon a time; he
knew how to drive.

"Are you sure you want to return to the scene of the
crime?" he asked.

Beams of light lanced the Saturday night Las Vegas sky,
announcing the strippers' competition to the very heavens. The colossus's diaper was the focus of a thousand
kilowatts of laser light every seventy-five seconds. A neon
sign boasted BABES . . . BODIES . . . BOYS.

"And miss Electra's debut?" Temple answered. "Your
landlady's not a stripping finalist every day. I hope you
don't regret skipping your stint at ConTact tonight."

He shook his blond head, which looked as gilded as Gypsy or June in the artificial light. "No regular client is calling now. Even though I said that knowing is worse than not knowing, I'm grateful that you managed to solve who she was. I won't have to wonder about what happened to her forever."

"Forever," Temple said, standing, "is a long time."

Matt nodded. "So is a day. Or a night. Why is Electra going through with it?"

"She's getting a charge out of it, what can I say? We can at least try not to laugh."

"I'm not in a laughing mood."

"Me, neither."

They entered the hotel, Temple bracing herself for passing the Sultan's Palace and The Love Moat. But Matt started asking her about the details of the case and she forgot to brood over these emotional landmarks.

"Molina says the case is cut and dried," Temple told him. "Wilma—Carter's her last name—has a history of mental illness, and there's no doubt her daughters were molested by her husband. They've all vanished, and she's left holding the bag of guilt. She'll be put away, but not in prison. It's harder to get out of a mental hospital than a jail, these days. Would you think I was crazy if I visited her?"

"I'd think you were a twenty-four-carat human being. I envy you," he said, as the velvet ropes parted for Temple's VIP pass. It was the least Ike Wetzel could do, and Ike Wetzel always did the least.

"Why?"

They were soon seated in a wine-velvet-upholstered banquet. An obsequious waiter dashed up with glasses of champagne on the house.

"Why?" she repeated after they had settled in.

" 'Friday's child is loving and giving,' " he quoted, toasting her with a tall, thin flute that sparkled like a yellow diamond.

"When were you born?" she asked, curious to the last.

"I'll tell you someday. Shhh. The show's about to start."

"Are you sure you really want to see something this risqué . . . ?"

"Shhh," he said. "Kitty did it. I want to know why."

The show began. There was the flare of prerecorded music, the parade of performers. The glitz, the glory, the get-down-and-dirty nitty-gritty of bump and grind. The grinning boys showing off muscles visible and invisible. The glorious girls with bodies a Barbie doll would die for. The Over-Sexty set, never saying die.

A vroom, vroom growled from the wings.

Temple clutched Matt's arm. "Holy hot rod, here comes Electra!"

"Moll Philanders," the man at the mike intoned.

Dry-ice fog drifted across the stage. Temple expected Dracula, and instead got a sleek silvery form that spit luminous flames—how the Hesketh had Electra managed that? The cycle was ridden by a dark, ambiguous helmeted figure. "Born to Be Wild" revved up on the sound system.

As the Vampire stopped with a batlike screech stage center, the leather-clad rider dismounted, kicked the stand into action, and began to peel leather from skin, and pose beside, atop and under the motorcycle. Temple especially appreciated her trick of lying back along the leather seat, her legs flailing in time to the raw beat.

For an old broad, Electra was pulling out all the stops. Except. After the chaps peeled away, and even as the jacket was tossed, she whirled it around her head. It became a fringed cape that swirled through the smoke and covered her like a Turkish towel. The audience saw a lot of discreetly bare shoulder and knee, but not much more.

A lot of flash, and very little flesh. Theater to the Max. Temple stood applauding at the end, tears of pride in her eyes. She understood Ma Bartles. Go, Electra! Give the lie to getting old and giving up. Matt was on his feet beside her, clapping sans tears.

It didn't seem right without Midnight Louie.

Chapter 34

Little Cat Feet

The muumuu came flying at Temple in the colors of hibiscus and orchid.

She regarded it dubiously. Ever since the strippers' competition, she was not about to buy Electra as a Grandma candidate.

"A policewoman left this off," Electra announced while still twenty feet down the hall.

Temple waited within the solid frame of her mahogany double doors, alerted by Electra's excited phone call, but leery.

"Is it something about the stripper case, dear?" Electra asked once she was at the condo door, huffing and puffing.

Temple regarded the thin roll of paper and shook her head. Just Molina returning the poster of Max she had borrowed, as promised.

"And the manila envelope" Electra prodded. "Honest Adonis, it looks like there are body parts in there!"

"Even Molina isn't that nasty," Temple answered.

But she opened the envelope with real curiosity. Then her mouth dropped. A black satin feline face emerged, pinned onto the shiny satin toe of a high-heeled pump. Two of them. A perfect pair.

"These are Kitty Cardozo's shoes!" Temple gave a macabre shiver. She pulled a piece of police memo paper out of the package.

"Kitty had a spare pair at her apartment," the no-nonsense handwriting read. "Lindy said you could have them. Looked like just your size. —Molina."

Temple turned them sideways to read the gibberish of letters and numbers on the lining. Molina was, as too often lately, right on. Size five-and-a-half, double A.

Temple swallowed. "I wish Kitty could have these."

"Maybe," Electra suggested, "she'd be happy to know you inherited them, dear."

"Maybe. I wish that we'd found out who was hassling her. None of the other strippers knew. He's still out there."

It was almost noon on the Monday after the competition. Molina hadn't wasted any time. Maybe Temple shouldn't either. She remembered Matt's reaction to the notion of her calling him.

Why not? Women were supposed to take risks these days.

After Electra had left, she sat in the blinds-drawn dimness of her bedroom, Midnight Louie lying like the world's largest lump of Christmas coal across her bedspread. Matt would be about ready to get a wake-up call.

Temple picked up the red-shoe phone, its sleek plastic shape curving to her hand. She remembered Matt's sudden confusion when she had jokingly threatened to give him a mash-call. These were perilous times, and a woman sometimes had to be bolder than her upbringing suggested. Max . . . Max had fixated on her; had seen her and decided. Had bent all his resources and concentration upon her. He was an irresistible force, but he was gone.

Maybe she would have to be a little irresistible herself. Matt wasn't Max. He was a man in hiding, too, but he didn't dare be as open about it as Max. He had to be teased along. Someone, some woman, had to care enough to take a risk.

Temple dialed the number Electra had given her.

She would wake him up. She had a purring, slightly smoky phone voice. Some people thought it was sexy. How far do you go to break down someone else's barriers? Maybe she'd find out. It wasn't much different from those long, coy teenage conversations. Boy/girl, girl/boy, practicing for the real thing.

The phone lifted. "Hello," Matt said in his best professional hot-line voice. Not a bad voice, but she'd rather hear it less controlled, and more surprised.

"Hi. This is your neighborhood hot line calling," Temple purred. "This is your wake-up call. Are you ready to give some lessons?"

Midnight Louie lounged on her bed, watching with calm, catlike neutrality. But when she caught and captured his glance, she winked.

It was night, and Matt picked up the phone, as he always did at that hour.

"ConTact?" the woman's hesitant voice asked anxiously.

"Yes."

"I—I feel I should give my name, but—"

"Names aren't necessary. Make one up if you like."

"Really? That simple? Mary Smith, then. Do you buy that?"

"It doesn't matter what I think, only what you do."

"Oh, God. I don't know what I think. I met a man. He was so sweet—now . . . what do I call you? I can't talk to you about this without a name."

"How about 'Brother John'?"

"Why do you use that?"

"Because I am your brother, and everyone's a John, or a Mary."

"Yes. I can't understand. He's so thoughtful. So sweet. He hit me, Brother John. I don't know what to do. It only happened once. Only . . . it's never happened to me before. You should see the candy and flowers he sent. But he hit me. It made me feel bad . . . wrong. But I liked it when he apologized. I kinda got a kick out of it. I don't understand why he has to say I'm so stupid, why I have to feel so superior and inferior at the same time. Brother John—? Are you there?"

"I'm here. I'm listening. What do you want to talk about?"

"Him. I'll call him Jim. That's not his name. But I'll call him Jim. I just met him—"

Midnight Louie Lets His Hair Down

Now that I have a literary reputation to consider, it is time to get a few facts straight.

An ugly rumor is circulating that I have a ghost writer. This is what I get for being magnanimous and not demanding a co-author byline. I am not against those of a spectral persuasion, but state here that I am fully responsible for every word attributed to me. (Not to discredit my collaborator, but I must report that some observers have even suggested that I should take over the entire narrative. Suits me.)

Although I am now something of a literary lion, having been critically embraced to a heartwarming degree for my debut piece, a limber little four-paw exercise called *Catnap,* there is also some confusion about my literary antecedents. (There has always been confusion about my biological ones, a hazard of my species.)

I have been compared to such divergent dudes as Mike Ham-

PUSSYFOOT

mer, "an aging mobster with a checkered past," and a "hep cat" who "fancies himself another Philip Marlowe but writes . . . like a pulp novelist who's been force-fed a dictionary."

Listen, I come by my expressional elegance the same way I do my uncanny sense of balance—naturally. Forget all those has-been dudes like Marlowe and Hammer: there is only one Midnight Louie. It is true that I have dozed off over a few tomes in my time and left my marks on a book or two. (I particularly recommend hardcovers; the corners are unsurpassed as a scent deposit site and double as a good muzzle scratcher. Fortunately, my associate author has plenty of those lying about the office library.) Anyway, these so-called critics are getting my influences all wrong, as usual. Even Miss Carole Nelson Douglas puts it about that my origins blend generic gumshoe with Damon Runyon, Charlie the Tuna (the TV ad huckster, not the comic) and Mrs. Malaprop.

I do not know this Malaprop individual from atom, but I have a bone to pick with this oversized Tuna dude (in fact, I would be delighted to discuss our differences over a long literary lunch—yum-yum). And, speaking of good taste, Mr. Damon Runyon had some admirable trends in that direction regarding the fair sex, so I will accept that comparison. As for the generic gumshoe charge, I do not share Miss Temple Barr's affection for footwear, whatever the height.

As long as I am on the subject of petty annoyances, the same critical dude who compared me to a regurgitating dictionary accused me of having "a fatal dose of the cutes." What can you expect from someone who will not even scratch his initials on a review? At least I mark my deposits. I have not been called cute since Reno Ravioli tried it in nineteen-eighty-seven and has been known as Scarface ever since. Not even little dolls so presume. And nothing has been remotely fatal to me but charm since birth, with the possible exception of Free-to-be-Feline.

Speaking of little dolls, I am told that the purpose of these mutual "About the Author" assignments is to mention a thing or two about my necessary associate. (I am physically challenged and need a little help in transcription, but she puts it down like I tell her. Period, semicolon, asterisk, et cetera.)

Carole Nelson Douglas

So here is some skinny about Miss Carole Nelson Douglas's private life, and I am in a unique position to know plenty. (After all, she did find me in the Classified "Purrsonal" column under "Pets.") I am sure you have been dying to know: the only thing she has in common with my delightful roommate, Miss Temple Barr, is a shoe collection that would choke a trash-removal vehicle (in my humble opinion all they are good for). Imelda Marcos is an amateur. As for the literary significance of such a fact, I leave it as a fit subject for the critics.

Carole Nelson Douglas Untangles a Few Snarls

Midnight Louie is like the Force: he is always with you. I am indeed supposed to shed some biographical insight here on Louie's life and times, but he seems to have taken that over, too.

There may be a misconception about Louie and me that I should correct before the ugly rumor he is so concerned about crops up on another front. Our association is not physical (though I would hesitate to call it spiritual). Perhaps metaphysical is the word. He does not cohabitate with me and mine, and never has. Our relationship is purely platonic, for good reason. We have not seen each other since 1973.

My introduction to Midnight Louie was a brief encounter that, nevertheless, made such an indelible impression that years later I found myself drafting him as a part-time narrator for a series of novels. Like all cats, Louie is eternal in a psychic sense. To put it in New Age terms, we communicate despite barriers of time and space. I may even be channeling Midnight Louie's parallel life, or lives both past and to come.

Louie would scoff at such trendy theories. Yet how can he explain away the fact that the only feline presence in the author photo on the hardcover dustjacket is "a stuffed shill," as he once described the soft-sculpture substitutes for the missing corporate cats, Baker and Taylor, in *Catnap?*

This substitute Louie (an oxymoron in the extreme: there is no substitute for Louie his own self) is, by the way, a cat-shaped, black velvet evening purse (a zipper at the back reveals a coral satin lining) with rhinestone eyes and a midnight satin bow-tie. It's my favorite evening bag (of a massive collection; so there, Imelda!), being convenient and even comforting to hold—and easy to stash under my arm when going through buffet lines. (Louie would much approve of aiding another's food consumption in any form.) I also adorn the bag with a rhinestone "Author" pin when attending crowded "Meet the Author" events that make it hard to tell who is what.

That purse gets a lot of comment and coos, so it was only natural that I should start calling it Midnight Louie, and even more natural to let it stand in for Louie.

Come to think of it, I know exactly how Louie would explain his lack of physical presence in the photo: because of his semi-shady past ("expeditions of a law-deriding nature") he must remain anonymous despite his new literary fame. That's why he allows me to maintain my self-deluding little fiction about him keeping his distance. He has also hypnotized me with his deep, emerald, Mystifying Max eyes into overlooking his very real presence. After all, a dude who is his own witness protection program can't afford to be too noticeable.

See what I mean? In person or in print, Midnight Louie maintains a feline Force field all his own.

CPSIA information can be obtained at www.ICGtesting.com
Printed in the USA
LVOW08s1459100913

351830LV00001B/128/P